I0682354

# Rescue Me

Nikki Rittenberry

"Love is the ultimate expression of the will to live."

—Tom Wolfe

# Rescue Me

# Prologue

MEMORIAL DAY

Randall Burns sat on his back porch with the remote to his stereo in one hand, a frosty bottle of Miller Lite in the other. It was ferociously hot today; the kind of heat that could fry an egg—or a person's flesh—in two minutes flat.

The thick humid air nearly smothered his lungs as he inhaled a deep breath, but that was the least of his worries. Kendall Porter, one of his best friends—and the woman he was in love with—was set to arrive in a few minutes. She called earlier and asked if she could stop by this afternoon, hinting that she had something important to talk to him about.

He had a pretty good idea that the "important topic" had to do with her return to full-time status at Porter Pharmacy. Rumor was she'd resigned from her position in Jacksonville last week at a large-chain pharmacy to return to the small drugstore her father opened nearly thirty years ago.

Question was: why?

It'd always been her plan to live in a big city, to blend with the crowd. And yet she was back...

Don't get him wrong—he wasn't complaining. The thought of her living four hours away in the state's biggest city had been a tough pill to swallow. And unfortunately his gut told him her reason for remaining in Butler Island was going to be an even bigger one.

The sultry breeze carried a hint of salt from the nearby

Gulf as Jimmy Buffet sang *Cheeseburger in Paradise*. The song reminded him of Kendall; the girl loved bacon cheeseburgers (and onion rings, of course). His thumb hovered over the SKIP button just as Kendall appeared along the side of the yard.

"Figured I'd find you out here", she uttered as she moved toward the covered patio.

Randall stood from his cushioned patio chair and wrapped his arms around the woman he loved. He held her a few seconds longer than he probably should have, taking the opportunity to breathe her in. And when she pulled away, the look in her amber eyes confirmed what he'd feared most.

She was in love with another man.

"You want a beer?" he finally asked, suddenly uncomfortable with the awkward silence.

Kendall shook her head. "I...I can't stay long. Um... I'm sure you've heard by now: I'm staying in Butler Island to run Porter Pharmacy."

He nodded. "Yeah, surprised the hell out of me. Leaving this place was all you used to talk about."

Kendall stared at her flip-flops as if the right words were scrawled along the jeweled straps. "Things change. People change", she uttered softly. She lifted her watery gaze, her eyes settling on his. "There's something you need to know, Rand. And I wanted to make sure you heard it directly from me... I..."

*God, here it comes...*

"I'm moving in with Ty."

Randall scrubbed his palm down his face, praying the action would temporarily disguise the agony that'd colonized just below the surface. He drew in a deep breath—difficult on a humid day like today—prepared to tell the biggest lie he'd ever told. "I'm happy for y—"

"There's more", she interjected. "I'm... well, I'm pregnant. The baby's due mid-November."

Wow. He hadn't seen that one coming. "You don't have to move in with the guy, Babe. We can make this"—he gestured between them—"work."

Shaking her head, she blurted, "We're in love with each

other, Rand... We're *sort of* engaged."

He was rendered speechless. Kendall was pregnant with Ty's baby, and they were... *in love*. A bitter ache unlike anything he'd ever experienced before speared his already fragile heart, making his chest feel heavy. Wounded.

"Rand?"

Briefly he closed his eyes, allowing the grief to pummel through him. Why was this happening? Why couldn't she love *him*?

"Rand, say something, please. You have me on pins and needles, here."

"I don't really know what to say", he managed as his eyes settled back on hers. "A small part of me is naturally happy for you. But the biggest part is...is... shit, Kendall!"

"Please, don't be angry with me. The last thing I wanted was to hurt you."

Pacing back and forth, he intertwined his fingers behind his head, desperately trying to keep his cool. "I'm not mad at you—I'm mad at the situation." Halting in front of the small table that housed his stereo, his temper flared. Randall swiped his hand, and in one swift motion, shoved the audio equipment over the edge.

Kendall cringed as it tumbled to the ground, pieces shattering, scattering at their feet.

He stood with his back turned, his hands low on his hips, trying to figure out how he was supposed to move on with his life. How he was supposed to watch the woman he loved start a family with someone else. "Why, Kendall?" he uttered softly. "Why couldn't you love me?"

"I wanted to, Rand. So very much, I wanted to. I'd do anything for you—you're one of my best friends! I don't want to lose you!"

Randall chuckled softly, although he didn't find the conversation to be the least bit humorous. "You'd do anything for me except give us a chance... Things could've been different, Babe. But you never gave *us* a real chance."

They'd been down this road a hundred times—a road that led to nowhere. It was utterly pointless contemplating what might've been. Randall loved her, and she'd lain awake many nights wishing she could reciprocate those feelings. "It wouldn't have worked between us, Rand."

"And you know this because...?"

"Because I found the person I was meant to be with."

"Ty", he stated flatly.

"Yes." Kendall slowly walked toward Randall, his back still turned. "There's someone out there for you, too, Rand; someone far better than me."

"Forgive me if I don't share your optimism."

Kendall's forehead thumped against his back. "Rand, please—I'm so sorry", she whispered. "Please don't—"

The on-call phone beeped twice, indicating the presence of an emergency. Randall couldn't have been more thankful for the sudden interruption. He walked several paces to his left and reached for the device he'd haphazardly tossed onto the patio cushion earlier and pressed the SPEAKER button.

Static filled the small patio for several moments before the dispatcher's voice came over the line.

"Deputy District Ranger Rodgers from the Apalachicola National Forest has just confirmed the presence of a brush fire located approximately twelve miles Northwest of State Road Sixty-five in Tate's Hell. The fire is currently burning forty acres and with breezy conditions expected over the next several days, he's estimating the fire will continue to spread. At this time, he's requesting assistance from neighboring fire departments to contain the brush fire."

Randall reached into his front pocket for his keys and then turned to face Kendall. "I've gotta take this."

"I'm so s-sorry, Rand", she murmured as a single tear slid down her cheek.

As much as he wanted to be angry, he couldn't—not when she was visibly upset. That tear did him in. "Come here", he said as he opened his arms. Without hesitation she stepped forward, allowing him the opportunity to hold her, comfort her, like he'd done so many times before.

Randall kissed the top of her head, stroking her hair as her body shook with grief. "You'll never lose me, Ken. I'll always be here for you—no matter what. I just... I just need some time, all right? Time to digest this."

Kendall pulled back, gazing into his steel-colored eyes, assessing the sincerity of his affirmation. "Okay."

With a final nod, Randall withdrew from the embrace, knowing if he didn't get away from her at that moment, he'd likely find himself on his knees, begging for another chance.

Love could make a man do crazy things.

"Please be careful out there", she pleaded as he slid the patio door open.

"I'm always careful, Babe", he called over his shoulder. "Take care of yourself...and that baby."

How appropriate, he thought as he climbed into his black Ford F-150. Today was Memorial Day. A day when the country celebrated and honored fallen soldiers. A day renowned for recognizing the deaths of thousands of men and women who'd died before their time.

And a day when any chance of a happy future with the woman Randall loved died, too.

# Chapter 1

"Okay, guys, here's what we know", Chief Handler began as he leaned his large derriere against the small brush fire truck. "The fire is believed to have been set unintentionally by a cigarette tossed from a car traveling along one of the small access roads that run through the forest.

"As you know, we're in the midst of a drought and conditions out here are brutally dry. That, coupled with fifteen mile per hour winds, is causing this brush fire to spread faster than a fleeing cockroach looking for a hiding spot under a bright light! The Deputy District Ranger in charge is Ben Rodgers. He's asked us to border the Southwest portion of the fire. The goal is simple: hold our ground and prevent the blaze from moving toward the town of Apalachicola. Any questions?"

"Has the area been evacuated?" Jimmy Phillips asked.

"According to Rodgers: yes. But Tate's Hell encompasses over two-hundred thousand acres—kind of makes it difficult to say for certain. So, be on the look-out for potential hikers and tourists."

The smell of burning brush filled Randall's lungs as he listened to Chief Handler call out instructions. Visibility wasn't bad. Yet. But he knew that a sudden wind-shift could change conditions in a flash.

Per Chief's orders, they were to pair-off and head North by foot about a half-mile into the brush until they reached the blaze.

Sounded easy enough.

Randall grabbed his tools from the small truck and ventured into the pine forest with the man he thought of as the brother he never had.

"Think we'll end up like the legendary Tate?" Jimmy asked as they ventured into the woodland.

In the late eighteen-hundreds, a local farmer by the name of Cebe Tate, journeyed into the swamp-laden forest with nothing more than a shotgun and a small pack of hunting dogs. His mission: kill the Black Panther that'd been feasting on his livestock. Lost in the swampland for seven days and seven nights, he was separated from his dogs, snake bitten, and forced to survive by drinking the murky swamp water. When he finally came to a clearing near the town of Carrabelle, he lived long enough to utter one last sentence: *'My name is Cebe Tate, and I just came from Hell.'* Since then the area became known as Tate's Hell: the Legendary and Forbidden Swamp.

"Nah, it's just a legend." At least he hoped that's all it was...

Trekking underneath rows of towering Longleaf and Slash Pines, Randall listened to the crackle of bone-dry pine needles under his feet, the snapping sound no match for the conversation replaying in his head.

*I'm moving in with Ty... I'm pregnant... We're in love with each other... We're sort of engaged.*

"You all right?" Jimmy asked as they moved deeper into the forest. "You're unusually quiet."

"You trying to hint that I talk too much?" Randall teased.

"No hints—you do talk a lot. You can pretty much strike up a conversation with anybody. I'm tellin' ya—I think you're Chatty Debbie's long lost son!"

"Fuck you, Phillips! That's taking it a bit too far, don't you think?" Chief Handler's wife, Debbie—*Chatty Debbie,* as she was often referred as—could strike up a conversation with a complete stranger (not that there were many of those around these parts). It wasn't so much that she liked to talk, but rather the odd subject matter she chose to talk about.

Jimmy shrugged as he stepped around a patch of Palmettos. "Probably… But I *did* get you talkin' again."

Roughly fifteen minutes later they arrived at their destination, ready to begin the tiring process of establishing a defense line. Over the crackle and roar of the flames, chainsaws revved and buffeting helicopter blades bellowed above.

It'd been nearly three months since the area had received any significant rainfall, and the typical sponge-like ground was uncharacteristically parched. Randall and Jimmy had devoted time and muscle digging a firebreak along a narrow dirt road while another group cleared the firebreak of flammable dead brush. It wasn't a foolproof plan: the flames were still capable of leaping through the canopies of the eighty-five foot pine trees towering overhead. But cutting the two-hundred-year old pines was a last resort.

"This is not how I expected to be celebrating this holiday", Jimmy uttered as he shoveled sand, dirt, and crisp pine needles from the trench. "I should be at home with a pair of tongs in one hand and an ice-cold beer in the other, manning the barbeque grill."

"Afraid of a little hard labor?" Randall questioned with a tinge of amusement.

Jimmy stuck the tip of the shovel in the ground and leaned one of his forearms against the butt of the wooden handle. "You mean, you're actually enjoying this?"

"Not particularly." Pretty bad when the muggy heat and back-breaking labor weren't enough to distract his mind away from Kendall. Nope, it was safe to say he wasn't enjoying a damn thing about today thus far.

"Yeah, that's what I thought." Jimmy picked up his shovel and resumed digging. "Hope Lana won't be upset about me not wanting to dig-up the flower beds this week; after today I think I might retire my shovel for the rest of the year!"

"How 'bout I help you? We'd get done in half the time and then we could head to The Saloon for a pitcher of beer."

"I like the way you think, Brother!"

The sun was minutes away from sinking beneath the tree line, causing the exhaustion from the debilitating workday to nearly cripple their tired bodies. In the distance, Grant and Tommy were dragging the last bit of flammable brush across the trench, looking equally drained.

Randall reached for his radio and informed Chief Handler that the fire break was in place and all ignitable debris had been moved to its new location within the trench border.

"How're the conditions lookin' in your neck of the woods?" Chief asked.

Randall scanned the area and then spoke into the radio. "Relatively calm at the moment."

"Well, let's hope it stays that way. Ranger Rodgers just informed me there's a wind-shift expected as nightfall settles in. That means there's a pretty good chance the blaze will be headed in your direction. Helicopter's gonna be dousing your location in about twenty minutes, so gather everyone and head back."

"Yes, sir."

Randall fastened the radio back onto his belt just as Grant and Tommy approached. "They're expecting a wind-shift soon; helicopter's on its way to drench this area as a preventative measure. We need to head back."

With tools in tow, the group retraced their steps toward the access road approximately one half mile south of their current location. Radiance faded as the day transformed into night. They walked in silence; the crunching of boots colliding against dry pine needles lulling their tired bodies, their pace noticeably slower than it had been hours earlier.

Randall's body shook with exhaustion, but his mind was restless. It'd been ten months since he'd made love to his best friend—ten months, eight days, to be exact. And he'd spent every day since optimistic about a repeat encounter.

Sure, she'd been seeing Ty for a while, but truthfully Randall hadn't expected the newly single guy to fall head-over-heels in love with her. But then again, Kendall Porter was incredibly easy to love. And now she and Ty were moving in together, *sort of* engaged, and expecting a baby by year's end.

How the hell had this happened? Okay, so he knew how it'd happened, just didn't really understand *why*.

The group had been hiking for roughly ten minutes when the first wave of dark smoke wafted by, announcing the arrival of the impending wind-shift. Buffeting helicopter blades echoed above them in the distance, in route to the destination the guys had just abandoned. The wind speed had increased as well, causing the pine canopies to sway, bend.

Randall's motions were automatic, placing one foot in front of the other, his thoughts solely focused on the catastrophic state of his personal life, instead of his environment. He barely heard the loud snap above him.

The next five seconds played out in slow motion. There was a steady drum of footsteps behind him as Jimmy hollered in warning. Two hands forcibly shoved Randall from behind, causing him to launch forward. His hands instinctively stretched outward in an attempt to cushion the fall. And as he collided against the parched earth, there was a loud cry behind him—a howl Randall felt deep in his bones—followed by a thunderous crash. The impact vibrated the ground beneath him. And as Randall turned he realized his day had gone from bad to worse.

"Jimmy!" Randall cried as he stumbled back to his feet.

A large pine trunk pinned Jimmy's body against the brittle forest floor, his body face down, not moving. Clumsily Randall surged toward his fallen friend, collapsing onto his knees as he halted beside him. "Jimmy! Damn it, answer me!"

A low guttural groan fled Jimmy's lips just as Grant and Tommy surrounded them. Randall quickly rose to his feet motioning for help with the fallen trunk. The log was approximately eight inches in diameter—not terribly heavy—but awkward to handle as numerous small branches and sharp pine needles bit into their flesh. The three of them removed the timber with relative ease as adrenaline coursed through their veins. And after tossing the tree aside, the three attended to their injured friend.

"Stay with us, man; you need to tell us where you're hurt", Randall declared.

Jimmy's breathing was shallow and erratic. Another

animal-like growl escaped his mouth as he desperately tried to suck air into his lungs. "Can't... feel my... legs", he managed softly, panting.

Grant reached into his med pack for the small oxygen tank and mask, and like a well-oiled machine, the three men carefully flipped Jimmy onto his back making sure to keep his spine in alignment. Dark smoke and poisonous gases carried by the steady torrid breeze would asphyxiate all of them if they didn't get out of there soon. Grant covered Jimmy's nose and mouth with the mask and turned the valve on the oxygen tank to the left, allowing their injured brother to breathe clean air.

Tommy reached for his radio and informed Chief Handler that Jimmy was injured, reciting the approximate location of where the rest of the department would find them. "Help's on the way, Jimmy", he uttered reassuringly. "Just try to relax and concentrate on your breathing."

*Fuck! Why was this happening?*

Randall knelt beside his best friend, carefully taking his vitals, inwardly panicking at the results. Jimmy was suffering from tachycardia—an increase in heart rate—and his breathing was still rapid and shallow. His hands were clammy and his blood pressure was slowly dropping. In other words, Jimmy was going into shock.

"This is one hell of a way to get out of digging up those flower beds, Jimmy. I told you I'd help out", he teased, attempting to keep Jimmy's mind off the pain and keep him conscious.

Dirty fingers slowly reached for the mask as Jimmy slid the plastic away from his mouth. He was still struggling to breath, fighting to draw air into his lungs as he looked into Randall's eyes. "Please..."

"Don't talk, Brother—just focus on breathing." Instinctively, Randall tried to replace the mask, but Jimmy weakly swatted at his hand.

Feebly, he shook his head. "Take care of... Lana and... Conner... for me—"

"Huh-uh—don't you dare! Don't you dare start telling me goodbye! You hear me?"

"Tell Lana I... love her and... Conner. Tell... them I'm sorry..."

"No, Jimmy, stay with me, man! You're talkin' crazy—just breathe. No more talking", he demanded soothingly.

"Promise... me, Randall. Promise me you'll... look... after them."

Randall briefly closed his eyes, knowing deep down his best friend wasn't going to make it. Accepting the bone-chilling fact that he was moments away from witnessing Jimmy's last breath. What he wouldn't do to trade places with him—hell, this was supposed to be Randall lying here—not Jimmy. Not the man with a five-year-old son and loving wife.

*Not Jimmy...*

The next minute was torturous to watch. Jimmy's breathing become more rapid, shallow.

Irregular.

His heart rate accelerated as his blood pressure plummeted.

In the distance, Randall heard the crunch of heavy, hasty footsteps as help arrived. "I promise", he uttered as his vision clouded with moisture.

And as if Jimmy had been hanging on to hear those two words, he took one final breath. And then...

Silence.

# Chapter 2

For as long as Randall lived, he would never be able to erase the image of Lana Phillips collapsing in his arms on her front porch as Chief Handler informed her that Jimmy had been injured—fatally injured. In an instant the color had drained from her pretty face as her body went limp with grief.

He held her while she wailed, gripping his shirt as though it were her only lifeline. And then as if a surge of strength erupted from her core, she straightened and uttered in a small voice, "How?"

Chief Handler cleared his throat. "The top portion of a pine tree snapped as the guys were hiking out of the brush. It fell approximately seventy-five feet—would've hit Randall—but Jimmy pushed him out of the way just in time..."

Lana stiffened in Randall's arms when she'd learned the specifics about how her husband's passing came to be.

"...The force of the impact caused internal injuries and... possibly severed his spinal cord... He, uh, complained he couldn't feel his legs..."

Lana gasped, covering her mouth as another sob fought for escape. And then she turned her mournful gaze toward Randall, searching for truth?—regret? And something else he couldn't quite pinpoint.

"...Jimmy saved Randall's life, Lana", Chief Handler declared soothingly, earnestly. "He's the epitome of a true hero..."

Confusion settled upon her face for a moment, her forehead trenched, her lips parted. And as if suddenly realizing the man supporting her grieving body was the same man rescued by the throes of death by her late husband, her somber expression turned angry. Lana's midnight-blue eyes swirled with fury, narrowing, focusing on Randall like two dangerously intense laser beams.

She raised her palm, striking his left cheek with such force his head snapped right, the crack of the blow echoing off the front porch with near-deafening precision.

Taking a step back, Lana turned her attention back to Chief Handler. "I want to see him."

"I don't know if that's such a—"

"I want to see my hu-husband!" she sobbed.


Randall stared at his pale reflection in the small mirror adorned to the sun visor of his truck, straightening his black tie. He hated this shirt—his light blue, long-sleeved B.I.F.D uniform shirt. He was a casual kind of guy, more than happy to wear his navy department tee to work. His dress uniform had always been reserved for special events like the Winterfest Parade or promotion ceremonies. But today he was wearing it for a different purpose. Because today Jimmy would be laid to rest.

Inhaling a fortifying breath, he flipped the visor into position and slowly emerged from his truck. The parking lot of Apalachicola Christian Church was filled to capacity, forcing cars to line the narrow street in two parallel rows along the road's edges.

The entire town of Butler Island was here to say goodbye and Randall had already spotted six fire engines from neighboring departments parked amongst a sea of cars and over-sized trucks. He'd bet his next paycheck that most of the firemen here had never clapped eyes on Jimmy Phillips when he was alive, but then again that's how the brotherhood worked. Firefighters shared a unique bond and when one of their "brothers" passed, unexpectedly or otherwise, the posse came together to pay their respects to one of their own.

Forging through the crowded parking lot, Randall pointed his work boots toward the heavy wood doors at the front of the church, anxious and hesitant over his final goodbye.

Jimmy's parents greeted arriving guests as they entered the historic brick building, exchanging polite, yet trivial, pleasantries. After all, what does one say to a grieving loved one?

*How've you been?*—or—*Did you catch the game last night?*—somehow seemed inappropriate.

Today would prove to be a day chocked full of hurdles, and as Randall stepped under the threshold he conceded that this moment was only the first of many.

"Randall", Mrs. Phillips acknowledged as he stepped forward. She placed the palms of her hands on either side of his face and focused her watery orbs on his. "It's good to see you", she uttered earnestly.

Randall opened his mouth, only to shut it moments later. Mrs. Phillips had lost her son—she was but an hour away from witnessing his casket being lowered into the ground—*and she was happy to see him?*

By all accounts it should've been him—today the crowd should've been gathered for Randall's funeral. Not Jimmy's.

His eyes skimmed over her features searching for contempt, anger, disgust. But ironically there was no trace of blame on her distraught face.

Only appreciation and... love.

"You, too", he managed feebly. Suddenly uncomfortable with her praise, he stepped back out of her reach, offering Mr. Phillips his hand. Jimmy, Sr. firmly shook, placing his free hand on Randall's shoulder. Unable to find his voice Randall tilted his head once in a hard nod and then set his sights on his fellow brothers already seated in the packed church.

On wobbly legs, he drifted down the single aisle toward the front of the crowded room, his eyes briefly landing on Lana's ghostly-pale face. Her eyes were tired and sunken and red, and she appeared to be several pounds thinner than she had been days earlier, her black dress hanging loosely on her small frame. The moment her gaze landed on Randall her eyes quickly averted to the young man standing beside her:

her five-year-old son, Conner.

He was dressed in his Sunday best: A pair of navy trousers and a matching navy vest, his sandy-blond hair gelled and spiked in the front just like Jimmy's.

"There you are—I saved you a seat", Kendall uttered softly as she wrapped her arms around his neck.

Randall swaddled her body with his arms, feeling her heave beneath his hands. And when he started to pull away she held him tighter.

"I can't stop thinking about how this could've been you", she mumbled as her voice cracked. "When you left for the fire you were so upset and—"

"Shhh."

"The last few days have been a nightmare", she whispered.

"I know." That was putting it lightly.

The music faded as the preacher took to the podium, signaling the beginning of the ceremony. Taking his hand, Kendall led Randall to their seat along the second row, next to Ty and the rest of the department.

The preacher began by thanking the crowd on behalf of the family—for the meals, beautiful flowers, heartfelt cards, and condolences. Randall's eyes traversed the front of the church, skimming over droves of floral arrangements and wreaths in scores of color combinations flanking both sides of the white casket. To the right, a wooden tripod showcased a large picture of Jimmy, flashing his signature ear-to-ear grin, reminiscent of happier times. And to the left lay Jimmy's bunker gear, positioned as it would be at the fire station, ready at a moment's notice for him to put on.

Movement at the podium snagged his attention as the preacher stepped aside, allowing Chief Handler to proceed with his prepared eulogy. The man looked every bit the fifty-eight years he was as he nervously shuffled his index cards. In fact, Randall inwardly acknowledged Chief had probably aged another ten years in the last four days alone.

"How many ways can one praise a hero?" Chief Handler began. "How many ways can one say 'thank you' for saving another's life? The truth is: there is no number. There aren't enough sunrises and sunsets in this lifetime.

"Jimmy Phillips loved being a firefighter. He joined our department ten years ago at the age of nineteen, fresh from the academy and wet behind the ears. The first year of any probie firefighter's career is a rite of passage: learning the procedures, training... and in Jimmy's case: fine-tuning his prank abilities."

The guys from the department chuckled softly, recognizing the playful side their fallen brother possessed.

"No doubt about it, he was a hard-working, levelheaded, skilled firefighter with a particular fondness for practical jokes. In fact, that's how he earned the nickname *The Joker*..."

Randall's eye's shifted toward the row in front of him where Lana and Conner sat, bravely listening as Chief Handler praised Jimmy for his service. Conner sat surprisingly still for a five-year-old, and he couldn't help but wonder if the boy fully grasped the concept that his daddy wasn't coming back. The thought sent a piercing jolt through his chest. Conner was going to grow up without a father...

*Damn it, Jimmy. Why couldn't you be more selfish?*

*Why did you have to push me out of the way...?*

"...There's only one thing Jimmy loved more than his life at the firehouse... and that was the two of you", Chief uttered softly as he turned his gaze toward Lana and Conner. "Let me assure you, *you* were the loves of his life. His eyes shined bright when he spoke of the two of you..."

Randall allowed his gaze to settle on Lana as Chief continued his heartfelt eulogy. From where he sat, he could see a portion of her profile. Her stone-like, vacant expression gave nothing away. It was as if her body was here, but her liveliness and vitality were gone—like her spirit had died along with Jimmy.

Lana's weary eyes bored into the glistening white casket as if she could will Jimmy's lifeless body to resurrect. Her long, light brown hair was pulled back into a loose ponytail and she wore a simple strand of white pearls and matching stud earrings. She looked every bit of the grieving widow she was.

A twenty-seven-year old widow...

Damn it!

He wasn't sure how much time had passed, but when his eyes returned to the podium, Chief Handler was gone, replaced by the preacher as he said a few words in closing.

Guess Lana wasn't the only one that'd slipped into a daze during the ceremony.

The preacher slowly abandoned the podium and descended down three steps, wandering toward the side of the church embellished with brilliant stained glass. There were a few moments of silence while he made the transition and then the familiar sound of three musical tones, like the ones heard at the fire station when dispatch alerted the department with an emergency, came over the loud speaker.

"Last call..." The dispatcher began. "Last call for firefighter James Phillips, Jr."

Chief Handler's voice came over the loud speaker. "Firefighter Jimmy Phillips, Jr. has answered his last call and has entered into eternal rest... He will be missed—"

"No!" Lana wailed as she covered her mouth, rocking back and forth on the pew. "No! Please... d-don't leave us! *No!*"

Hearing her desperate plea, her heartbreaking sobs, was more than Randall could bear. This was his fault—he was the reason this woman was experiencing unspeakable agony.

Randall was to blame.

Standing, he quickly stepped into the aisle, wiping his palm down his face as he scurried toward the exit. There wasn't a dry eye in the room as Lana's breakdown continued.

He needed to get out of here. Now.

Bursting through the heavy wood doors, his strong façade cracked as the emotions from the previous four days rushed over him—through him.

*Damn it, Jimmy... It should have been me...*

A single hot, wet tear slid down his cheek as he climbed into his truck and started the ignition. He needed to get away, needed to be far from prying eyes.

Needed to grieve for his best friend on his own terms. Alone.

Squealing out of the packed parking lot he glanced at the

gauges along the dash. He had a full tank of gas. Good. He'd head East on I-10.

His destination was unknown.

His return date: yet to be determined.

# Chapter 3

Lana Phillips quietly closed Connor's bedroom door, torn between falling to bed in a heap of exhaustion, or enjoying the silent solitude that followed tucking her five-year-old in bed.

Well, maybe *"enjoy"* was a bit of a stretch, and the *"silent solitude"* was anything but peaceful.

It'd been roughly five months since she'd buried her husband. Five months since the weight of the world fell solely upon her shoulders. There were bills to pay, groceries to purchase, school functions to attend, and a myriad of other duties to perform. She was now a single parent—a twenty-seven-year-old woman attempting to raise a boy into a man.

All by her lonesome.

Conner hadn't quite adjusted to life without Jimmy. Guess it was safe to say neither of them had.

She worried about her little boy. She tried to make extra time for Connor, but that was problematic considering she was now assuming the roles of both mommy *and* daddy.

Trudging into the kitchen, Lana snatched the bottle of white zinfandel she'd opened last night from the fridge and filled her wine glass half-full—or rather, half-empty. Yeah, that sounded better—sort of summed up her life the last five months.

Half-empty.

Taking a sip of crisp wine, she drifted into the living room. Jimmy was her high school sweetheart: her first boyfriend, her first real kiss, her first... *everything*. He'd been a senior when they began dating, Lana a freshman.

She still remembered every detail of the day they'd met. She'd been walking down the crowded halls of Butler Island High when someone had bumped into her from behind, causing Lana's books and papers to scatter recklessly along the speckled linoleum floor. Dodging droves of feet scurrying by, she began gathering her belongings, aware that the delay would likely make her late for her third period algebra class.

Unexpectedly, a good-looking blond with broad shoulders and delicious milk chocolate eyes swooped down to her rescue.

"You all right?"

"Um, yeah... Just a little embarrassed, I guess."

His laughter was warm, soothing—no hint of ridicule what-so-ever. "Well, good to know even pretty girls like you get embarrassed from time to time. Here you go", he re-marked as he handed her a stack of books.

"Thanks", she uttered, rising to her feet. Mirroring her movement he stood as well, his six-foot frame towering over her. It was then she noticed his jersey. "You're a football player", she stated flatly. *Weren't jocks supposed to be mindless, arrogant assholes?*

"Did the jersey give me away?"

His tone was playful, unmocking. She regarded him warily, silently for a stretch. They stood in the middle of the hallway, the crowd bisecting around them as though Jimmy was Moses parting the Red Sea. His body shielding her from another collision. Nervously she tucked her light brown hair behind her ear and smiled. "I suppose. What position?"

"Receiver."

"And that means...?"

He smiled. "I catch the ball; make touchdowns."

"So you're one of those guys that do those silly dances in the end zone?"

"Why don't you come to the game tonight and find out?" he proposed.

And that's precisely what she'd done. She'd sat in the bleachers, chanting the Marlins to victory along with her peers. And when her football hero caught the winning touchdown, he dropped the ball, celebrating the team's six-point gain with a spur-of-the-moment back flip.

The home crowd went wild as the band played a victorious tune. And as he returned to the sideline, Jimmy's milk chocolate gaze sought and found hers. She couldn't deny the shiver of excitement that'd surged down her spine; his performance had been choreographed with her in mind.

Lana gained a boyfriend and encountered her first *real* kiss that evening. The rest was history.

Collapsing onto the weathered tan recliner Jimmy had spent countless hours lounging in when he was alive, she took a gulp of white zinfandel and sighed. She desperately needed a change. Everywhere she looked she was accosted with memories of Jimmy and the promise of what might have been.

In the beginning the familiarity of his belongings brought an odd sense of comfort. Like he was away on shift at the fire station (a very long shift) and was expected to return home at any moment. Sometimes, after she'd put Connor to bed at night, she'd sit in this chair, listening for the sound of Jimmy's keys rattling... Of course, that'd never happened. Her husband was buried in a white casket six-feet below ground.

He wasn't coming back.

More than anything she wanted to wallow in her despair. Wanted to curl up in a ball and cry until her body shriveled from dehydration. But she couldn't. She refused to surrender to the insanity nipping at her heels. Connor had already lost his daddy; he didn't deserve to lose his mommy, too.

Glancing around the room, she conceded that the "change" she so desperately needed had to begin with her environment. Maybe she needed to purchase new furniture or redecorate. Yeah, that was a good place to start.

It was time to forge ahead with life on her own two feet. Time to take charge as the head of the household. Time to cease her procrastination.

Time to begin healing.


"Okay, let's put your Spiderman mask on and then we'll be ready to go", said Lana as she reached for the thin spandex material lying on the coffee table. She carefully placed it over Connor's head and fastened the Velcro along the back. "There. Can you see?"

"I don't gotta see good, Mommy; I can use my spider sense", he assured her.

Lana smiled at her little superhero. "You're right—I keep forgetting. Grab your trick-or-treat bag and let's go."

If it were up to her, she'd forego the whole trick-or-treating thing altogether this year. She was more than happy to stay in, stuff her face with buttered popcorn, and watch reruns of old scary movies. Every time Lana left the house— for groceries, PTA meetings, for work—she was bombarded with inquiries from nosy residents.

"How're you holdin' up?", or "How've you been?" or "Can we do anything to help?" became tiresome rather quickly.

She fully understood the repetitious questions, and the concerned residents that fielded them, meant no malice. People were just curious and were only trying to be nice. But just once she'd like to answer truthfully, explain how she struggled to get out of bed every morning and typically cried herself to sleep most nights.

That was one surefire way to end the curious inquisitions.

As tempting as it was, she was raised to be polite. And so she'd paste a grin on her face tonight as she accompanied Connor—ahem, Spiderman—through the neighborhood, even if it killed her. Connor had lost so much this year already; faced an unspeakable tragedy no child should have to endure. It was past time for his childlike innocence to return.

Gripping her flashlight, Lana locked the front door, making sure her fake smile exuded cheerfulness, strength, and confidence. "C'mon, Spiderman, let's save the city's supply of candy from the evil Green Goblin."

"Yeah!"


The radiant sun burned a path in the sky, leaving vibrant hues of violet, coral, and magenta in its wake, another twenty minutes and the colorful heavens would be replaced by inky darkness.

They'd been at it for well over an hour, Spiderman's bag practically bursting at the seams with enough candy and chocolate to last until next Halloween. They really needed to head back home; Connor still needed a bath and Lana desperately needed to lose her shoes.

"Mommy, look!" Connor shouted excitedly as he pointed toward the black Ford F-150 up ahead.

*So the rumors were true...Randall was back.*

"Can we go say hi?"

"I don't know, Connor. We really need to head ba—"

"Please? I'll be real quick! Pretty please?"

"All right, fine", she conceded softly.

Lana's heart hammered against her chest, the swooshing sound of her rapid pulse blaring in her ears. With knees aquiver, she climbed the front porch steps as Connor eagerly pounded on the front door. Swallowing hard, Lana braced herself. She hadn't seen Randall since the funeral—hadn't spoken to him since the night she'd learned of Jimmy's accident.

Refusing to return to that dark memory, she pushed it aside. "Connor, honey, I don't think he's home."

"But his truck's in the driveway", he whined.

Lana sighed. "Well, maybe he rode into town with someone, or maybe he's inside sleeping."

"Grown-ups don't go to bed this early, Mommy. And I really, *really* wanna show him my costume! Can I knock again?—just one more time—please?" he begged.

She hadn't seen her son this excited since he found the golden egg during Butler Island's annual Easter egg hunt. Every year one golden egg was strategically hidden along the boardwalk and the person lucky enough to find it was first in line to meet the Easter Bunny.

Truthfully she wanted to run as far away from this house as possible—not because she was angry with Randall. She knew it wasn't his fault Jimmy had died. No, her reasons for running had to do with her embarrassing reaction to his death: specifically the part where her right palm had struck Randall's dirt-smudged cheek.

"One more time and then we have to go."

Connor pounded on the door with both fists and then took a step back, fidgeting while he waited for the door to swing open. But that never happened.

"See?—he's not home. C'mon, we have to go now."

"Okaaay", he acquiesced, hanging his head as he descended down the porch steps. "I just really wanted to show-off my costume."

"I know, honey. Maybe we can get the pictures developed this weekend and you can show it to him. What do you think about that?"

Connor nodded listlessly as they traveled down the sidewalk toward their home four streets over. She hated seeing him like this—especially when he'd been in such great spirits earlier in the evening.

Her son adored Randall. And now that he was obviously back in town, it was past time to apologize for her erratic behavior. Connor had lost his father; she didn't want him to lose Randall, too.


Randall removed his fingers from the wooden blind slats and drew in a deep breath. He'd lost track of how many times he'd heard a knock on his door tonight. So what possessed him to peek through his blinds this time?—he hadn't a clue. But when he'd separated the wood slats with his fingertips, the image of Lana, and who he presumed was Connor dressed as Spiderman, accosted the segment of his heart ravaged with grief. His heart was damaged, forever tarnished with sadness and guilt. But one look at Lana and Connor standing on his front porch had him feeling emotions he hadn't felt in months. A twinge of hope blossomed in his tainted chest as he peered through the window pane, his body frozen as the unfamiliar sensation flickered light into his dark existence.

He'd stood speechless, motionless—his legs heavy as though his shoes were constructed of concrete. Randall hadn't seen Lana and Connor since the funeral, since the day he'd hurriedly fled the congregation of grieving beings in route to his truck. That day seemed like a lifetime ago.

He'd pointed his Ford F-150 East along I-10, spending his five-month leave-of-absence near Steinhatchee, a small Gulf coast community located along Florida's big bend. He'd rented a rundown motel room along the river—the kind of place that offered rooms by the week, by the month, or in some cases, by the hour. There wasn't a lick of luxury in sight, but that didn't matter; its sole purpose was to provide a roof over his head, a bed to lie on, and a bathroom to shower in every night.

Upon his arrival he'd visited the local marina and leased a boat, haggling the owner down in price considerably. Randall's routine didn't change much from day to day. He'd wake up before sunrise and grab what remained of the Jack Daniels bottle from the night before, slowly winding down the river until he reached Deadman Bay. Cautiously he'd maneuver his small vessel around oyster beds until he was further into the Gulf, throwing his anchor overboard to watch the sun peek over the horizon. He couldn't explain it, but somehow watching the sun rise, feeling the warmth of the rays as they touched his tan skin felt... therapeutic. Like the streams of light flickered vivid color into his somber soul.

Like Jimmy's memory was shining down on him.

It sounded silly, really, now that he thought about it. But that hadn't stopped him from rising before the sun every morning to witness the birth of a new day. It'd become as necessary and routine as brushing his teeth—and he didn't see that changing any time in the near future.

Stepping away from the window, Randall shuffled into the kitchen, rattling ice against his almost empty tumbler. He may've started a tradition of waking before dawn, but his preferred method of ending each day involved another bottle of Jack Daniels poured over several cubes of ice. Reaching for the bottle, he poured the amber liquid over the remaining ice and took a satisfying sip.

Nights were the worst—when memories, should have's, and regrets haunted him. When the piercing pain of losing his best friend could only be dulled by ingesting eighty-proof liquor.

He'd escaped reality and now it was time to return. Randall's five month hiatus would officially end tomorrow morning at seven when he reported to the fire station for shift. Throwing his head back, he swallowed the remainder of liquid in his glass and slammed the tumbler onto the counter. Like a magnet, his eyes settled on the bottle of Jack Daniels, his mind debating whether or not to finish the remains.

Picking up his glass, he shook the empty tumbler, ice clanking against the sides. The familiar sound spoke to him, encouraging him to pour one more round to deaden the ache from within.

And Randall was more than happy to oblige.

Toddling into the living room, he sank into his favorite chair, making a mental note to contact Mr. Morgan in the morning about the old Boston Whaler he'd had for sale last spring. Restoring the neglected vessel was just the kind of distraction he needed. He just prayed the marina owner hadn't sold it to someone else in his absence.

And, of course, it went without saying that he needed to talk to Lana. He owed her an apology for walking out on her and Connor when they'd needed him most.

But not tonight.

No, tonight he hadn't been ready to face her.

Raising the tumbler to his lips, Randall took another satisfying sip, finding comfort in the warmth that trickled down his throat. He hadn't been ready, but he would be eventually. *Soon...*

# Chapter 4

"I just don't know if I'll have time to play catch tonight, Connor. I have to finish dinner and I still need to finish typing the minutes from last week's city commission meeting", Lana explained as she dumped a fistful of spaghetti into a pot of boiling water.

"But you promised!"

"I know I did, but I hadn't anticipated on getting a call from your teacher today when I made that promise", she uttered as she cautiously stirred the noodles. She'd learned the hard way during the first year of marriage that failing to stir pasta within thirty seconds often led to a gummy clump of starch, which wasn't the least bit appetizing.

Satisfied that the noodles were swimming gracefully and freely in the pot, she added salt to the boiling water and carefully laid her stirring utensil on the counter. "We've been over this countless times, Connor: leaving early from work means I have to bring home the work I wasn't able to finish. Which reminds me"—she said as she turned to face her son— "I thought we discussed you aren't to have Mrs. Wilkes call me to come pick you up unless you're *really* sick."

"But I *was* really sick, Mommy: I had a mega belly ache!"

"Well then, I guess it's a good thing I can't play catch tonight. You're sick, remember?"

"Oh—I feel lots better, now", he assured her.

"Really?" Lana crossed her arms and leaned her backside against the edge of the counter. It still amazed her how quickly Connor came down with an ailment (and how miraculously he'd recover once she picked him up and brought him home). "And when did that happen, huh?" she questioned, amused.

Connor shrugged his tiny shoulders and stared at an imaginary spot on his shoes like it was the most interesting thing he'd ever seen. "A while back ago."

"Uh-huh..."

The doorbell chimed just as a bubbly sizzle sounded from the pot. The pasta water boiled over, temporarily diverting her attention to the stove. "Shit!" Lana quickly reached for her kitchen mitts, scooting the pot away from the glowing red circle on the glass stovetop.

The doorbell chimed again. "Shit", Connor mumbled, "guess I'll get it."

*Seriously...?*

Yep, Lana's life could be summarized into one four-letter word: shit. She was a twenty-seven-year-old widow and her five-year-old son was a cursing hypochondriac. Needless to say, she was failing miserably as a single parent.

A low groan escaped her mouth as she glanced at the ring around the burner. She'd just cleaned the stovetop last week. Apparently scrubbing the burnt-on pasta water would be yet something else she needed to add to her growing to-do list tonight. Realizing there wasn't much she could do about it until the burner cooled, she returned her attention back to dinner, using her pasta utensil to transfer the cooked noodles into a waiting skillet of marinara sauce.

"You don't hafta play catch with me no more, Mommy!" Connor shouted from the living room. "I got someone else!"

"Really? And who might that be?"

"Hey, Lana..."


Randall hadn't meant to scare her. He'd been on his way home from the fire station and the next thing he knew, he'd been idling in Lana's driveway. It was past time to look her in the eyes and apologize. And he figured there was no better time than the present.

He'd stepped into her kitchen, the delicious aroma of Italian cuisine wafting through the familiar room, reminding him of the countless nights he'd stayed for dinner when Jimmy was alive.

At the sound of his voice Lana jerked, no doubt startled by his presence.

"Ouch!" she cried as scorching-hot marinara sauce splashed onto her wrist.

"Shit! Are you okay?" He asked as he dashed toward the stove. Carefully, he took her hand and led her to the sink.

Lana stood by, watching as Randall placed her wrist under the running faucet. The cool water eased the sting, but his presence still left her speechless. Stunned. She'd expected one of the neighborhood boys Connor sometimes played with—not Randall. His concern touched her, infiltrating a segment of her heart that'd been numb for nearly five months. She didn't deserve his kindness, tenderness—not after the way she'd treated him after Jimmy's accident.

He held her hand as cold water trickled over his finger-tips. And when he seemed satisfied that the remedy had alleviated much of her pain, he turned the faucet off.

Her eyes tracked his thumb as he gently caressed her wrist. "I'm fine. Really", she assured him. "It was just a minor splash." Silence enveloped them, for how long she couldn't say. But when Randall finally found his voice, the two words he spoke were the last two words she expected to hear.

"I'm sorry."

Lana tore her eyes away from her injured arm, her orbs settling on the two gray eyes staring back at her. "For what?" she asked confusedly.


Shifting his weight nervously onto his left foot, he leaned his hip against the counter and shrugged. "Where do I begin..."

"Randall, please—"

"Hey, Randall"—Connor shrieked excitedly a moment before his bedroom door slammed behind him—"can you eat wif us?"

"Um, I'm not really sure if—"

"—*Please?*"

Randall resettled his focus on Lana, attempting to gauge her reaction. She didn't appear appalled by the idea, but then again her five-year-old son was present. She'd been raised to be polite, and besides the slapping incident, he couldn't remember a time when she'd ever lost her composure. Randall figured she'd had good reason to lose her cool that dreadful day; he certainly wouldn't hold that against her.

His eyes continued their journey over her exhausted face. Dark circles cradled her midnight blue orbs, further substantiating that the transition to single parenthood had been tiresome.

"Stay... There's plenty", Lana reiterated.

There was no trace of disgust or contempt. Nor was there any hint of blame etched on her pretty face, which really surprised him. After all, if not for his weak, distracted mind, Jimmy would still be alive. She was offering him an olive branch, and although he didn't think he deserved it, he was going to latch on with a firm grip. "All right. I'll stay."


The cool November breeze gently swayed the bamboo wind chimes hanging just above her on the back patio as Connor and Randall took turns throwing and catching a neon orange Nerf football. They'd been at it for almost an hour—surprising since the yard was only lit by a meager flood light mounted on the back of the house. In fact, she was amazed the pair could actually see well enough to catch the darn thing. But she was grateful for the distraction it provided her son. Even more grateful that she'd managed to complete the work she'd brought home before Connor's nine o'clock bedtime.

Lana saved the document she'd feverishly created to her flash drive and closed her laptop. In the dim light, she could still see the intense concentration on her son's face. The bamboo wind chimes clanked together with a random, soothing beat, intermixing with the sound of Connor's laughter.

And just like that, she was taken back.

Back to a time when life was easy, good times were plentiful, and troubles were few and far between. Funny how she once thought she had troubles… there was nothing more troubling than losing the one person who knew you best.

"Mommy, watch this!" Connor shouted as he took off running. He ran in a straight line away from Randall, and just as Randall released the ball, Connor quickly darted to the right, the ball practically falling into his small hands. "Touchdown!" he yelled excitedly. "Did you see that, Mommy?"

"I saw it! That was amazing!"

"He's really good", Randall commented. "Not only can he catch—he's got one hell of a spiral, too."

"Uh…*a spiral?*" She asked as she stepped off the back porch.

"Yeah, you know, the way the ball spins in mid-air. I know grown men that haven't mastered that skill."

Lana rubbed her bare arms with her hands for warmth, coming to a halt in front of Randall. She was way out of her league. She knew nothing about football. Well, that's not entirely true—she did know the basics. The game was usually played with a brown ball, the quarterback threw the ball, and a receiver caught it.

*And the rest of the men running around on the field?*

Well, she figured they were there for moral support (you know, the occasional chest bump or swift slap on the ass). And to think: she'd thought a spiral was the latest victory dance. Apparently she had a lot to learn.

"So a *spiral* is difficult to achieve?" she asked, hoping her question didn't make her seem as though she'd been living under a rock for the last twenty-seven years. Because truthfully, it'd only been approximately five and a half months.

"For some, yes, but for others it just comes naturally. And Connor, here, is definitely a natural", he said as he rubbed the top of Connor's blond head.

"Well, he obviously got his athleticism from Jimmy."

"Don't sell yourself short; I've seen you dance", Randall remarked. He couldn't help but notice the way her cheeks turned a subtle shade of pink. Obviously he'd embarrassed her. Clearing his throat, he smiled, hoping to clarify what he meant. "I mean—you're plenty coordinated."

Lana prayed the darkness camouflaged the warmth that'd settled along her cheeks, because she was clearly blushing.

Question was: *why?*

It was no secret she loved to dance. When Jimmy was alive they'd spend two Saturdays a month at The Saloon: Jimmy would drink and play pool, Lana would dance.

Her body just naturally moved to music. In fact, Jimmy used to tease her, comparing her compulsion to move to a reflex. As soon as she heard a beat, her hips would sway. But something about the way Randall alluded to her ability was... different.

It wasn't a come-on or a seduction attempt. It was more like... appreciation.

Yeah. Like he recognized her finesse—her ability—as being impulsive. Instinct driven. Natural. And he would know; he was one hell of a dancer himself.

So if his flattery was nothing more than a genuine compliment, how exactly did she explain her rattled reaction?

# Chapter 5

"Lana...?"

Her cheeks were now stained a brilliant red; she could just feel it. What on earth was happening to her?

"I didn't mean to embarrass you", he reiterated, sincere, but amused.

Lana smiled, shaking her head as though doing so would jolt the quandary from escalating. "It's fine, really... Thank you."

"Randall"—Connor interjected excitedly—"I'm open!"

Across the yard, he waved his little arms in the air, enthusiastic about running another play. The backyard was bathed in subtle dim light and although Connor stood some distance away, she was still able to identify a certain buoyancy about him.

"One more and then it's bath time", she called out. She couldn't remember the last time her little boy had looked so happy, so carefree. She'd do just about anything to keep that contented expression on his face. Randall had managed to accomplish in two hours what had taken her nearly six months to achieve. And the jury was still out on how successful she'd actually been.

For the first time in ages, Randall felt like he was actually doing something productive with his free time. And it felt damn good. Connor's peppy little laugh caused the corners of

Randall's mouth to turn upward. He couldn't recall the last time he'd smiled. Hadn't really had a reason to for some time. And even in the dark he noticed the worry fade from Lana's angelic face...

He should have never left. He should have been here.

Maybe if he had, the healing could've begun sooner. Make no mistake—their wounds were all still painfully fresh, but there was power in numbers. "Go long!" he shouted to Connor as he pretended to take possession of the ball from the imaginary Center.

Lana watched as Connor hung on Randall's every word. His tiny legs took off running toward the fence as Randall reared his arm back and launched the ball (a perfect spiral, of course). Looking over his small shoulders, Connor tracked the neon orange Nerf, and then opened his arms just as the ball dropped from the inky night sky.

Air whooshed from Lana's lungs when her little boy finally turned around, the look of admiration clearly visible. He looked to Randall as though he were his idol.

And that's when she knew: It was time. Time to apologize for her rude and erratic behavior. Time to ask for a fresh start. She just prayed her plea for forgiveness wasn't too late.

"All right, that's it!"

"Aww, c'mon, mommy—just a couple more—please? I just got warmed up!"

She felt terrible breaking up the fun. Ever since Jimmy's passing, she was the sole disciplinarian—the bad guy. "I know, but you have school tomorrow."

"Just a little bit longer?"

Was she being unreasonable? What was so terrible about a few more throws? "I—"

"It's okay, buddy", Randall chimed in. "We can play again another night this week."

"Really?" Connor asked, hope filling his tiny voice.

"Really."

"All right!" he yelled as he hurried past, dashing up the porch steps.

"Go ahead and get undressed", Lana called over her shoulder. "I'll be there in a sec!" Crossing her arms, she turned to face Randall. "Thank you for that. I can't remember the last time he's been this excited."

Randall shrugged. Playing catch with Connor was a small drop in a large bucket, as far as he was concerned. It didn't even begin to make up for all the time he'd spent away. But he was here now. And he intended on making up for lost time. "He's a good kid."

Lana nodded. Connor was a good kid. Sometimes she forgot that he was just a child, learning to cope with life's unfair realities. And if spending time with Randall rescued him from the throes of grief, who was she to argue?

A gust of crisp wind sent wisps of long brown hair into her field of vision, forcing her to tuck the silky strands behind her ear. Her focus settled on Randall's steel-colored eyes, revealing his wounded and broken soul, an utter contradiction to the large, strong man they belonged to. "You mind stickin' around for a bit longer? I was sort of hoping we could talk."

"Um, yeah. Sure."

Together they turned toward the house, climbing the porch steps as another strong gust of wind rustled the trees. The breeze carried a hint of winter, causing the hair on the back of Lana's neck to rise. She convinced herself that the odd tingle had nothing to do with Jimmy's spirit, and everything to do with the arrival of the first cold front of the season.

Because she didn't believe in ghosts. No matter how badly she wanted to.


Rushing ahead, Randall reached for the screen door and gave it a tug, motioning for Lana to enter ahead of him. He may be dead inside, but he hadn't forgotten his chivalrous manners. His mother had hammered the importance of gentleman-like behavior into his brain from the time he was Connor's age. It was like second-nature; he didn't have to think about it. Which was good. Because the only thing that had been on his mind lately was how he didn't deserve to be breathing. He didn't have a death wish, per se; he just no longer cared either way.

"It'll only take a few minutes to give Connor his bath and tuck him in... Make yourself at home."

In a flash she turned away and headed down the hall, leaving Randall alone with the ticking clock and a room full of memories. He stood motionless for several moments as an eerie sensation washed over him.

Tick. Tock. Tick. Tock.

Wiping his palm down his face, he stepped further into the living room, the motion feeling as though he was stepping back in time.

Slowly he walked the perimeter of the room, his boots clapping against the pine floor in time with the tick-tocking of the clock. Everywhere his gaze landed he was reminded of his late friend: pictures, trophies—even spotted a pair of Jimmy's flip flops lying on the floor beside his favorite chair. It'd been five and a half months since his passing, and Lana was still unwilling to pack away her husband's possessions.

*She wouldn't have to if you hadn't been selfishly distracted that dreadful day.*

No matter how hard he tried, his thoughts always circled back to that premise.

He did this. This was his fault.

Being here wouldn't change what happened in Tate's Hell, but maybe it could make a difference in moving forward. After all, it was Jimmy's dying wish that Randall take care of his family. He hadn't made good on that promise, but he would. From this day forward, he vowed to spend every day he had left on this earth mending what he took away from Lana and Connor.

A picture on the wood mantel suddenly caught his attention. Inside the metal frame was a picture he and Jimmy had taken last year at the annual Oyster Festival. He plucked the heavy frame from the mantel, raising it for closer inspection.

They'd just competed in the oyster shucking contest—both losing miserably to a twelve-year-old little girl named Emmy. She'd cheated... okay, not really. But that was their story and they were stickin' to it. Her father owned The Saloon on the boardwalk and the girl had undoubtedly been shucking the damn things for at least half of her twelve years.

"That was a fun day", Lana commented as she entered the room.

He glanced over his shoulder at Jimmy's widow before returning his focus back to the picture. "Yeah...it was." Carefully, he set the frame back into position.

"Can I get you anything to drink? Don't have any beer, but I do have some leftover white zinfandel in the fridge."

Turning around, he shoved his hands into his front pockets and smiled. "You never did like beer."

"Some things never change, I reckon."

"And sometimes, everything changes..."


Lana got the inkling they were no longer talking about beverages. She glanced down at her hands, picking at her nails. It was a nervous habit, one her burgundy polish would likely not survive. Steeling herself with a deep breath, she set out to make things right. "Listen, Randall... I... Well, I owe you an apology."

"An apology?" he questioned incredulously. "For what, exactly?"

"For the way I acted, for slapping you... for causing you to run off—"

"My leaving had nothing to do with anything you did, Lana", he affirmed. "If anything, I owe you one... I should've been here, you know?—for Connor... for you."

Lana tore her attention away from her pitiful-looking manicure, allowing her eyes to scan the wounded man that stood several paces in front of her. Outwardly he appeared the same, but upon closer inspection she recognized it: on the inside he was broken and hollow, just like her.

Slowly, she was filling, swelling with purpose. But she knew she'd never return to normal. Never be the person she used to be. Randall was still nearly empty, but tonight while playing with Connor she saw a flicker of life in him. Maybe there was hope for him—for all of them.

"Connor really missed you, you know. I can't even begin to

describe how excited he was to see your truck parked in the driveway on Halloween. We stopped by, but—"

"I know", he confessed softly. He watched confusion settle over Lana's pretty face, making him feel like a fucking coward for hiding like he had.

"How?"

"I saw you."

"But, why didn't you—"

Randall shrugged. What could he say? He'd acted like a pussy; liquid courage in the form of whiskey hadn't even given him fortitude. "I needed more time, I guess. Wasn't quite ready to face you yet."

Wrapping her arms around her middle, Lana nodded. "Don't suppose I gave you any indication I wanted you around the last time we saw each other, huh?"

Randall rubbed his left cheek with the palm of his hand. "You have one hell of a hard hand", he teased, hoping to lighten the mood. "Remind me to never make you mad."

Embarrassed, Lana covered her face with both hands. "Gosh, I really am sorry about that!"

"Don't worry, you were forgiven the moment it happened."

She raised her head from her hands. "Really?"

Randall shrugged, still rubbing his cheek. "Well, maybe not at the *exact* moment..."

The edges of his mouth turned up. *Was he toying with her?* Yes, he most certainly was.

Lana snatched a throw pillow from the couch and tossed it at him (although she was incapable of a perfect spiral). She watched as he threw his hands up, blocking the sage-colored cushion from colliding with his head.

"All right, all right—I probably deserved that", he confessed, smiling.


Randall picked up the pillow and glanced at the woman that'd launched it at him. Her lips quivered for a moment, immediately followed by the sweetest sound he'd ever heard: Lana's laughter. In that moment, five and a half months of worry and concern faded from her face. He wondered how many times she'd laughed since the accident.

Probably zero.

But, damn, it looked good on her. And he'd be lying if he said that putting it there didn't thaw a small portion of his frozen insides. "It's good to hear you laugh."

Lana's cackle quieted. "Thanks", she uttered softly. "I haven't done that in a while."

Tossing the green pillow back on the couch, Randall took a seat, leaning his forearms against his knees. "So, how've you been?"

There was that question again. Funny how such simple words sobered her. "Good", she managed. And then he did it: he gave her *The Look*. Kendall often referred to it as a truth serum, because with one look, the truth typically started pouring out of his intended target. And right now, his gray eyes were intensely focused on her.

"C'mon, Lana, you don't have to bullshit me. How've you been? Really."

Sitting down in the chair across from him, she sighed. "I'm… managing. *Barely managing*" she emphasized just above a whisper. "It's a daily struggle, you know? I never realized how hard life actually was for single moms until I become one."

Randall nodded. He understood; his father had walked out on his mom when he was nine. He saw firsthand how unglamorous of a job it sometimes was. But of course his circumstances had been different. He hadn't been sorry to see the son of a bitch leave. Because after he left, the beatings his mother occasionally endured stopped. "And Connor?"

"He's had a hard time adjusting. His teacher calls at least once a week demanding I pick up my sick child—only he's not *really* sick. He's craving attention right now and he's not picky about it being good or bad."

Randall nodded again. He'd gone through a similar stage after his father left: acting out in class and talking back had been his M.O. It wasn't until the owner of the marina, Mr. Morgan, took him under his wing that his behavior improved. "Listen, maybe I can help."

"You don't have to do that, Randall."

"I know I don't, but I want to. Let me take some of the load from your shoulders. Please..."


Lana stared into Randall's sincere eyes, amazed to find that his face revealed no hint of pity—and for that, she was grateful. He had no ulterior motives; he simply wanted to be a guiding force in her son's life and ease the burden she'd inherited after the accident. "Okay. I'd really appreciate that."

It wasn't the first time someone had offered help. But it was the first time she'd accepted it. Randall was practically family.

And family stuck together.

For the first time in months, she felt the heavy weight she'd carried since Jimmy's sudden passing ease a bit.

And for the first time in months the road ahead didn't seem quite as dark and scary.

# Chapter 6

Sitting front row in the town's small auditorium, Lana patiently waited for the city commission meeting to begin. As Mayor Cliffburg's secretary, it was her responsibility to record the substance of each meeting and ensure the mayor and commissioners didn't stray from the proposed topics.

After corralling the town's residents into their awaiting seats, she reached for her digital recorder, allowing her to document the meeting in its entirety. Tomorrow she'd transcribe the dialogue and load it onto the town's new website.

There was a time, not so long ago, when she'd feverishly take notes, and then would spend the following day responding to calls from residents that had been MIA. Now she didn't have to. Typing the contents did cost her time, yes, but spending her days without her handset practically glued to her ear was a step in the right direction.

"Good evening, folks", Mayor Cliffburg began. "Thank you all for coming tonight. Let's see... for the record, today's date is November twentieth, two-thousand twelve. And let the record reflect that Commissioner Anthony and Commissioner Rhodes are both present.

"Okay, first topic on our agenda this evening is the old theater. As you all will recall, the building was condemned last year after an intentional fire caused the already debilitated brick building to partially collapse. Funds have been allocated to..."

Lana tried to concentrate on the contents of the meeting,

but her mind kept drifting back to her earlier conversation with Chief Handler. He'd suddenly appeared at her desk at city hall just before lunch today with a thirty-two ounce container of Coca Cola, a pleasant smile, and a personal invitation.

"Haven't seen you in a while, honey. How've you been?"
*Lonely, stressed-out, exhausted.*
Pick one.
"Pretty good, Chief—just really busy these days with work and Connor." *There, that sounded better.*
"Any plans for Thanksgiving?" He asked before slurping a gulp of Cocoa Cola through his straw.
"Think Connor and I will head to my parents'."
Although not because she expected a good meal. Everyone within a twenty-mile radius knew her mother was an awful cook. In fact, she was still amazed she hadn't suffered permanent damage from ingesting her mother's odd creations over the years.
Really amazed.
But the fear of yet another repulsive meal hadn't deterred her from declining the invitation. Because, truthfully, she was more terrified of spending the holiday alone than she was of her mother's latest surprise casserole.
"Good. Family's important—*especially* on Thanksgiving. Which is why I'm here... I know Jimmy's no longer with us, but you and Connor are still—and will always be—considered members of our fire department family. We'd really like it if the two of you stopped by."
Lana leaned back in her chair, resisting the urge to pick at her newly-painted nails. "Thanks for the offer, Chief. But I'm just not really sure if we should." She hadn't been to the fire station since before the accident. Just thinking about being there sent an uncomfortable shiver down her spine. "I just—"
Chief placed his palm in front of him, interrupting her mid-sentence. "You don't have to make a decision right now. This holiday season will be difficult for all of us. I just thought

it'd be nice if we all faced it together. Think about it, all right?"


And that's precisely what she'd been doing since he'd marched his large derrière away from her desk earlier today. Lana acknowledged Chief's explanation made sense. But she just wasn't convinced it was a good idea.

For the first time since Jimmy's death she was feeling a trace of optimism. She now knew the overwhelming grief wouldn't suffocate her (she couldn't say the same a month ago) and she was even hopeful that she was emerging as a decent role model for Connor.

She never wanted to go back. Never wanted to revisit the place in her mind where she felt hopeless, helpless. Alone. That deep, dark, bottomless trench she'd tumbled into six months earlier; a wild free fall that left her lost and scared. Never again.

Never. Again.

"Lana... Lana?"

Lana quickly snapped her head toward the front of the room where the mayor and city commissioners sat, staring at her. "Yes, sir?"

"How's the budget lookin' for our New Year's Eve fireworks display?"

Quickly, she thumbed through her notes until she found the information she was looking for. "Actually we came in under budget this year, sir. I found a wholesale supplier willing to give us a substantial discount if we agreed to purchase our Independence Day fireworks from them, as well."

"Lovely", Mayor Cliffburg uttered, smiling. "Isn't Ms. Lana, here, lovely?" he gestured with his palm as he addressed the small crowd. Nods of affirmation rippled across the auditorium, looking like a sea of bobbleheads.

Suddenly embarrassed by the mayor's public praise, she tucked her hair behind her ear and uttered a tiny, "Thank you." Mayor Cliffburg had always rubbed Jimmy the wrong way, suggesting he was a bit too friendly to his female employees—*especially* Lana. It'd never really bothered her much until recently. Now that she no longer had a husband, Mayor Cliffburg's subtle flirtatious mannerisms now seemed... not-so-subtle.

But she was a big girl. And if she could handle the loss of her beloved husband, surely she could handle a forty-something, sex-starved, smooth-talking politician.

Surely.

The meeting continued, and as soon as the focus was diverted away from her lovely self, she thought about Chief Handler's offer.

Would visiting the fire station trigger those dark feelings again? She didn't know. This was a big decision. One she'd debate over and over in her mind in the upcoming days; the consequences far too heavy to contemplate right here, right now.

"I still can't believe you haven't sold this thing yet", Randall uttered as his palm swept over the seasoned 1983 Boston Whaler Outrage.

Mr. Morgan tossed his rag over his shoulder and scratched the back of his head. "Yeah, well... I gave you my word, son. I knew you'd come back. And when you did, you'd still want her."

Randall could see through the wear on the finish to the bones of the vessel. It had potential; just needed a new layer of fresh gel coat, a little bit of TLC, and she'd look good as new. "She's a beauty."

"Yep. Needs some work, though."

Randall shrugged. The boat ran like a dream, its flaws merely cosmetic. "I've got nothing but time." And time spent transforming the boat that held so many pleasant memories from his childhood would aid in camouflaging the nightmares that plagued him daily.

This wasn't the first time this vessel had rescued his sanity. After his father left, Mr. Morgan had assumed the role of father figure, allowing him to help out at the marina. The man had passed along his love of the water, of boats, and had offered him something his father had never bothered to give: his undivided attention. Guess it was safe to say the boat held sentimental value.

And he was relying on the old Boston Whaler to save him once again.

Mr. Morgan reached into his front pocket, handing Randall a set of keys. "She's all yours. Can't wait to see her refurbished back to her prime."

Neither could Randall. Question was: what would be his next distraction after his latest project was complete?

"So what are you gonna do?" Olivia asked as she poured Italian dressing over her chef salad.

Lana shrugged, slowly stirring her chili as if the explanation to all her unanswered questions were hidden beneath the thick layers of minced onion and melted cheese. "Don't know yet."

It'd been a couple weeks since she'd seen Olivia. She'd been away, photographing the aftermath of a school shooting that'd taken place early last week in a rural town in Northern Idaho. As a freelance photographer specializing in documenting tragedies, Olivia fled the confines of Butler Island on a regular basis. She often compared living in the small island community to living on an ant farm, where every step taken, every word spoken was carefully observed by curious onlookers.

Funny how Lana used to be one of those meddling types. Now that she resided inside a glass house, she understood how intrusive the analytical observations could be.

Olivia stabbed a piece of iceberg lettuce with her fork and sighed. "Okay, let's put our heads together and list the pros and cons, shall we?" She waited for Lana's nod of approval, and then continued. "If you attend, what's your biggest fear?"

Lana glanced at her son beside her. "Chew with your mouth closed, Connor", she reminded him, knowing her correction had less to do with his table manners and more to do with stalling.

"Well…?"

Satisfied that Connor was busy concentrating on devouring his grilled cheese sandwich like a gentleman, Lana steeled herself with a deep breath. "My biggest fear is... taking two-steps back. I can't go back, Liv. I can't allow myself to fall apart again."

"And the best thing?"

"I don't know. I guess the best possible scenario would be closure. Aside from Jimmy's grave, it's the one place I've deliberately avoided since the accident."

"Okay, now we're gettin' somewhere", Olivia uttered as she pointed her fork at Lana. "As the reigning expert in loss, I can assure you that how you'll feel upon arrival will most likely fall somewhere between your worst and best case scenarios."

"Do you think I'm completely overreacting?"

"Absolutely not—in fact, I think your hesitancy is completely normal."

"You do?" she questioned, releasing an anxious breath she hadn't been aware she was holding. "I'm not crazy."

"You're not crazy", Olivia reiterated. She reached for her sweet tea and took a sip before stealing one of Connor's French fries. "Listen, grieving is... a process. A journey. Sure, you might make a few wrong turns along the way—might find yourself lost a time or two—but you have to keep goin'. You can't give up on your destination."

"And what am I supposed to do if I do find myself lost, huh? How do I find my way back?"

Olivia plucked a slice of garlic bread from the bread basket and swept the crunchy fare along her near empty bowl. "Simple: you just stop and ask for directions."

# Chapter 7

Having had her fill of her mother's all-in-one turkey dinner casserole, Lana made a spur-of-the-moment decision to accept Chief Handler's invitation. After crossing the Mainland Bridge, she took a left onto First Street, and then a right onto Palm Drive until she came upon the hidden entrance to the fire station.

Spending Thanksgiving with family in Apalachicola today had chased away the loneliness nipping at her heels. In fact, she hadn't shed a tear all day. That, she was truly thankful for. She maneuvered her small sedan between two mammoth-sized Ford trucks and shoved the gear into PARK.

Maybe she was high. Yeah, that had to be it. Because, clearly, ingesting her mother's latest casserole creation had affected her ability to make intelligent decisions. She gripped the steering wheel firmly with both hands while the engine idled, her mind teetering between taking the next step in the grieving process and throwing her Corolla in reverse.

"Why are we just sittin' here?" Connor asked from the backseat. "Are we gonna get out?"

Averting her eyes to the rear view mirror, Lana studied his innocent face. "Do you *want* to go inside?"

Connor shrugged his tiny shoulders. "Anything's better than eating Nana's Jell-o salad."

"Guess you have a point", Lana sighed. "All right, let's do it." After emerging from behind the wheel, she shoved her keys into her front pocket and reached for Connor's hand. Up ahead she could hear laughter and lighthearted conversation echoing from the bay garage, taunting her with memories of years past. With a fortifying breath she willed her feet to move beneath the open bay door, willed her body to continue down the road to recovery.

Cackles and idle dialogue ceased as the room became aware of their presence, practically daring Lana to flee. *What had she been thinking?*

Chief Handler placed his hands on his knees, rocking back and forth several times until he gathered enough momentum to rise from his chair. He walked several paces toward the front of the bay, enveloping Lana in a welcoming hug. "Hi, honey, glad you made it."

Lana smiled nervously. "Thanks, Chief."

"My goodness, Connor, you sure are gettin' big."

"That's 'cause I'm in kindergarten, now."

"Kindergarten, eh? Wow!" Chief shoved his hands into his front pockets and rocked back on his heels. "I remember when you were knee-high to a grasshopper..."

Connor wrinkled his nose in confusion. "What the hell does that mean?"

"Connor!" Lana chided.

"Sorry." His eyes scanned the crowded garage, finally landing on Randall's. "Can I go say hi to Randall?"

"Of course."

Chief placed his hand on the small of Lana's back, and with weak knees, Lana moved further into the bay, burrowing into the inquisitive crowd.

*You can do this. You can do this...*

She chanted the mantra over and over again, willing the slogan to be true. For half an hour she immersed herself in hollow chat, reciting the same answers to the same questions she'd been asked for months.

It didn't take long for Chief Handler's wife, Debbie, to corner her. She didn't know whether to snatch Connor by the collar for a quick getaway, or throw her arms around the woman. *Chatty Debbie*, as she was often referred as, was a legend around these parts (mostly for her peculiar conversation topics). But right now, Lana couldn't be happier for a subject change. Couldn't be happier to standby and listen to one of Chatty Debbie's crazy stories, instead of convincing everyone she was okay.

"Well, don't you look gorgeous!" Debbie announced as she wrapped her arms around Lana.

"Thank you—"

"Love that nail polish you're wearin'."

Lana looked at her newly-painted purple polish. It was no secret she had a bit of a nail polish fetish. Her collection included pigments ranging from the lightest frosted silver to the opaqueness of pure black. She still remembered how Jimmy would shake his head from side to side, and then ask, "How many shades of pink polish does a woman need?"

"One for every occasion", she'd always reply.

"It's called Diva of Geneva, by OPI. You're more than welcome to borrow it."

"You know—I just might take you up on that offer. I have a pedicure appointment on Monday. Barbara Dennison and I started goin' to that new salon that just opened next to Mainland Cottages..."

Instinctively, Lana's eyes sought the whereabouts of her little boy, finding him sitting comfortably behind the wheel of the fire truck on Randall's lap.

"...It all started last summer. Barbara took off her polish and her toe was yellow! I swear, it looked like she'd dipped her big toe into a container of French's mustard..."

It was difficult to pay attention—not because of the unusual subject matter (lord knows the woman had no reservations when it came to sharing personal information about herself or loved ones). No, it was difficult because she was experiencing a strange bout of déjà vu.

"...It's a good thing she has insurance; that ointment would've cost seventy-three dollars!"

It was a strange phenomenon: everything was the same, yet different all at the same time. Suddenly she began to feel that familiar twinge swell inside her chest. It started as a dull pang, but quickly expanded, snuffing her optimism, crushing her lungs with a force so strong she struggled for breath.

"...Could've been worse, though; they could've amputated.

That actually happened to my Aunt Gerdy when I was a kid, bless her heart. She had diabetes, you see, and her big toe became black and wrinkly. Anyhow, she had it amputated. But that didn't stop her from wearing her favorite flip flops. She'd have to drag her left foot behind her in order to keep the darn thing on."

This was too much. Watching Connor hang on Randall's every word, pretending she wasn't suffocating, was too much. She couldn't do this. She could no longer deceive the crowded room. "I'll be sure to drop the polish off to you this weekend. Excuse me, will you?"

Lana stepped around Chatty Debbie, her eyes stinging with unshed tears. She made it all the way to the kitchen before the first sob escaped. She covered her mouth with the palm of her hand, but it was no use. She couldn't stop them.

*What if she couldn't make them stop...?*


"This switch turns on the lights. And this knob right here turns on the sirens", Randall added as he gestured toward the dash.

"Can we turn 'em on?"

"Don't think so, buddy. They're pretty loud and we might scare some of the younger kids."

Randall stole a glance at Lana, she was still held captive by Chatty Debbie. He still couldn't believe she was here. Olivia had mentioned earlier Lana was thinking of stopping by, but he hadn't believed she'd actually show. He was in awe of her courage—lord knows he hadn't shown any six months ago when he'd squealed out of the Apalachicola Christian Church parking lot. He'd left her and Connor to fend for themselves, allowing the guilt he harbored to this day to gnaw at his conscience.

"Say cheese", Olivia advised as she aimed her camera at Connor and Randall, twisting the long lens for optimal focus.

"Cheeeese!"

Lowering her camera, Olivia examined the picture on the small LCD screen. "Perfect! Let's do a few more, okay? Connor, I want you to grip the steering wheel like you're driving." Raising her camera once again, she pointed the lens toward the driver's seat. "Look straight ahead."

" 'Kay."

Olivia pressed her finger down on the button, the rhythmic click-click-clicking of the device slicing through the steady humdrum chatter behind her. "Great job, kiddo! Your cute lil' face was made for the camera."

"That's what my Nana always says."

"Smart woman", Olivia reiterated.

"Not when it comes to cookin' stuff."

Randall and Olivia howled with laughter. They'd heard the epic tales about Mrs. Crawford's culinary talent—or rather, the lack thereof. He'd never had the privilege to taste her infamous casseroles, thank God. But if they were half as bad as everyone claimed, he'd rather eat dirt than subject himself to that kind of torture.

His eyes wandered over the crowd once again, the sight of Lana's fleeing back zigzagging through the crowd reminding him of a marble's jagged journey in a pinball machine. "Shit", he mumbled softly.

Olivia followed his gaze, catching a glimpse of the back of Lana's black sweater as she hurried toward the solid metal door that led to the interior of the fire station.

"Listen, Connor, why don't you and Olivia get in line for dessert. I hear Jenny made cookies 'n cream cupcakes."

Pivoting in his lap, Connor's brows drew together, wrinkling his tiny forehead. "What about you?"

"I'll meet you over there in a few minutes."

"Okay!"

Carefully Randall lowered Connor down the side of the cab until he was low enough for Olivia to reach. When his feet finally touched concrete, Randall began his descent, landing with a heavy thud after hopping from the bottom rung. "If I don't make it back in time" ,he called over his shoulder, "make sure to grab a cupcake for me, too!"

"We will!"

Randall pointed his work boots toward the door Lana had disappeared behind minutes earlier, his even gait never wavering. It didn't appear as though anyone else had noticed her speedy departure. Good. Guess if it had to happen, at least she'd held off until the crowd had become distracted by the allure of the dessert table.

Tugging on the heavy metal door, he stepped over the threshold, allowing the distant echoes of Lana's sorrow to navigate him. The clank of his boots hitting the linoleum floor should have announced his arrival, but sadly she couldn't hear them—not over the volume of her cries.

His feet came to a halt at the entrance to the kitchen, and although he had a pretty good idea of what he was walking into, the picture in his mind didn't begin to prepare him for what he stumbled upon. Her petite body trembled, her left hand braced along the countertop likely the only thing keeping her upright. Her right hand was positioned over her mouth, most likely in an attempt to muffle the shrill of her sobs.

It was a small peek into the pain she struggled to suppress daily. A glimpse at the agony he'd created. Suddenly he felt like an imposter, feeling as though he was spying, invading on what seemed like a very private moment. Scrubbing his palm down his face, Randall decided to make his presence known. "Lana..."

Startled, Lana spun around, eight trembling fingertips frantically swiping at the moisture cascading down her face. "Where's C-Conner?"

"With Olivia. Getting dessert." Her head bobbed up and down several times before another wave of grief fought for release. She bit her bottom lip, but she was far too weak to curb the cries from escaping again. Her eyes clamped shut while her hand masked her mouth.

Listening to the sounds of a wailing woman wasn't one of his favorite pastimes—and he didn't know of any man that would disagree—but retracing his steps back to the crowded bay wasn't an option, either. Stepping forward, he opened his arms, offering security to her unanchored emotions.

He held her while her small frame quivered, supporting her grieving body as she wept for the husband she missed and the father Connor had lost. Weeping for the memories that'd surfaced of the years she'd spent with Jimmy. And the many years ahead she'd endure alone.

Lana's tears had soaked through the heavy cotton of his navy department T-shirt, but he didn't care. Offering his uniform as a handkerchief was the least he could do. He waited until the volume of her sobs softened, stroking her hair as he urged her to confide in him. "Talk to me. What's going on?"

Lana sniffed, her head still buried against Randall's solid shoulder. "I made a mi-mistake."

"A mistake?"

Lana nodded, then raised her head. "I shouldn't b-be here. And Connor... What if he s-sees me?" Gripping the front of his shirt, she focused her watery gaze on two gray eyes swirling with concern. "He c-can't see me like thi-this, Randall. I made myself a promise a-after Jimmy's funeral that I'd n-never let him see m-me like that again."

"Look at me", he commanded softly as he cupped the sides of her face. "You're going to take the back door to the parking lot and get in your car. You're going to drive home—"

"But, Connor will—"

"Connor will stay here with me. My shift ends in an hour. When it's over I'll bring him home—"

"I c-can't ask you to do that, Randall."

"You didn't. I offered, remember...? Go home. Pull yourself together. Connor never has to know about this."

"And what about everyone else?" she asked as she briefly closed her eyes. "If I l-leave, they'll—"

Randall brushed a fleeing tear from her cheek with his thumb, wishing he could offer her more than a spur-of-the-moment babysitter. "If anyone asks, I'll tell them you weren't feeling well. You *did* eat dinner at your momma's..."

Despite her grief, Lana laughed softly. "Yeah, I did."

Randall smiled, feeling as though he'd accomplished the impossible: he'd made her laugh. He was unprepared for the sense of satisfaction that pummeled through him, unprepared for the flicker of light expanding in his dark heart. "Go. I'll see you in a bit." Hands still cupping her face, Randall leaned forward and placed his lips against the top of her forehead.

Lana closed her eyes, feeling a glimmer of hope for the

first time in months. She wasn't alone. She didn't have to carry the burden by herself any longer. "Okay", she whispered softly. "Okay."

Beams of light danced across the white mantel, followed by the low hum of Randall's truck pulling into the drive. Rising from Jimmy's favorite chair, Lana tucked her still-damp hair behind her ear. Near-scalding water had cleansed the overwhelming gloom from her body, the shower's drain thirsty for her tears. She'd become accustomed to crying in the shower, hiding the anguish from Connor behind a palm-tree-printed curtain.

She felt better—exhausted, but better. The amount of energy leached from her small frame by way of her tears still amazed her. Sometimes after a good cry she felt as though she'd competed in a marathon. In fact she was pretty damn certain she could make a sport of it. And if the Olympics recognized table tennis and badminton as a sport, she didn't understand why *Mourning Marathons* couldn't be included too.

Heavy footsteps thudded against the porch steps as Lana reached the front door. Randall greeted her on the other side, carrying a sleeping Connor.

"He passed out before we even made it to Main Street."

Lana moved aside, making room for Randall to enter. Once he'd cleared the threshold she gently closed the door. "He had a busy day today", she uttered quietly.

Motioning for Randall to follow, she journeyed down the narrow hall lined with pictures of Connor, all framed in white wood and randomly positioned in a collage. Jimmy never cared for the casual appearance, arguing that it looked as though she'd hung the pictures with her eyes closed. She hadn't, of course. There was a method to her madness. She'd seen it done on HGTV once. It was supposed to command attention, luring one's eyes to journey over the images in a sweeping motion, allowing the still shots to tell a story.

Randall followed Lana into Connor's room, light from the hall spilling onto the green area rug patterned with thin white stripes: yard lines like the ones painted on a football field. Careful not to trip over any toys, he gently placed Connor in his bed, backing away while Lana removed his sneakers. Feeling as though he was intruding on a precious, private moment, Randall slowly backed away, wiping his palm down his face as he strolled into the kitchen.

Walking up the porch steps moments ago he hadn't known what to expect; she'd been a mess at the station. Now puffy red eyes were all that remained.

"Thank you", Lana uttered just above a whisper as she joined her rescuer in the kitchen.

Randall shoved his hands in his front pockets, bewildered by her gratitude. "It was nothing, really."

"Don't do that. It meant a lot to me." Wrapping her arms around her middle, she continued, "You saved me from falling to pieces in front of Connor tonight."

Shrugging his broad shoulders, he leaned his hip against the counter, allowing his gaze to wander over her face. "I told you before, I want to help."

Two gray eyes staring back at her revealed pain—like a festering wound that refused to heal. She recognized the weariness, the despair, the discontent. Looking into his eyes was like looking in the mirror. And if there was any truth in the eyes being the windows to the soul within, their depths divulged his vitality had suffered an immeasurable blow. The agony was camouflaged well behind his poker face, but she still saw it. He couldn't hide it from her.

And although his pain wreaked havoc on her already fragile heart, the comfort of knowing she didn't have to heal alone rescued her from the black hole she'd stumbled into nearly six months ago. "I'm glad you're here."

It felt damn good putting her mind at ease. For the first time in months it felt like Randall was doing something positive and productive with his time, instead of spending it pickling his liver with eighty-proof whiskey. He'd been numb for so long feeling seemed foreign to him. But as his eyes settled on the healing woman before him, he had to admit it felt good.

It felt good to be here. Good to see her smile again. Hell, it just felt damn good to feel. "Me too."

# Chapter 8

The first weekend in December had been reserved for Winterfest for as long as Randall could remember. The annual celebration began on First Street as eager spectators lined the road's edges for the Christmas Parade. And after the Winterfest Queen rode by on the back of the mayor's blue 1966 Ford Thunderbird Convertible, residents migrated to the boardwalk, sampling some of the best Christmas cookies available this side of the equator. But the biggest attraction, by far, had to be the carnival.

Fried funnel cakes dusted with powdered sugar, Polish sausages smothered with grilled peppers and onions, cotton candy sold in pairs of red and green tempted the masses in droves. And when bellies were sated, thrill seekers binged on rides that spun, twisted, dropped and lifted. Large stuffed animals hung from tent ceilings near the exits, beckoning folks to spend the remainder of their hard-earned cash for a chance to win a coveted Christmas prize.

But Randall wasn't interested in parades, Christmas cookies, or the thrill of a carnival ride. It was Saturday night—which meant two dollar domestic drafts at The Saloon.

Yeah, that was something worth celebrating.

Pushing his way through the heavy wood door, the familiar scent of stale cigarettes and Pine Sol accosted him immediately, filling his nose with a strange sense of comfort. He waved at the bartender, Dan, as he wound his way to the back of the room. Grant had managed to snag their favorite pool table in the back corner, and was already arranging the billiard balls inside the triangular rack for their first round.

"About time you got here", Grant teased as he carefully lifted the triangle from the table. "I was beginning to think you weren't going to show."

Randall slapped his hand against Grant's, pulling him in for a manly shoulder-bump. "What're we wagering tonight?" he inquired as he turned his attention to the wall, meticulously analyzing the display for a cue stick before selecting the one on the end. Pointing the tip toward the ground, he studied the wooden rod, checking for any signs of warpage.

"Loser buys the next round."

"Olivia have you on an allowance or something?" Randall asked as he stepped away from the wall.

"Only when I'm playing pool with you."

Randall chuckled under his breath. He didn't like to brag, but he was damn good at the game. He'd taken Grant's money on more than one occasion over the years—a fact Olivia was obviously well aware of. "Where is she, by the way? Figured she'd already be parked on a stool for moral support." The waitress arrived with their first round, placing two frosty mugs on a nearby table. "Thanks, Rachael."

"You bet", she answered with a wink, then scurried toward the neighboring table to collect another order.

Grant hovered over the billiard table, allowing the cue stick to glide back and forth over his thumb several times before he struck the cue ball. The perfectly-aligned billiard balls scattered violently along the green felt. "She's at Lana's; should be here anytime now." He studied the arrangement, looking for an easy solid-colored ball to sink.

"Lana coming, too?"

"That's the idea." Grant struck the cue ball again, attempting to sink the solid number three ball into the corner pocket—of course, he missed. "*Damn.*"

Swallowing a large gulp, Randall placed his beer on the high bar and grabbed his cue stick. He stalked the table, slow and confident, studying the whereabouts of each striped ball. Once his selection was made he got into position, pocketing number ten with ease. "What about Connor?" he questioned, altering his stance for his next shot.

"Her parents are taking him to the carnival, then keeping him for the night."

Randall eyed the cue ball as it bounced off the side rail, smacking into number twelve with a loud clank before disappearing in the left corner pocket. "Think Olivia can talk her into it?"

"Don't know. She said Lana seemed onboard earlier. Guess we'll find out when they get here."


Olivia pressed her thumb against the doorbell and waited. And waited.

"Lana"—she yelled as she pounded on the door with her fist—"it's me, Olivia!" Moments later the door swung open, revealing her friend still wrapped in an ivory satin robe. "Why aren't you dressed?"

Turning on her heels, Lana left the door open for Olivia and wandered into the living room. "Probably because I'm not going."

"Why not?"

Lana shrugged. "I don't know. I can't really put it into words, really. It just... doesn't feel right."

"Lana, Connor's gonna be gone until tomorrow afternoon; this only happens once a month. You can't just sit here all night by yourself and—"

"I'll go next time."

Crossing her arms, Olivia eyed her from across the room. "That's what you said last month", she politely reminded her.

"I know, I know. It's just... I don't think I'll be very good company tonight. It's probably best if I just, you know... don't go."

"Huh-uh, you're not sittin' here tonight by yourself—I'm not havin' it. If you're plannin' on stayin' in, then so am I." Olivia plopped down on the couch, arms still crossed.

"No!" she pleaded. "Grant's expecting you to be there and—"

"He's expectin' *you* to be there, too", she reiterated. "Listen, sugar, this is an all or nothin' kind of situation: either we both go to The Saloon together, or we both stay right here. Your choice."

Lana ran her fingers through silky hair she'd spent twenty minutes straightening. Olivia was right: Connor wouldn't return until tomorrow afternoon. Her parents kept him overnight once a month, and once a month she'd savor the much-need break it provided her. Alone.

It wasn't that she didn't want to move forward—she did, *she really did*. But sadly every step she took toward the future meant she was one step further from her past. She knew it probably sounded silly, she'd buried her husband almost six months ago. He was gone. Forever. But moving on somehow still felt like she was leaving him behind.

Abandoning him.

Two months in a row, Olivia and Grant had invited her to join them at The Saloon. And two months in a row she'd declined, always hinting she'd likely accept their invitation the following month. Lana understood what they were trying to do. They were nudging her to take that next step.

Was she ready? Would she ever find herself in a place where she felt prepared for life's curveballs? She didn't know. But one thing was certain: she couldn't decline the invitation a third time. "Anyone ever tell you how incredibly stubborn you are?"

The corners of Olivia's mouth turned upward in a grin as if recalling a fond memory. "Yep, my husband likes to remind me daily. So… what's it gonna be?"

Even though taking the next step felt like a frightening leap, Lana finally obliged. "All right, all right. Let me just get out of this robe." She pivoted and headed down the hall to her bedroom, but not before noticing the victorious expression plastered on Olivia's face.

Maybe Olivia was right. Maybe it was time to take advantage of the parenting pause her mom and dad offered once a month. Maybe it was time to stop merely existing and start actually living.

After all, that's what Jimmy would have wanted.

Lana tossed her robe on the bed and tugged on a pair of denim jeans. She slipped on a green plaid flannel, leaving the ends unbuttoned so she could tie the soft material at her waist. She finished her ensemble with her favorite pair of brown cowgirl boots, distressed and worn in from countless hours on The Saloon's dance floor. Glancing in the mirror a final time, she nodded in approval.

Tonight Lana would rejoin the living. Wishing her life had turned out differently wouldn't change a damn thing.

Because no amount of wishing was going to bring Jimmy back.


Grant bought the next round after Randall effortlessly sank the eight ball into the called right corner pocket. Again. "Man, Livvey's gonna kill me if I keep this shit up."

Stifling a smirk, Randall glanced at his watch. "Maybe not; they should've been here an hour ago. Maybe they changed their minds."

"To do what?"

He shrugged. "I don't know—chick shit, I guess."

Grant slurped a sip of beer and then ran his tongue over his mouth to capture a segment of froth that'd settled on his upper lip. "Chick shit, eh? And what might that be?"

"Nail painting, purse swapping"—leaning forward, he braced his hands along the edge of the pool table—"pillow fighting... You know, shit like that."

"Pillow fights?" Olivia asked as she sidled up beside them. "What type of fantasy land do you reside in, Randall?"

Tugging at her waist, Grant pulled his wife against him. "What took you so long?" he questioned as he nuzzled his face in the crook of her neck. "

"Well..."

"It was my fault", Lana began. "I—"

"Almost won the pillow fight. Yep, and you know Lana: Mrs. Competitive", Olivia emphasized teasingly as she gestured at Lana with her thumb. "She demanded a rematch."

Laughter rippled around the pool table. Olivia's rundown of the events that'd taken place prior to their arrival couldn't have been more contradictory in nature. Lana was sweet. Compassionate. She didn't have an antagonistic bone in her body.

"Well, I'll be... I thought that was you", said Dan as he came to rest next to Lana. "Sure is good to see you in here." The longtime bartender/owner swung one of his arms around her shoulders and smiled.

"Thanks, Dan. Looks like you're in for a busy night tonight."

"Yes, ma'am. Winterfest always seems to draw a big crowd—plus I heard it's supposed to rain later. When that happens, folks will likely stop in here. What're you lovely ladies drinkin' tonight?"

"I'll have a glass of merlot", Olivia announced. "A *full* glass."

"I think I can manage that. And what about you?" he asked as he turned his attention back to Lana. "The usual?"

"You mean—you still remember? It's been ages since I've been in."

"Of course, I do. It may've been a while, but I wouldn't forget. Malibu and pineapple juice, three maraschino cherries", he gestured with his fingers.

Stifling a shy smile, Lana nodded.

"All right. Be right back."

Randall placed his half empty mug on the nearby table, gathering Lana in his arms in a friendly greeting. "Hey, girl, I was beginning to think you weren't going to show. Good to see you."

"Thanks, good to see you too", she said as she stepped out of his arms.

"Grant mentioned your parents were taking Connor to the carnival."

Lana nodded. "They usually keep him overnight once a month to give me a break. Just so happens it fell on Winterfest this month." She forced herself to smile—nobody wanted to be around a Debbie Downer. "I'm sure he's milking them for ride tickets and a load of junk food as we speak."

"Yeah, he's a smooth-talker, all right. Talked me into buying donuts at Anderson's Bakery last week."

"Wait—he talked *you* into it?" She emphasized as she pointed a finger in his direction. "Am I hearing this correctly?

Because I don't recall anyone ever having to talk you into that before."

Anderson's Bakery was a family owned establishment that'd been opened for nearly three generations. They sold everything from bread to pastries to pizza dough. The bakery specialized in unconventional donut flavors, and if customers timed their arrival just so, the gourmet creations were served warm.

"Touché", Randall replied, attempting to hide a growing grin. "I do have a weakness for key lime glazed donuts."

"Who doesn't?"

Dan appeared again—this time with drinks. And when his delivery was complete he wove around the growing crowd, returning to his position behind the wood-shellacked bar.

"Now that the girls have their drinks, you ready for another round of pool?" Grant asked.

Randall smirked, revealing an easy confidence. "Depends: Are you up for buying the next round of brew?"

# Chapter 9

Enveloped in a thick cloud of haze, Lana sat at a high bar table wedged in the corner of the smoke-filled room, alternately chatting with Olivia and sipping her mixed drink while Grant and Randall rivaled in another round of eight-ball. She'd fought the urge to phone her parents to check on Connor numerous times in the hour since her arrival. She knew he was in capable hands, but relinquishing control—even for one night—was still difficult to do.

Losing Jimmy had been out of her control. And somewhere deep inside the recesses of her mind she concluded that as long as Connor was within sight, she'd be able to keep him safe. Her theory was probably unrealistic, she knew. Because when a person fulfilled their time on this earth, no amount of careful observation could save them. But that certainly didn't obscure her half-baked rationale.

Music spewed from the speakers, an eclectic mix of classic rock and fast-paced country tunes, causing Lana's toes to tap against the bottom rung of her wood stool. It took a conscious effort not to squirm in her seat as Luke Bryan's voice serenaded, requesting country girls to shake their tushes. God, she missed dancing. Missed how her mind would go blank and her body's sixth sense simply took over.

To her right, Olivia sat with her arms raised above her head, snapping her fingers to the melody, mouthing the lyrics to the catchy chorus.

"We should dance!" Olivia suggested over the roar of the

music.

"Maybe later." She'd purposely kept her response vague—that way, she wouldn't feel guilty when it was suggested again. And she knew it would be at some point.

"Okay."

The lights dimmed as the upbeat rhythm transitioned into a slow country ballad, beckoning couples to the rectangular dance floor like moths to a flame. "Hey, Womack", Olivia shouted, "you 'bout done yet?" Hopping off her stool, she sauntered up to Grant and pried the cue stick from his hands.

"Livvey, baby, we're in the middle of a game, here."

"Oh, quit actin' like you've got a chance in hell at winnin'." Olivia latched onto the front of his shirt and tugged. "C'mon."


Randall laid his cue stick along the edge of the pool table and plopped his rear end on the stool Olivia had vacated moments ago. He took a healthy gulp of Miller Lite, then turned his attention to the pretty brunette to his left. "Having fun?"

"A lot."

He eyed her over his glass while he took another sip. "That so?"

"Uh-huh."

It was a whopper of an answer. And he wondered if her response was meant to put his mind at ease, or her own. He wasn't going to call her out on her obvious lie—not yet, anyway. Changing the subject, Randall gestured over his shoulder at the dance floor with his thumb. "Think I might've lost my pool partner."

Lana diverted her attention to Olivia and Grant, locked in a lover's embrace. They'd married in early spring in a simple ceremony along the stretch of surf behind Grant's beach house. They'd looked so in love that day, and as Lana observed them swaying on the dance floor tonight, she sensed their feelings for one another had only continued to ripen. "They look really happy..."

He didn't need to look over his shoulder again to know the two newlyweds were mashed up against one another, practically hypnotized by their close proximity. Just like he didn't need to look at Lana's angelic face to know she was thinking of Jimmy. "Yeah, they're a good fit." Propping his elbow on the table, Randall rubbed the course stubble along his cheek with the back of his fingers. "Surprised you haven't ventured out to the dance floor yet."

Chipping away the teal polish painted on her nails, she shrugged. "Guess I just, you know… haven't had the urge."

"Are you shittin' me?" He asked incredulously. "I saw you over here squirming in your seat, your boots just-a-tappin'—it's in your bones."

"You're crazy, you know that? You saw no such thing, you've been busy playing pool. Or don't you remember…?"

"Trust me, I *definitely* remember." And he was likely to never forget how her body had subtly swayed to the melody, her bottom fidgeting about on the hard wooden stool. A man would have to be damn near blind not to have noticed.

The soothing sound of steel guitar faded, replaced by a heavy thump of beating drums, followed by an unmistakable electric guitar intro. Randall stole a quick glance over his shoulder at the dance floor as John Mellencamp's *Hurt So Good* began, stirring a craving deep in his gut he couldn't quite name. Standing, he offered his hand. "C'mon."

"What?—*no!*"

"Huh-uh, I'm not taking no for an answer. Dance with me…"


It'd taken every ounce of courage she owned to be here tonight. In fact she was quite proud of the forward progress she'd made thus far—albeit a tiny baby step. Panic coursed through her veins, but one look into Randall's gray eyes shoved it down.

*You're not alone, you can do this…*

Lana accepted his offer with trembling hands, allowing Randall to guide her down from the stool she'd occupied since her arrival, to the adjacent crowded dance floor.

It took a few moments to loosen up, but when she finally let go, allowed her tense body to unravel, something magical happened: questions, doubts, worry, and fear dissipated. And in its wake, Lana saw a glimpse of the lively woman she used to be.

Randall spun her around as they traveled the dance floor. He was a really good dancer—taking the lead, yet still allowing her an opportunity to unleash her creative finesse. He was right: dancing was in her bones. And she had an inkling it was just the kind of therapy her body needed to mend itself.

She was blossoming before his very eyes, a contented smile spreading across her pink lips. Admittedly, Randall had done a lot of wrong things in his life. But this?—this felt good. His heart quivered when he realized what he'd managed to do here tonight. Lana had taken another step, entrusting him to lead her.

He hadn't known until that very moment how much her trust would mean. How the simple gesture of taking his hand moments ago would rescue him from the arms of anguish.

*"...Hey baby, it's you, come on, girl, now, it's you*
*Sink your teeth right through my bones, baby..."*

Randall spun Lana around, then firmly gathered her in his arms. This no longer felt like a one-sided arrangement. Holding Lana while their bodies swayed patched the gaping hole in his heart. And while he still felt considerably empty, he couldn't help but wonder if this woman was his ticket to contentment.

*"...Hurt so good*
*Come on baby, make it hurt so good..."*

Maybe he didn't have to be tough all the time. Maybe this incredibly strong woman could be his rock, too.

A slap on the back startled him as the song came to an end. Randall turned to find Grant by his side.

"Hate to skirt out early, but I just got a call from Ty.

Kendall's water broke. They're already at Mainland Hospital. We're heading over there now."

"Oh, wow", Lana began. "I'm sure Ty's probably freaking out right about now!"

"Yeah, that's an understatement! Listen"—Grant shouted over the music as he turned to Lana—"we can drop you off at your house if—"

"That's not necessary. I'm sure I can catch a ride home with somebody."

"I'll drive you home", Randall offered.

Lana turned to face him, baffled by his generous offer. "Wait—you're not heading over there with Grant and Liv?"

"Nope, wasn't plannin' on it... Your call: I can either take you home now, or we can stay." Randall eyed her for a few long beats. He could see the gears-a-turning in her brain as she carefully considered her choices. He figured she'd probably call it a night. After all, she'd conquered many firsts tonight.

"I think I'll stay for a bit—I mean, if you're sure it's okay."

"Of course, it is."

Lana turned to Grant. "Give Kendall and Ty my best."

"Will do. I'll have Olivia call you once we have some news." Grant squeezed through the crowd toward the bar where Olivia stood waiting for him. She gave a quick wave to Lana and Randall before disappearing behind a sea of line dancers near the front segment of the dance floor.

"Are you sure you're okay with this? I'm sure I can find someone else to—"

"I'm positive", he reassured her.

"But she's one of your best friends. Figured you'd want to be there, you know?"

Randall shrugged. What could he say? He'd bared his soul, as well as his naked body, to Kendall two summers ago, confessing how he'd fallen for her. He'd done all he could— short of begging her—to give him a chance. But she hadn't wanted that. Instead, she'd pursued a friends-with-benefits relationship with his lieutenant, Ty Everitt.

"It's complicated." There was no need in rehashing the past. Their friendship had withstood the blow of her marriage to Ty, but he'd be lying if he said it hadn't suffered irreparable damage. "How 'bout we get another drink?"

"Only if you promise to dance with me again later", Lana countered.

"I think I can manage that."


The crowd had thinned considerably by the time Randall and Lana ordered their last shot of tequila. "Okay", she uttered, wincing as liquid warmth swam down her throat. "I think I'm done, now."

Slamming his empty shot glass on the shellacked bar, he smiled. "I think that'd be wise." Randall raised his hand above his head, motioning for the bartender. "Cashin' out, Dan."

"Be right with you." Dan appeared moments later, placing the check face down on the bar.

Lana reached into her purse for her wallet. "Here, let me—"

"Hell, no—put your money away! Tonight's on me."

"Randall, we drank a ton of tequila! The tab's gonna be—"

"The tab's taken care of", he assured her as he placed his credit card on the bar. "Don't worry"—he winked—"I'll let you buy me a beer next time."

*Next time...* Lana tucked her hair behind her ear, unsure what to do with her hands, knowing her cheeks were probably ten shades of pink. *Why was it suddenly so hot in here?*

Dan swiped Randall's card from the table and slid it through a groove along the side of the register. He waited for the receipt to finish printing before returning both paper and plastic to the bar top.

She watched as Randall scribbled his name on the receipt, returned his credit card to its rightful slot, then shoved his wallet into the back pocket of his faded blue jeans.

"Ready?" Randall asked.

Lana tore her eyes from his backside, praying he hadn't noticed. "Uh, yeah. I'm ready."


The short drive from The Saloon to her small home on the

west side of the island was driven in near silence. Good. Because she wasn't entirely confident she'd be able to hear him much anyway over the roar of her rapid pulse.

The headlights illuminated the cold wet pavement, puddles near the road's edges glistening like twinkling stars.They made a left onto her street, kicking her nerves into overdrive—although why she couldn't say. She glanced at her hands just as Randall turned in to her driveway, flecks of teal polish scattered along her lap.

"And we're here", he announced as he shoved the gear in PARK. "You okay? You're not gonna throw up in my truck, are you?"

"No, I-I feel"—*restless*—"fine…" The steady hum of the idling engine surrounded their bodies, which ironically only seemed to further enhance the silence lurking between them. Butterflies assaulted her insides, her heart galloping to a hasty tempo.

God, she was nervous. *Why was she suddenly so nervous?* "Well, um, thanks for the ride."

"Anytime."

She stared at him a moment longer, laid back in his seat, completely unaware of the static currently wreaking havoc on her brain. "Okay, so… yeah, guess I'll see you later." Clumsily she reached for her purse, only instead of gripping the leather bag, she somehow managed to knock it over. A medley of items spilled from the cleft, finally coming to rest along the floor board. "Shit", she mumbled.

"And the mystery of what you girls carry in these damn things are finally revealed", Randall uttered as he picked up a small spool of black thread. After tossing it into her purse he gathered more items, desperately trying to suppress his growing grin.

This was beyond embarrassing— it was downright *humiliating*! Why did she have to be so darn clumsy? Hadn't she suffered enough? The sudden need to grab the rest of her belongings and flee the confines of Randall's truck washed over her.

Stretching her body over the console, she reached for a tube of pink gloss that'd settled near the gas pedal, completely oblivious that Randall was reaching for the same item, until his fingers covered hers. His hands were rough, big, dwarfing her dainty digits. Slowly her eyes traveled up his chiseled forearm, past his broad shoulders, finally landing on two curious gray eyes. His steel-colored orbs were focused on hers, their faces inches apart. They sat motionless, frozen, breathing the same air—so close she caught a hint of tequila on his breath.

Lana swallowed hard, then licked her suddenly dry lips (something Randall had clearly noticed, seeing that his eyes had averted to her mouth). Energy charged between them, pure, electric, rooting their bodies. She waited for the moment when the strength of it became too powerful, when the pull weakened their resistance. And just when she thought he'd close the distance between them, Randall did something completely unexpected: He nudged the tube of gloss into her palm, clearing his throat as he quickly pulled away.

"There you go."

"Uh, thanks", she managed feebly. Shoving the gloss in her purse, she scrambled to find the door handle with quaking hands.

"Let me walk you to the—"

"No! I'm fine. I'll be fine." With the passenger door finally open, she carefully climbed down. "Thanks again..." Shoving the heavy door she pivoted, allowing Randall's headlights to guide her up the weed-filled path to her front porch. Once inside she let go of the breath she'd been holding, leaning her back against the front door until her wobbly knees could support her weight.

She'd mull over the details of tonight in the morning, when the sun's splendor focused light on what'd almost happened moments ago in Randall's truck. She didn't want to think about it right now. Right now she wanted her flannel pajamas and a big bowl of Cap'n Crunch. And then a good night's sleep in her lonely king-size bed.

# Chapter 10

A pounding headache and a throbbing hard-on greeted Randall the moment his weary eyes opened. Neither was an unusual occurrence, really. But the pretty brunette with eyes like the midnight sky who'd starred in his lascivious dream had certainly been a first. Lana had seeped into his unconscious mind with her plump pink lips, spellbinding curves, and fuck-me boots. Closing his eyes, he briefly replayed the vivid fantasy in his mind again.

*"I want you, Randall Burns."*
Lana suddenly appeared before him, fingers twirling the ends of her long brown hair. His eyes lowered to her breasts, barely contained in a blue lace bra, down the contours of her stomach, to the shimmering rhinestone dangling from her navel.
*God, help him. He was a sucker for pierced navels.*
His eyes continued south, caressing the sweet curve of her feminine hips, adorned with matching panties. Honey clung to her inner thighs, glistening in the dim light. His mouth watered—eager for a taste.
She seemed to move in slow motion, her boots lazily clicking against the floor as she ambled toward him.
Tap… Tap… Tap…
His cock twitched. *Ah, hell… those cowgirl boots were his undoing.*
*"Do you want me, too?"* Her words were breathy, raw,

glazed with desire.

Randall licked his lips. *"God, yes."*

*"How bad?"*

*"Really bad."*

*"Yeah?"*

*"Yeah."*

Lana straddled his lap, running her red-painted fingertips up the solid wall of his chest. The sweet scent of her arousal was intoxicating, flooding his body with endorphins.

*"Well, now that you have me, what are you going to do?"*

Randall smirked as his fingers tugged the delicate lace blanketing her round breasts. *"This..."* His mouth covered her hard pink nipple, extracting a faint moan from her luscious lips as his tongue continued to tease.

*"Don't stop. Please, don't stop..."*

Randall groaned, scrubbing his palm down his face.

*This* was a complication he didn't need: X-rated visions of a woman he couldn't have. Lana was Jimmy's wife, for heaven's sake. What kind of man lusted over his dead best friend's woman?

Rolling out of bed, he trudged into the kitchen and reached for the bottle of whiskey beside the fridge. Foregoing a glass, he drew the bottle to his lips, swallowing a few healthy gulps of his favorite poison. It was a hangover remedy he'd stumbled upon during his stay in Steinhatchee. In fact, it'd worked so well, he hadn't purchased a bottle of Advil since early spring.

He took another swig from the bottle, finding solace in the fiery amber fluid as it slid down his throat. Then bracing his hands along the counter's edge he lowered his aching head, trying to make sense of the unfathomable.

It wasn't that she was unattractive—hell, Lana was the best kind of beautiful. She had a pure heart, an angelic aura about her, combined with a girl-next-door exterior. Her allure wasn't intimidating, but rather, *approachable.*

Last night she'd looked so carefree on the dance floor. And idling in his truck in her driveway she'd looked... fucking delicious.

Randall blew a puff of air from his lungs, wishing the action would expunge the vivid fantasies from his body. He needed to pull himself together. He needed to stop thinking about Lana. Forget about the way she'd felt pressed against him last night on the dance floor. Obliterate the memory of those deep blue eyes staring back at him.

He couldn't have Lana Phillips.

Not now. Not ever.

"Well, aren't you a pretty lil' thing." Lana sat next to Kendall, holding baby Tenley in her arms. "How'd the labor go?"

"Well, this being my first, I don't really have anything to compare it to", Kendall began. "But according to Dr. Gillard and the nurses, it was about as good as one could hope for. I had virtually no pain once the epidural was in place."

"She barely broke a sweat", Ty commented as he entered the room.

Lana raised her gaze from the tiny bundle in her arms to the man standing to her right. Ty's expression was that of a proud husband, proud father. "You two sure do make pretty babies. What on earth are you going to do when she's fifteen?"

"I don't even want to go there—I'm still workin' on getting through the first week!" Ty explained.

"Well, enjoy every minute of her while she's young; they grow up too fast. Connor's turning six in March. I honestly don't know where the time went!"

"Is he still at your momma's?" Kendall inquired.

Lana nodded. "I'm headed that way after I leave here."

"Olivia said she'd managed to talk you in to going to The Saloon last night. How was it?"

"It was... weird at first, you know? Jimmy and I spent so many Saturday nights there... Anyhow, Randall sensed my hesitation, practically dragged me onto the dance floor and... well, I think that helped chase the awkwardness away." For a while, anyway; the discomfort had returned later on in his truck.

"Speaking of Randall, have you heard from him yet this

morning?" Kendall questioned. "I've left several messages, but he hasn't returned them yet."

"No, I—"

"I wouldn't expect to hear from him till at least noon", Ty shared. "Especially if he was out late last night drinkin'."

"You're right", Kendall softly agreed. "It's just... It's just... I miss my best friend!" Tears traveled down her face as a sob broke free. "I guess I j-just figured he would've visited by now."

"Your wish is my command", Randall announced as he stepped into the room, bearing a small bouquet of pink roses and a to-go order of onion rings. His eyes quickly averted to Lana, holding who he assumed was Tenley, then back to Kendall. "Don't cry, Babe", he soothingly appeased, moving further into the room.

Kendall swiped at her eyes, then threw her arms around Randall's neck when he was within reach. "I was w-worried you weren't going to show."

"C'mon, now—you actually think I'd purposely steer clear of you on one of the happiest days of your life?"

Pulling away, Kendall shrugged. "Deep down I knew you wouldn't, but when I didn't hear ba—*are those onion rings?*"

"You are so predictable", he teased.

"Yeah, I suppose. Sorry", she uttered as she gestured toward her tears, "I'm a little hormonal at the moment."

Lana felt a bit uncomfortable sitting there holding Tenley, like she was intruding on a very private conversation between two people with oodles of history. "I should probably get going; my parents are expecting me for lunch." Carefully, she transferred Tenley back into her mother's arms and stood.

"Not a casserole, I hope", Randall chuckled.

"Sandwiches", she confirmed, meeting his gray gaze from across the hospital bed. "Pretty hard to screw that up—at least, I hope." Lana turned her attention back to Kendall. "Congratulations, again. She's absolutely precious."

"Thanks, I think she's pretty adorable, too—but then again, I'm sort of biased."

"I'll walk you out", Ty offered as he placed his hand on the small of Lana's back.

"Oh, you don't have to do that—I'm quite capable of finding my way back to the elevator. Stay here with your new family."

Ty waved off her suggestion. "I'm headin' to the cafeteria, anyway. Besides, it'll give them time to catch up", he explained as he reached to open the door.

She was moments away from stepping into the hall, when the sound of Randall's voice halted her feet. "Tell Connor I'll stop over later today to play catch."

Lana looked over her shoulder, attempting to gage whether that was secret code for I-think-we-should-talk-about-what-almost-happened-last-night. But unfortunately his mundane expression gave nothing away. "Um, okay. I will."


Lana lay restless on her back that evening, staring at the ceiling fan blades as they slowly whirled. She'd been lying there for nearly two hours, plenty of time for her eyes to adjust to the darkened room. Plenty of time to reflect.

Guilt gnawed at her conscience. She'd had an astonishingly good time last night, laughing, dancing, drinking. She'd felt... *alive.* A glimmer of hope had trickled into her heart, allowing her to take her first real, deep breath since the end of May.

What did that say about her, exactly?

Selfish: that's what she was—her husband was buried in the Apalachicola Cemetery while she'd been twirling on the dance floor. And then, of course, there was that awkward moment in Randall's truck—that incredibly intense moment when his mouth was centimeters away from caressing her lips...

Lana shivered as she recalled the memory. Of all the times for her libido to rekindle, it'd chosen *that* moment. With *that* man.

Turning onto her side, she vigorously fluffed her pillow, then nestled her head against the cotton sham. She'd spent a better part of the day combing over the details of their almost-kiss, trying to figure out if the allure had been one-sided. Because there was no sense in denying there'd been a small part that'd wanted him to kiss her.

Yeah. What was she supposed to do with that admission?

She wasn't quite sure.

Clearly, she'd spun too many times on the dance floor and had become too friendly with Jose Cuervo.

As promised, Randall had stopped by just before dinner. He and Connor tossed the football back and forth in the backyard while she'd pretended to read a magazine on the patio. She'd carefully watched Randall for any signs of discomfort or remorse—if there were any, she hadn't seen them.

Neither had spoken about what'd almost happened last night in the cab of his truck. Maybe she was worrying over nothing. He'd had an awful lot to drink last night, too; maybe he didn't even remember their near-kiss.

And if he didn't remember, then she clearly needed to forget.

Lana allowed her heavy lids to close, drawing the comforter over her shoulders for warmth. Thank goodness he'd probably been too drunk to remember.

Thank goodness for Jose Cuervo.

# Chapter 11

"Looks like it's going to be a late one tonight."

Lana's eyes veered from her computer monitor to Mayor Cliffburg, hovering next to her with a worried expression. "Why? What's going on?"

The mayor braced one hand on her desk, the other on the back of her chair. His blue and yellow striped tie caressed her forearm, causing her to flinch slightly.

"Just got a call from the company we ordered our fireworks from for the New Year's Eve bonfire. Seems their warehouse was burglarized early this morning."

"Let me guess: they can't fulfill our order."

The mayor shook his head. "We need to put our heads together; find a replacement company—and quickly. We've got less than a week to make this happen."

"Yeah, of course… I'll make some calls."

"Great", he sighed as he pushed away. "Buzz me if you get any leads."

Mayor Cliffburg disappeared into his office, leaving Lana alone with two monstrous dilemmas: finding a company with enough inventory to supply fireworks before the bonfire next week, and locating a last minute babysitter to pick Connor up from day camp and remain with him until the riddle that'd been tossed at her moments ago was solved.

Glancing at the clock on the wall, she made note of the time: half past four. Connor had to be picked up from day camp by five—or else she risked having to pay a hefty late fee.

She couldn't afford that; she'd barely scraped enough money together to place him in the special two week program to begin with.

It was times like these she wished she would've saved her vacation days, instead of wasting them crouched into a fetal position grieving after Jimmy's accident. In the end it hadn't changed anything. Jimmy was still gone. She could've used the five-hundred dollars she'd spent on the two-week Christmas Break program on gas and hotel accommodations, establishing a new holiday tradition with her son far from Butler Island, far from curious onlookers and last-minute pyrotechnic emergencies.

Panic, thick and thriving, mounted inside her chest.

*What was she going to do?* Lana ran her fingers through her light brown hair, wracking her brain for a solution. Because after all the heartache she'd endured this year, she figured a miracle was long overdue.

Then suddenly it occurred to her. Reaching for her phone, she dialed Randall's number, relieved when she heard his voice come over the line.

"Hello."

"I have to work late! My parents are in the Keys—Kendall's busy with a newborn—Olivia's still in Denver—and I'm freaking out, because—"

"Whoa, whoa, slow down, Lana", he soothed. "Take a deep breath and relax, okay?"

Lana sucked in a cleansing liter of air, releasing the breath through her pursed lips.

"Better?"

Lana's head bobbed up and down several times.

"Are you still there?"

Crud. Had she actually nodded as though he could see her? "Sorry. Yeah, I'm still here."

"Okay. Tell me what you need, Sweetheart."

Lana twirled the phone cord around her finger, feeling a sense of calmness suddenly wash over her. "I… I need a favor. A big one… Connor has to be picked up from day camp in"—she glanced at the wall clock again—"twenty-five minutes. I'm stuck here at work dealing with a major setback in the New

Year's Eve celebration. I don't know how long I'm going to be..." Switching the handset to her other ear, she sighed. "I hate to ask, but—"

"It's not a problem, Lana. Really. I'll pick up Connor. We'll hang out at the marina for a bit, maybe grab a pizza or something, and then head back to your place. I still have a key."

Lana closed her eyes. "Thank you so much", she whispered. "I'll be home just as soon as I can."

Hours later Lana sat at her desk, her phone wedged between her right shoulder and ear, waiting for the customer service rep from the latest pyrotechnic company to return to the line. She'd been put on hold roughly ten minutes ago by the kind gentleman. Apparently there'd been a ferocious storm in Atlanta where the company was located, temporarily zapping their computer system. He'd gone to the warehouse to check inventory the old fashioned way with his eyeballs.

Lana peered through the large picture window to her left, the normally serene view of the small courtyard now swallowed by opaque darkness. Crickets serenaded as she mindlessly tapped the top of her pen against a yellow legal pad. She would've picked the polish from her nails if she had any left, but unfortunately the last remnants of frosted-pink enamel had disappeared a half hour ago.

"Any luck?" The mayor inquired, appearing from his office.

Lana shook her head from side-to-side. "You?"

He moved to stand beside her, leaning his backside against the edge of her desk. "Nope, looks like we may be lighting sparklers this year."

"Yes, I'm here", she spoke into the phone when the gentleman returned to the line. She then displayed the universal hand gesture to Mayor Cliffburg to indicate she'd be with him in a moment. "Uh-huh... *They canceled*? How many are we talkin'?"

With his secretary distracted, the mayor pushed off the

desk, using the rare opportunity to look his fill without shame. Lana Phillips had been his secretary for nearly seven years.

And for seven long years he'd wanted her.

Truthfully it was her looks that'd landed her the position. One glimpse of her sinfully sweet smile and the gibberish printed on her one-page resumé had no longer mattered.

But he'd been wrong about her. The woman was courteously resolute when it came to her job: The perfect blend of aggressiveness and grace; an angel with an ambitious agenda; the will of a lioness with a heart of a cuddly kitten.

She had people eating out of the palm of her hand—himself included.

"...Well, we usually aim for double that amount for a fraction of the cost", Lana explained as she spoke into the handset. "But since you're the first person I've spoken to today with inventory left, I guess we can't afford to be picky."

*Hmm, this sounded promising.*

The Mayor tore his attention away from the lavender bra strap peeking out of her sleeveless sweater and carefully listened to her end of the conversation.

"...Well, Henry, we need those fireworks just as much as your company needs to quickly unload the inventory so you won't have to eat the cost. Make us a deal we can't refuse and it's a win/win situation for everyone..."

Mayor Cliffburg stroked his chin with his fingertips, marveling at her bold, yet dignified approach. She was charming the pants off the man on the other end of the line—*no surprise there.* In fact, if she pushed hard enough, they'd probably get the damn fireworks for free."

"... How soon can you get 'em to us? We're located in the Florida Panhandle... *Really*? Well, I think you've got yourself a deal!"

She recited the city's credit card information, as well as the billing and shipping addresses. "Thanks, Henry. Happy New Year to you, too."


After placing the handset back into position, she slumped,

allowing her head to thump against the desk. "I'm not sure how we managed this", she began, her voice slightly muffled, "but we'll have twenty-four fireworks delivered by Saturday at half-price."

"Half-price?" he questioned as he stepped closer, reaching out to touch her shoulders. "That's definitely something to celebrate..."

Lana tensed the moment she felt his hands. It wasn't necessarily that he was touching her—she'd been his secretary for almost seven years, now. And when you worked closely with someone you were bound to accidently touch.

But this wasn't accidental.

This was more than a simple, nonchalant touch—this was a caress. His fingertips grazed her bare arms, raising the hair on the back of her neck. Lifting her head from the desk, she quickly glanced over her shoulder. "I have to go. It's late." He must have sensed her discomfort, because suddenly the unpleasant sensations of his fondling fingertips were gone.

"You mean, you don't have time for a celebratory cocktail? C'mon, this is a big deal, Lana; we just dodged a bullet! Just one drink", he gestured with his finger.

"I'm sorry", she uttered as she collected her belongings. "I can't. Randall's watching Connor... He's waiting for me."


The mayor unclenched his jaw and shoved his hands in his trouser pockets. He thought even less of Randall Burns than he had Jimmy Phillips. The man was a hothead, a smartass, and a drunk. "Randall?—not sure that was such a good idea, Lana."

"Why do you say that?"

He shrugged, buying time while he carefully chose his words. "He's... ill-mannered. Is that really the kind of influence you want on your son?"

Lana slid her other arm into her black blazer and then ran her hands under the collar to free her long brown locks. "He's been nothing but kind to me and Connor over the years. And besides, I didn't have much choice considering the circumstances."

Mayor Cliffburg opened his mouth to say something, but quickly thought better of it. If he pushed she'd only get defensive, and if there was one thing he did know, it was that Randall Burns didn't deserve one ounce of her blind devotion. "Fair enough. So about that celebratory drink... Maybe some other time?"

"I don't know. We'll see." Lana tossed her purse over her shoulder and turned to go. She was several paces from the front entrance when she heard his voice again.

"Good work tonight, Lana. As usual, you never cease to amaze me..."

"Hey, I'm really sorry it took so long", Lana spoke as she carefully nudged the front door closed behind her.

Clicking the TV off, Randall rose from the couch and shoved his hands knuckle-deep into the pockets of his denim jeans. "You get everything straightened out at the office?"

"After spending hours on the phone on a wild-goose chase, I managed to find a company in Atlanta with enough fireworks to get us by this year." She quickly glanced around the room, noting how uncharacteristically quiet it was for eight-thirty in the evening. "Where's Connor?"

"He fell asleep about twenty minutes ago watching cartoons."

"Really?" she asked incredulously as she lowered her purse from her shoulder. She gently placed it on the entry table she'd faux-finished earlier this month and tucked a strand of hair behind her ear. "That early?"

Randall nodded, scratching the back of his head. "He helped me on the boat for a bit before we grabbed pizza. Think I wore the little guy out."

"You are just full of surprises", she mumbled softly, smiling. "Let me just check on him. I'll be right back."

Slowly pacing back and forth, Randall tried to convince himself her praise meant nothing, that her angelic and genuine smile held no significance.

But then he'd be lying. Because it had.

And somehow just knowing he'd been the one to ease her

weary mind tonight—that he'd been the person she'd turned to—created emotions he'd long forgotten. A sense of warmth, along with something he couldn't quite name, quickly multiplied and unfurled deep in his chest. It was a feeling he feared he'd become too fond of if he wasn't careful.

"You were right. He's exhausted—didn't move a muscle when I kissed him good night!"

*Lucky kid.* Randall cleared his throat. "Anything else you need before I go?"

Lana crossed her arms as she studied him from across the room. "Yeah, you can have a drink with me. After the day I had, I could use one."

He wavered for a moment or two. It would probably be better if he left; it'd taken every ounce of control he possessed not to act on his feelings when she'd walked through the front door. He didn't really understand them, and it was *that* admission that scared him most.

His fascination with Lana had only intensified since the night in his truck nearly a month ago. It seemed she'd gone from Jimmy's sweet, innocent wife to the beautiful woman starring in his graphically-erotic fantasies almost overnight.

And that's where she had to stay, because acting on them would only complicate matters.

Being alone with Lana would only test his resistance—something he knew would fail him when she looked at him like that: her eyes pleading, her teeth nibbling on that plump bottom lip. Randall opened his mouth to decline her invitation, except when the words materialized on his tongue, he couldn't seem to voice them. "Yeah, sure."

Lana smiled nervously, surprised by the jittery reaction her body had. "Okay, be right back."

Moments later she reappeared from the kitchen carrying two wine goblets filled with white zinfandel. "I'm sorry. I know you're not much of a wine drinker, but this is all I have." She placed his glass on the coffee table and sat beside him, tucking her legs underneath her.

As the clock on the mantel steadily ticked, they engaged in casual conversation, neither rehashing the difficulties of celebrating Christmas just two days earlier. Randall couldn't help but notice how their somewhat meaningless exchange was in direct contrast to her rigidness. She seemed... ill at ease. He eyed her for a few long beats as she spoke about the mass invasion of weeds smothering her Autumn Joy plants.

"With it getting dark earlier now, I haven't really had much time to stay on top of it, you know? And lately it's been raining so much, even the weekends are a complete bust."

Was it her?—or was Randall carefully examining her? She'd put a lot of effort into duping him, wanting him to believe she was at peace: her mind, body, and spirit coexisting in complete harmony. Apparently he wasn't buying it. "Okay, what?" She finally asked. "You're looking at me like you're trying to figure something out."

"Guess I'm busted. So... is everything all right with you?"

Lana captured the edge of the wine glass between her lips and took a small sip. "Yeah, why do you ask?"

"You just seem kind of...*tense*. Probably more so when you first came home, but you're definitely still keyed up about something."

Tilting her head slightly, she regarded him. "You weren't paying attention to a single word I've said in the last five minutes, were you?"

"Sure I was—I can multi-task—and quit trying to change the subject."

"Multi-tasking? Didn't think men were capable of something difficult like that!" she teased.

But then he gave her *The Look*: his bullshit detector. It shouldn't have surprised her, really. She was knee-deep in it and he knew it. With a defeated sigh, she answered, "It's just my job. I'm finding it more and more difficult to handle these days... for a lot of reasons—too many to go into right now."

"If it's making you *this* unhappy", he emphasized with his hand in a sweeping motion, "then why don't you just quit?"

"Because I need this job. I can't afford to lose it."

"Okay, so in the meantime search for something else."

"I never finished college, Randall. And there isn't exactly a high demand for secretaries in Franklin County, at the moment."

Lana swirled the glass in her hand, watching as the blush liquid climbed the sides of the goblet, taking on a whirlpool-like form. "By the way, if I didn't mention it before I really appreciate your help tonight with Connor. I honestly don't know what I would've done if you hadn't stepped in and rescued me again."

"Glad it worked out."

"Me, too." Drawing the glass to her lips, she swallowed another sip, eyeing Randall's wine still sitting on the coffee table where she'd placed it half an hour earlier. Gesturing toward his glass, she finally asked, "Aren't you going to drink that?"

He didn't really want to. The damn wine was...*pink*, for heaven's sake. But she was so damn alluring, looking up at him with those midnight eyes, long lashes fluttering—hypnotizing him. In fact, he was pretty damn certain he'd stand up and hop on one foot right now if she asked him to. Lucky for him, she was only suggesting he take a sip.

Reaching forward, he gripped the dainty glass filled with pink alcohol in his large hand and brought it to his lips. He swallowed a meager portion, wincing as though he'd sucked the juice of a sour lemon. "Ugh. How the hell do you drink that shit?" He questioned, setting the glass back on the coffee table.

"*Shit*...? I'll have you know this is a high quality white zinfandel. And really, I could say the same thing about that god-awful whiskey you like to drink."

Randall allowed his weight to settle back onto the sofa. "First of all, Sweetheart, that high quality shit you're referring to is pink—not white. And drinking whiskey is practically in the man code."

"All right, well is there something in the 'man code' about the color pink?"

Randall rubbed the coarse stubble along his jaw with the back of his fingers, trying desperately to suppress his growing grin. "No, we happen to like the color pink."

Somehow Lana didn't think they were still discussing wine. "So since I obviously don't have any whiskey, what're you gonna do? I wouldn't want anyone to revoke your man card or anything."

God, she was pretty. And the best part was: she had no idea the affect—the power—she had over him. He was spellbound, lured by the longing in her eyes, captivated by the fiery spark spontaneously ignited whenever they were near one another.

Right now he wasn't worried about his fucking man card. Nope, and she wouldn't be either if she'd noticed the massive bulge expanding behind his zipper.

Unable to control the impulse to touch her, Randall reached behind her head, palming the back of her neck; noting how his hand seemed to fit perfectly there. His eyes raked over her delicate features, and it was then he noticed the light sprinkling of freckles scattered along her nose.

Lana's heart raced.

*Kiss me. Kiss me...*

She'd been here before: her face inches from his, staring into steel-colored eyes, silently pleading for him to narrow the distance until their mouths collided.

*Kiss me, please. Just kiss me...*

Gazing into her midnight orbs, Randall sought confirmation that she was feeling this pull between them, too. And when the answer in her eyes reflected the yearning in his, he inched forward until his mouth landed against her soft pink lips.

He clung to his restraint for a few long beats, his lips lightly grazing over hers, giving her time to push him away if she was having second thoughts. And when that didn't happen, he swept his tongue inside her mouth, finally tasting what he'd been dreaming about for nearly a month.

The moment their tongues collided, he was a goner. Even knowing how wrong this was he didn't stop—couldn't stop.

And judging by the faint moan that'd escaped from the back of her throat she didn't want him to, either.

Their unhurried kiss continued, tongues waltzing in harmony, slow and steady; delicately crossing uncharted boundaries by testing the unspoken attraction that'd unintentionally blossomed between them.

Randall's left hand remained on the back of her neck as his right slowly began wandering. His fingertips lightly grazed her shoulder, down her arm, and almost immediately he felt the ripple of goosebumps beneath his fingertips, temporarily marring her satiny skin. Just knowing he had that effect on her created a reckless hunger within him. Desperate to get closer, he gathered her in his arms and hauled her onto his lap.

Lana settled onto his lap the best she could in her black skirt, straddling his powerful thighs while he feasted on her mouth. God, she was burning up, ablaze with need, so raptured by the thrill of the moment that her hands trembled against his solid chest. His strong hands kneaded into her backside, pulling her closer still. But when she felt the pressure of his rigid length against her aching center, she panicked.

He was a crazed man, his desire for Lana eating him from the inside. Blood roared in his ears as his heart pounded, quickly draining south to his painfully-throbbing cock. Palming her sweet ass, he raked her body over his dick, realizing immediately that he'd taken it too far. Lana's malleable body suddenly stiffened, and the next thing he knew the pressure of her sweet mouth was gone as she scrambled to her feet.

Lana backed away, wrapping her arms around her middle. "I-I think you should go."

"I'm sorry. I shouldn't have... I didn't mean to..." Randall scrubbed his palm down his face. "Christ", he mumbled. "Maybe we should talk about what just happened."

Lana's head rapidly shook from side-to-side. "No, I... Please, just go."

He sat motionless, staring at her, his desire and his conscience waging a brutal battle. He didn't want to leave things like this—not when he knew he was the cause of her rattled state.

"*Please*", she pleaded again just above a whisper. She didn't know how much longer she could suppress the growing wave of hysteria mounting inside her chest. She closed her eyes as though doing so would magically make him disappear, as if it could erase the reality of what she'd done.

No good would come from him staying, and yet knowing this, he didn't want to go. But this wasn't about what he wanted. "Okay." Rising from the couch, Randall stood and journeyed to the front door. He was halfway through it when he suddenly stopped, gripping the jamb. He looked skyward for a moment before turning back to glance at her over his shoulder one last time. "Good night, Lana."

And just like that he was gone, leaving Lana alone with the ticking clock and a whale of a guilty conscience. The sound of his ignition caused a cold shiver to work its way down her spine.

She couldn't help but feel like a tease. God, what Randall must think of her...

She'd wanted him to kiss her; he'd known that. And when he'd acted on the impulse she'd felt alive, consumed by unbridled desire—so consumed she'd lost sight of who she was—who *Randall* was.

Randall was Jimmy's best friend, for heaven's sake! He was the *one man* on the planet she wasn't supposed to be kissing! She didn't believe in ghosts, but she wondered if Jimmy's spirit was spitting nails right now, having witnessed the two people he'd trusted so implicitly, kissing on his sofa.

Because it'd been wrong.

Hadn't it?

Lana ran her trembling fingertips over her lips, still slightly wet and swollen from their kiss. If it had been so utterly wrong, why had it felt so right? Why had the sensation of Randall's lips pressed against hers felt so reviving?—like she had suddenly wakened from a deep sleep?

She'd never get over the heartbreak of losing Jimmy.

Ever.

But she was so tired of being lonely. So tired of lying awake at night wishing she could change the past. Wishing she had the courage to carve a new future.

Wishing for a different life.

If only there was a formula to follow, some semblance of guidance printed clearly in black and white designating each part of the grieving process; a model to guide her, indicating the appropriate time to start thinking about moving on with her life.

She'd worry about that another time, because right now she needed to wash away the agony, the despair.

And the embarrassment.

Covering her mouth, Lana suppressed a fleeing sob as she trudged into the bathroom. Turning the faucet to the hottest setting, she slowly removed her clothes.

She had more tears to cry and a shower drain more than willing to collect them.

# Chapter 12

The sound of the local weatherman's voice greeted Randall as his lids slowly fluttered open. He'd finally fallen asleep on the couch about three-thirty this morning, and judging by the time displayed in the lower right hand corner of the television, that'd been roughly three hours ago. No wonder his lids felt akin to coarse sandpaper.

He'd gone to The Saloon after leaving Lana's last night, hoping the consumption of Jack Daniels would siphon the memory of that kiss. And when that hadn't happened, he'd come home to a quiet, empty house, the memory of Lana's soft lips in tow.

Damn, he'd really made a mess of things.

He probably should've left the moment she returned last night, but there was just something about sweet, beautiful Lana he couldn't resist. Something about the way she looked at him.

Something about the way she made him feel.

Randall slowly swung his legs over the sofa cushions until his feet made contact with the knotted-Pine floor. Resting his elbows on his knees, he hung his head, running his fingers through his jet-black hair. He'd made a promise to Jimmy, agreeing to take care of Connor and Lana in his absence. The man had saved his life, and in return Randall had skipped town for five months and made-out with his wife…

What kind of man did that to his best friend?

A no-good, worthless, selfish son of a bitch, that's who.

For Chrissakes, Jimmy died saving him! The man had sacrificed precious years with his son, decades with the woman he loved, without hesitation. And knowing the kind of man Jimmy was, he'd probably do it again if given the opportunity. Randall figured the very least he could do was keep his hands to himself.

Rising from the couch, he quickly changed his clothes and brushed his teeth. He had to make this right. Lana needed to know she could count on him, that he wouldn't take advantage of her like he had the night before. With a hasty step he moved outside, carefully loading the tools he'd need for the laborious job that lay ahead.

Randall was going to honor his promise to Jimmy, keeping his hands off Lana—even if it killed him. And now that he knew the texture of her soft lips, experienced the perfection of her body under his fingertips, tasted heaven in her kiss, he conceded that it just might.


Lana poured a splash of milk into the steaming bowl of cinnamon instant oatmeal she'd made for Connor and gently placed it in front of him on the kitchen table. "Be careful stirring that up; it's really hot."

"Thought you said we were havin' French toast?" Connor whined.

"Don't have time this morning. I woke up late. Maybe tomorrow, okay?" Lana stole a glance at Connor over her shoulder before pouring her coffee. She felt guilty about nixing the French toast menu this morning. But after spending most of the night tossing and turning, reliving every blessed moment of kissing Randall, then silently scolding herself for having enjoyed it, she'd been too tired to get moving this morning.

"I need to finish getting ready. We're leaving in twenty minutes, okay?"

Connor never said a word, just kept shoveling spoonfuls of instant oatmeal in his mouth. The kid sure could lay the guilt on thick. As if she hadn't had enough to feel guilty about already...

Moving into the master bath, Lana quickly pulled her long brown trusses into a loose bun and applied a thin layer of mineral foundation, paying particular attention to the dark circles under her weary eyes. After a few sweeps with her mascara wand and a light coat of nude lipstick, she selected a winter-white pant suit from her overstuffed closet.

She really needed to think about packing Jimmy's stuff. It would solve the cramped conditions in her closet, giving her ample room to store her clothes and accessories. Funny how she'd often complained to Jimmy about sharing the small space. Lana couldn't recall how many times she'd suggested he store his clothes in the guest room, and now that she was capable of acting on her frequent request, she wasn't entirely certain if she still wanted to.

Refusing to allow her thoughts to travel down that road this morning, she stepped into a pair of taupe heels, surveying the ensemble in the mirror while she fastened a pair of simple pearl studs to her ears.

To her relief, she looked the same.

Good.

Because on the inside she felt…different. She wasn't entirely sure whether different was a good thing or a bad thing just yet, she was still trying to figure that out. But at least there were no scarlet letters adorned to her blazer; no outward visible signs illustrating the scene that'd unfolded last night between her and Randall.

Satisfied with her overall appearance, she headed to the living room where Connor sat watching cartoons. "Did you brush your teeth?"

"Yeah."

Lana grabbed her purse on the entry table and flung the strap over her shoulder. "All right, turn the TV off. It's time to go." Connor begrudgingly did as she asked, then joined her at the front door.

After days of overcast skies and misty rain, she was delighted to find the golden sun beginning its climb over the horizon. And as she scaled down the porch steps, she was shocked to find something—*or rather, someone*—else: Randall kneeling in her flower bed, tossing weeds into a neat pile beside him.

Her body froze in mid-step as her eyes drank him in. The thin cotton t-shirt clung to his broad back, brawny muscle rippling underneath. Oh boy...

"Whatcha doin'?" Connor asked excitedly as he zoomed down the steps.

So much for being discreet.

Randall's head snapped up at the sound of Connor's voice. His eyes quickly averted to Lana before returning to Connor. "Just a little bit of yard work for your mom. Careful", he warned when Connor reached down to pull a nearby weed, "I don't want you to get your nice clothes dirty."

"Can I help?" Connor asked hopefully.

Lana finally unfroze and found her voice. "You have to go to day camp, remember?"

"I think I'm gonna just stay here with Randall."

"I don't think so."

"Randall don't care, do ya?" he uttered confidently as he turned to him.

Lana didn't give Randall an opportunity to answer before interrupting, "I paid a lot of money for this two-week program, Connor. You're going."

"But you let me hang out with him last night" he whined.

She could feel Randall's eyes boring into her, assessing the extent of the damage he'd inflicted last night. Feeling as though she needed to kill two birds with one stone, she chose her response carefully, leaving Randall to sort the hidden meaning as she returned his inquisitive gaze. "Last night was...a one-time deal."

Lana glanced at her watch, then back at Connor. "Go get in the car, okay? I don't want to be late." Shoulders slumped and head hung low, Connor shuffled to the driveway.

Glancing over his shoulder, Randall called out, "I'll stop by on Sunday. Maybe we can head to the beach and throw the Frisbee around, if it's okay with your mom."

Connor turned on a dime, searching Lana's pretty face with hopeful eyes. And when she nodded, the boy threw his hands in the air in celebration before sprinting to the car.

With her son out of earshot, Lana turned her attention

back to Randall. "What are you doing?"

"Pulling weeds", he answered as he stood, dusting his dirty hands on the side of his legs. "Told you I was paying attention last night."

She tried to suppress her grin, but the corners of her mouth disobeyed. She was relieved he wasn't angry with her for leading him on, then kicking him out. But then, that was Randall: flexible, always friendly, and forgiving. "I stand corrected; guess you *can* multi-task. A little.

"Among other things", he remarked with a wry grin.

Lana's cheeks took on a rosy hue, recalling the *other things* they'd done last night.

"Thought I'd even trim your hedges while I'm here too."

"You don't have to do this, Randall, really—any of this", she kindly emphasized as she swept her hand in the air.

"It's okay. I want to…"

Seconds ticked by as they both silently dared one another to be the first to acknowledge the kiss. Shifting his weight, Randall finally cleared his throat. "Look, I'm, uh… I'm sorry about last night. I crossed the line and I shouldn't have. It won't happen again."

Lana's eye's quickly found her feet. She didn't know whether to be relieved or disappointed. That kiss had knocked her completely off her axis. "You're forgiven. It was…a crazy, one-time incident, you know? No need to dwell on it."

"Yeah…" He wasn't entirely sure who she was trying to convince at the moment, but either way she was right. It couldn't happen again; he needn't forget that.

# Chapter 13

Winter's grip loosened on the Florida Panhandle by early March, high temperatures rising into the low eighties for the first time since late November. Spring was Randall's favorite time of year. Mild daytime temperatures and refreshing Gulf winds made favorable conditions for boating, and a breath of chill was still detectable upon nightfall.

His life had settled into an almost predictable routine, consisting of work, restoring his boat, and quality time with Jimmy's family. And at night when he returned to his quiet, empty house, he turned to an old trusted friend: Jack Daniels. The amber liquid had become his M.O., a fundamental part of who he was. Guess he was more like his old man than he wanted to admit.

Nearly two months had passed since he'd thoughtlessly kissed Jimmy's widow. So far he'd managed to keep his hands—and lips—off Lana Phillips.

Barely.

There were times he'd clench his fists so hard to keep from touching her, he feared he'd shatter the bones in his hands. He wondered if maybe the allure had to do more with hungering for something he couldn't have, rather than...

*Ah, shit, who the hell was he trying to fool?*

He wanted her. Wanted to hear his name fleeing her luscious lips as he buried himself deep in her beautiful body; learn all the places she liked to be touched and kissed...

But just because a person wanted, didn't mean they had a

right to have. Most folks wanted to be a millionaire. That didn't give them the prerogative to enter a bank and demand a slew of cash. It was the nature of our species: always wanting something more, something extraordinary.

And extraordinary didn't even begin to describe Lana Phillips.

Randall parked his truck along the narrow street. He reached for the wrapped gift on the passenger seat, then strolled up the path, up three porch steps, until he came upon a familiar red door. He let himself in, something he'd been told to do on numerous occasions over the last month or so, and gently nudged the door closed behind him.

He was immediately accosted with the sound of rambunctious shrills likely emanating from the backyard. With a cautious gait, he followed the squeals and laughter into the kitchen, stumbling upon a pretty woman with long, light brown locks and graceful curves even the great Michelangelo couldn't recreate.

She hadn't detected his presence yet, and like a deer caught in a blinding beam of headlights, he froze, too stunned to move. Too stunned to do anything other than watch as she swayed and sang quietly to herself while clearing paper plates from the kitchen table.


The stressful portion of Connor's birthday party was now complete. The kids had devoured the cake, watched excitedly as Connor ripped into his presents, and were now all outside beating the life out of a Spiderman piñata. Needing a break away from the mounting chaos caused by an overdose of sugar, no doubt, she'd put Grant and Ty in charge of the affair, and Olivia and Kendall in charge of photographing the event.

It'd been a rather tough day celebrating her son's sixth birthday without the man that had aided in his creation. There wasn't a day that went by she didn't think of Jimmy, but the piercing anguish she'd experienced immediately following his death had lessoned into more of a steady ache. Most days.

At least once a month there was a special day that would remind Lana of her late husband. Last month she'd encountered her very first St Valentine's Day without a valentine since she was fifteen. That day had been spent painting her newly decorated living room—anything to keep her mind busy. Holidays and milestones like these were particularly difficult to endure. Days like these—like today—Jimmy's absence was ironically palpable...

Refusing to allow her mind to be sucked into a vortex of sorrow and despair, she shifted gears, humming the melody of a Katy Perry song she'd heard earlier in the day on the radio. She tossed paper cups printed with spider webs in the trash, and began stacking used paper plates on top of one another.

*"Let's go all the way tonight*
*No regrets, just love..."*

Lana twirled around, then nearly fell when she realized Randall was leaning his shoulder against the wall, watching her.

"*Omigod!*" she gasped as she smacked her free hand against her chest, soothing her racing heart. "You scared the daylights out of me! How long have you been standing there?"

"Long enough to be serenaded by your pretty voice", he responded with a wry grin. "Sorry I'm late. Got carried away workin' on the boat and lost track of time."

Obviously Randall was amused by her performance. She wasn't so much embarrassed by the fact he'd stumbled upon her dancing and singing in her kitchen as she was about the lyrics she'd mouthed. Those lyrics had been sung with him in mind, something she was afraid he'd detect if she didn't regain the upper hand.

And quickly. "Hmm, unable to glance at his watch *and* sand his boat at the same time", she uttered as she stroked her chin. "Guess you're not as good at multi-tasking as you once thought."

Randall shook his head at her witty remark, feeling the

corners of his mouth rise once again. The woman was determined to prove to him that men were pretty much incapable of dividing their focus amongst more than one thing at any given time—which was often true, but not always. He could think of one activity in particular he excelled at.

*Exploring the female form...*

"I take it I missed the cake and presents?"

"Don't worry about it; he can open your gift later once everyone leaves. Which"—Lana glanced at her watch—"should be in about thirty minutes, thank goodness."

"Rough day?" He asked as he placed Connor's gift on the counter.

Lana chuckled under her breath. "I think *rough* is a bit of an understatement."

"Too much of a good thing never hurt anyone."

She tossed the last paper plate into the trash, then crossed her arms. "Define 'good', because there are currently ten six-year-olds' in the backyard that have probably binged on two pounds of sugar a piece, beating the crap out of a Spiderman piñata. Go ahead", she gestured with a tilt of her head, "see for yourself."

Ambling toward the small window he peered through the glass at the pandemonium unfolding several feet from the back fence. Grant and Ty were doing their best to curb the mass disorder while Kendall and Olivia documented the sugar-induced debacle with their clicking cameras. "I might need a beer for this", he mumbled under his breath.

Lana laughed as she gathered the plastic Spiderman tablecloth in her hands. "I bought you some Miller Lite. It's in the fridge."

Randall walked several paces to the refrigerator, trying to convince himself that Lana's thoughtful gesture didn't mean anything. That keeping his favorite beer on hand, even though she couldn't stand the stuff, was of no consequence. Opening the fridge he reached for the bottle, twisting the cap as he moved toward the back door. "If I'm not back in twenty minutes, come rescue me."

The sound of Lana's laughter echoed in his ears as he closed the door behind him and began the fearless trek across the yard. Well, maybe *fearless* was a stretch; ten six-year-olds' cracked-out on sugar was a pretty scary thing to be walking into.

He was roughly halfway when Kendall spotted him. "I was wondering if you were going to show!" She called out, coming toward him.

Randall pulled her in for a hug, surprised when he didn't feel that familiar jolt of unease. He'd fallen for Kendall two years ago—had even spent one night loving on her body—but she hadn't felt the same way about him. She'd wanted to remain friends. He'd gone along with it for a while, hoping she'd change her mind, but as soon as Ty had come into the picture Randall hadn't stood a chance. "Where's Tenley?"

"With my mom. We're heading over there as soon as the party's over to pick her up. You should stop over some time and visit. She's three months already; you wouldn't believe how big she's grown since the last time you saw her a few weeks ago."

Kendall slipped from his embrace. *Hmm, that was odd...* He didn't get that empty feeling, the one where his chest ached where his heart used to sit when she'd stepped away. "Yeah... I'll come by soon."

"Hey, you gonna stand there and paw at my wife, or are you gonna help us?" Ty shouted teasingly.

"Ignore him", Kendall mumbled, cupping her hand to cover her mouth. "This is his first glimpse into what we're in store for in a few years. At this rate, I think Tenley might be an only child."

Randall laughed and then swung his arm over her shoulders. "C'mon, Babe, guess we'd better get back over there, then."


This was ridiculous, ludicrous, and just about every other synonym that ended in *o-u-s*, Lana conceded as she peered through the kitchen window at Kendall and Randall. So they were hugging—big deal. Kendall was married to Ty, head-over-heels in love with her husband, she might add. And Randall...? Well, Lana had no claim on Randall; he wasn't hers.

*Then why are you spying through your kitchen window like a jealous girlfriend?*

Lana began picking at her lilac nail polish, suddenly overwhelmed with where her thoughts were taking her.

Randall had been there for her and Connor—maybe not at first—but he'd certainly made up for his five-month absence in stride. He'd call to check on them at least once a day, and stop over four or five days out of the week to play with Connor, giving her a break. He'd sort of stepped into the role of man of the house, becoming the primary male influence in Connor's life, even though Randall didn't live here.

She was becoming fond of his regular presence—maybe too fond. And that was both exciting and frightening. Because she wasn't supposed to feel this way about the man that'd been almost like a brother to her late husband. She wasn't supposed to stock his favorite beer in her fridge, look forward to the sound of his work boots thumping across her wood floor, nor search for him in a crowded room.

She wasn't supposed to want the one man she couldn't have.

With a frustrated sigh she pushed off the counter, poured a glass of sweet tea, then willed her feet to take her to the backyard. She needed to get over these... these...*feelings* she was having. Stuff it down until later when she'd be alone. Because right now she needed to brave the rest of the party, as well as the quality time she'd spend with Connor and Randall after the celebration ended.


Dusk was swallowed by darkness by the time Connor finally mellowed from his sugar high. Lana sat on the couch watching Randall assemble a Lego toy Connor received for his birthday. The scene seemed so ordinary to the naked eye, but it was far from conventional.

It was remarkable to witness, actually, which explained why her Cosmo magazine lay open and neglected on her lap. The scene was reminiscent of years past when Jimmy was still alive. He'd been a phenomenal father and when he died

Lana struggled to fill the void he left behind. She tried to be everything she was and everything good that Jimmy had been and had somehow managed to lose her way. She'd been drifting—simply existing—until Randall came back last October. He'd stepped in and rescued her.

Randall had become her rock, lending his strength to her battered soul—never asking for anything in return. She'd even noticed a positive change in Connor. His bad language had improved, she no longer worried about ill-timed four-letter obscenities, and she couldn't remember the last time Connor's teacher had phoned indicating he was sick.

The colossal wake created after Jimmy's death was finally beginning to settle. Their lives would never be the same, but slowly they'd established a new "normal." A new family dynamic.

Of course, she'd seen the looks—overheard the whispers—from some of the folks in town. There were several overly judgmental people that believed her family dynamic was a bit unorthodox; that Randall's regular presence was odd. Strange. Peculiar, even. She tried to ignore it, tried to tell herself that the feelings she harbored for Randall Burns were purely platonic.

But with each sunrise and sunset, she was becoming less sure...

"I almost forgot", Randall said as he rose from the floor, "You have one more present to open."

"From who?" Connor inquired excitedly.

"From me. Sit tight, I'll be right back." Randall disappeared into the kitchen, returning moments later with a flat box, clumsily wrapped in Spiderman paper. He placed the gift on Connor's lap, and within a nanosecond Connor tore into the paper like a piranha during a feeding frenzy.

"Cool!" Connor removed the last remnants of paper, then rotated the box in his little hands. "What is it?"

"Twister... You've never heard of Twister before?" Connor shook his head from side-to-side.

"Damn, I feel old", Randall mumbled to Lana, wryly. "Okay", he said, turning his attention back to Connor, "It's real simple. One person spins while the others play. When the spinner calls out, 'left foot on red', everyone puts their left foot on red, but you have to keep it there until you're told to move your left foot somewhere else. Understand?"

Connor's head bobbed up and down. "Can we play?"

"Sure", Lana answered, snatching the box from Connor's grip. She opened the game and spread the polka-dotted mat on the floor in front of the coffee table, then tossed the spinner board at Randall. "Think you can spin and call out the combination at the same time, Mr. Multi-tasker?" She asked, smiling.

Randall chuckled under his breath. "I think I can manage."

It didn't take long for Connor to become distracted by the allure of the spinner, leaving Lana behind in a rather compromising position: bent over with her ass in the air.

"Can we trade places?" he asked Randall. "I wanna spin now."

Maybe he should've purchased Monopoly instead, he thought to himself as he approached the tangled woman on the mat. There was nothing sexual about nudging a thimble around a board. "Let see what we have here", he mumbled as he deciphered what color each of his extremities were to be placed. Hovering above her, Randall stretched his limbs until his hands and feet mirrored Lana's.

Connor began shouting combinations, laughing as the two struggled to move, while Lana and Randall bantered back and forth.

Who knew a simple game of Twister could incite so much trash talk?

Randall had never seen this competitive side to her before. Her taunts were sort of weak and unoriginal, but that made the whole experience that much more enjoyable. Her walls were down. She was being silly, having fun. And Randall thought she'd never looked more beautiful than she did at that very moment.

Concentration severed, Randall's foot slipped and his sturdy frame suddenly warped. His knee came down to cushion the fall causing his hip to nudge into the back of Lana's leg, and like a house of cards, they both collapsed.

Howling with laughter they remained on the mat until their cackles quieted, suddenly aware they were lying next to one another, limbs still tangled.

Their eyes met and held for several moments before Randall cleared his throat, unwinding their coiled extremities. He then stood and offered his hands.

Lana stared at his calloused palms for a few long beats before placing her trembling hands in his. In one swift motion, she found herself on her feet staring into two hungry gray eyes. His stone-like expression may have been neutral, but the intensity of his heated gaze spread warmth across her skin like a sweltering summer's day.

"I'd better go before this kid gets me injured", Randall uttered, tilting his head slightly toward the sofa behind him.

*Holy cow*, she'd been so wrapped up in Randall—the way his perceptive eyes bored into hers, the sensation of his powerful body blanketing her small frame—she'd all but forgotten her six-year-old son was still in the room. "Um, yeah...that would probably be smart..."

His thumbs lightly scaled over her knuckles, almost as if instinct had overpowered reason. Such an insignificant touch, yet overwhelmingly endearing. She couldn't help but wonder if he'd meant something by it, if his modest caress had been a way to communicate the unfeigned pleasure he experienced by merely touching her.

Because she was reveling in the simple brush of his fingertips.

As if he'd read her thoughts, Randall released her hands and turned to Connor. "See ya tomorrow, kiddo", he declared, rustling the boy's blond hair before snatching his shoes from the floor.

"Can we play this game again next time?" Connor questioned excitedly. "It makes me laugh when grown-ups' fall!"

Randall finished sliding his feet into his shoes and straightened his large six-foot frame. "Guess we'll see what happens."

His eyes skittered to Lana one last time before he turned to go, leaving him to decipher the irony of Connor's parting words. Because falling wasn't funny—not when he feared he was beginning to *fall* for his best friend's widow...

# Chapter 14

"Man, what's gotten in to you tonight, huh?" Grant asked as he leaned his hip against the edge of the pool table.

Randall straightened his upper body and reached for his mug of Miller Lite after missing another clear shot. It couldn't have been a more perfect set up: the solid number three was perfectly aligned with the center pocket, but he'd managed to miss it.

Why? Well, it may have been a mystery to everyone else, but not him. Nope, the person responsible for his uncanny performance stood roughly seven inches shorter than his six-foot frame, with long light brown locks and lethal curves, wearing a white cotton dress and those damn fuck-me cowgirl boots...

"Maybe I'm feeling guilty about takin' your hard earned cash every weekend", Randall shouted over the music. "Until tonight, I can't remember the last time I actually bought myself a beer here...Thought maybe I'd give you a break."

Grant laughed with such intensity, he had to grab hold of the billiard table to keep his balance. "C'mon, man, are you shittin' me?" he finally asked once his cackles quieted. "You're one of the most competitive people I know. You can't stand to lose! What's going on with you? *Really*."

Grant followed Randall's gaze, which just so happened to be on Lana, swaying with newly-single Tommy Carson on the dance floor.

Tommy worked with the guys at the station. He was

younger than Randall; graduated with Lana back in '03, and had joined the fire department about five years ago. He'd been married to Jenny for nearly three years now, but rumors of Jenny's infidelity had surfaced just days into the new year. He didn't seem too torn up about their separation at the moment, Randall acknowledged—considering how he held Lana's body close on the dance floor.

"Lana's a big girl—a *good* girl", Grant emphasized. "No way would she let Tommy—"

"That's not what I was thinking", Randall retorted as he stepped around Grant to align his next shot.

"Really?—'cause you looked nearly rabid a minute ago. In fact, you still kind of do! Listen, at some point she's gonna move on, you know? You can't stand guard just because you think Jimmy would 've been—"

"That's not what I was doin'. Just drop it, already, okay?" Randall hovered over the table, stretching his body over the green felt to gain better access. He ran the cue stick over his left thumb several times to get the feel of it, then forced the chalked-tip against the white cue ball. The white cue accelerated, striking the orange number five ball, the clank of the collision rising above the blaring melody of music.

Number five barreled down the table at near lightning speed, charging toward the right corner pocket. He watched as the orange sphere vanished from view, followed by the white cue as it, too, disappeared into the pocket.

"*Fuck!*" Scratching was a beginner mistake—something he hadn't done in years—at least, not on purpose.

Randall straightened, then glanced over his shoulder at the dance floor, feeling helplessly enraged by the image of Tommy's hands on his sweet Lana.

*His?*

Since when had he laid claim on Lana Phillips?

Reaching into his back pocket for his wallet, he fished a crisp twenty dollar bill from the hidden groove. He laid it on the table and shoved the wallet back into his rear pocket, then swallowed the remainder of his Miller Lite in one massive gulp. "Beer's on me tonight. I've gotta go." He started to walk away, but Grant's baffled tone stopped him in his tracks.

"Wait!—where are you going? It's not even ten o'clock yet!"

Randall turned back to Grant, speaking through clenched teeth. "As far away from the temptation of beating that sorry bastard—" he gestured toward Tommy "—as I can get." Pivoting, he weaved through the growing crowd, his vision almost tunnel-like as he focused on the heavy wood doors that led to the boardwalk.

He barely remembered climbing into his truck, let alone the short five-minute drive home. When he finally emerged from his deranged daze, he was still sitting behind the wheel in his driveway, the radio quiet, his engine idling.

Fuck, he was so screwed... The familiarity of the situation couldn't be overlooked. He was on the verge of falling for an unavailable woman. Again.

Randall climbed out of his truck and shoved the front door open. The house was dark. Silent. Empty. Kind of like his life.

Kicking off his leather flips flops he reached behind his head and grabbed a fistful of his white polo, then tugged it off, tossing it onto the tan sofa on his way to the kitchen. Flipping the light switch, his eyes immediately darted to the bottle of whiskey perched on the counter next to the fridge.

He needed the comfort the amber liquor provided. Needed to feel the instant gratification of fiery warmth as it trickled down his throat, burrowing deep until the heat cauterized his open wounds. Trekking across the kitchen he reached for a tumbler in the cupboard, poured three fingers of eighty-proof whiskey, then drew the glass to his lips.

Almost immediately his mouth and throat were ignited in feverish bliss. The feeling was so soothing—so fucking incredible—he swallowed another mouthful, certain he'd be too drunk to feel anything at all if he kept this up.

And that's precisely what he wanted: *to stop feeling.*

Randall wasn't exactly sure when it'd happened, but somewhere along the way he started viewing Lana Phillips as the seductively beautiful woman she so obviously was, instead of his best friend's grieving widow. Somewhere along the way the platonic nature of their friendship had shifted on its axis.

Somewhere along the way he began wanting more.

And the scariest part: the pain of chasing Kendall for two

long years, only to lose her to Ty Everitt, didn't begin to touch on the intensity of how he felt about Lana—which was completely crazy considering he and Lana had only shared one brief, incredible kiss roughly three months ago.

Eyeing his glass, Randall swallowed the remains. He feared there wasn't enough whiskey left to mask the overwhelming need mounting in his gut tonight. Maybe there'd never be...

Reaching for the bottle, he poured another round, then returned to the couch. Light from the kitchen spilled into living room, just enough to allow angular shadows to distort the silhouettes of the sparsely-placed furniture.

Seeing Lana on the dance floor tonight, her body swaying in time with the music while Tommy Carson held her close had infuriated Randall beyond reason—which was rather surprising, since he'd never considered himself the jealous type. Sure he'd been upset by Kendall's fascination with Ty Everitt last spring, but he'd never pictured beating the life out of his lieutenant. Much.

He couldn't say the same about Tommy Carson at the moment.

Tommy was a good friend of his—that was one of the things that made this entire situation odd. Hell, Randall was a groomsman in Tommy's wedding three years ago, for crying out loud! Yet just thinking about how his hands had settled on the small of Lana's back on the dance floor had Randall fantasizing about all the ways he could murder the guy.

Randall caught the edge of the tumbler between his lips, ready to drain the remnants of poison he'd poured minutes earlier in hopes of numbing the ache that resided in his chest, when the sound of the doorbell halted him. He sat motionless for several moments, praying the person on the other side would get the hint and simply go away. But when the sound came again he slammed his tumbler on the coffee table, brown liquid sloshing over the edge of the glass as he stumbled to his feet.

He hurried to the door, ready to scare the britches off the little shit on the other side. He expected to find one of the teenage boys that lived in the neighborhood, hustling to find a good hiding spot. This was Butler Island, after all. And a group of teens mischievously roaming the neighborhood on a Saturday night, ringing doorbells on a dare, then sneaking away, wasn't an uncommon occurrence.

Damn pussies. When he was their age, he and Olivia had caused quite a ruckus with the stunts they'd pulled. In fact, he was partly responsible for her Jet Ski fiasco now chronicled as the crime of the century. Yes, Olivia's three-hour joyride had caused quite a stir. In fact, that's how she'd earned the nickname DD in the first place: Daredevil. He probably should've known better than to dare her into driving off on Mr. Baker's Jet Ski that summer—he knew she'd never back down from a dare.

And he'd been right.

The doorbell rang again, jolting him from his adolescent reverie. Randall was ready to bolt through the door and run the little shit down, but standing on his front porch he didn't find a pimple-face teen.

Nope. It was *her*.

"Lana... What're you doing here?—is everything all right?"

"I-I don't know. Can I come in?"

"Yeah." Randall stepped aside, allowing her access to his sparsely furnished living room, then gently nudged the door closed behind him. "What's going on? Is it Connor?—did something happen?"

Lana shook her head, swallowing hard as her eyes dipped to his bare chest, then lower to his rippled abs. "No, Connor's with my parents. As far as I know he's fine."

Randall stepped closer, his hands nestled low on his hips. "Then what is it? What's wrong?"

"I don't know", she uttered as her focus skittered back to his analytical gaze. The room was poorly lit, light from the kitchen casting shadows along his angular face. But even in the dim light she recognized genuine concern in his somber gray eyes. "I saw you storm out of The Saloon earlier. And when I asked Grant where you went—what happened—he just said you got angry and left."

Shifting his weight onto his left foot, he answered, "I

sucked at pool tonight. It..." Randall shrugged his broad shoulders. What could he say? He could practically play eight ball with his eyes clamped shut and tonight he'd managed to lose four games in a row. "It just pissed me off, that's all."

"Is this a multi-tasking thing?" She asked smiling, trying to make light of the bleak air surrounded them.

Randall scrubbed his right hand down his face while he half-groaned, half-laughed at her playful dig. "Yeah, guess you could say that." Because what man in his right mind could witness what he'd seen on the dance floor and still be expected to be competent at another task? Hell, even something as simple as breathing had proven to be difficult while he'd stood by and watched.

"So that's it? You left because you lost a game of pool?"

"It wasn't just one loss—it was more like four—and the other reasons...well, they're complicated."

"Okay, so...explain it to me, then."

Randall shook his head. "It's not important."

"Well, it sure didn't look that way from my vantage point. Don't shut me out, Randall. You've been there for me; let me be here for you, too."

The worry in her eyes tore him to shreds. He didn't want her to waste one second fussing over him. Her midnight orbs glistened in the dim light as the uneasiness lingered. He fought the urge to reach out and touch her, reassure her, but he didn't trust himself. He was losing grip on his self-control, slipping, sliding. Fearing his restraint would fail him, he interweaved his hands behind his neck and stared skyward at the ceiling. And when the silence stretched on, Lana made the next move, taking a step forward; launching inquiries in rapid succession.

"Is it Grant?—Kendall?"

"No."

"Work?—your boat?"

Randall subtly shook his head. "No."

Lana placed her palm over her chest and asked, "Is it *me*?" She waited a few long beats for Randall to dismiss her as the subject of his fury, and when he didn't outright deny the notion immediately, she knew she was getting closer to the core of his anger. "Did I do something wrong?—something to offend you? Because you barely spoke two words to me tonight—I just don't get it! Please, Randall, *talk to me...*"

Randall groaned deep in his throat, running his hand through his black hair before placing it low on his hip again. "You really want to know?" he questioned gravelly. "Because once it's out there, I can't take it back."

She hesitated for an instant. "Yes."

Taking a deep breath, he gathered his courage, ignoring the whisper of forewarning clutching his tongue. He couldn't live like this anymore, couldn't pretend he wasn't feeling what he was feeling.

"You drive me crazy", he began. "It takes every ounce of will power I have to keep my hands off you. Every time I'm with you, I want to touch you...

"I want you, Lana—so bad, sometimes it's hard to breathe. I want to do things to you", he murmured as he slowly walked toward her, halting when their bodies were inches from colliding. "*Dirty things...*"

# Chapter 15

Lana drew in a rapid breath. He eyed her carefully, searching for any signs of anger or disgust. Shock had widened her eyes a bit at first, but mere moments after the words had left Randall's mouth her expression softened, revealing she was not only curious, but eager about what he had in mind.

When the massive lump finally dislodged from the back of her throat, she swallowed hard, whispering her plea. "Show me…"

She was killing him—*fucking killing him*—nibbling on that plump bottom lip, her eyes clouded with so much desire he went instantly hard. More than anything he wanted to scoop her up and devour every inch of her beautiful body, but he needed to know—without question—that this is what she truly wanted.

No regrets.

"Are you sure about that, Sweetheart?" "He asked as the pad of his thumb caught her bottom lip, tugging it downward. "Because once I start, I won't be able to stop…"

Their eyes met and held, the sound of their heavy breaths echoing, curling around them. This was it, he thought to himself: the moment of truth.

Randall had finally confessed the depth of his desire for this beautiful, fascinating woman. She was now aware of the anguish he endured when she was near and no matter what she decided tonight, he'd have to accept it. Steeling his spine, he waited, aware that the course of his future lay in the hands of a woman he didn't deserve.

Lana's mouth opened then closed. She couldn't find her voice, couldn't seem to move her mouth to form the words and enunciate them. The need to feel Randall's hands on her body was so intense, it nearly paralyzed her. She was frozen, yet so incredibly ablaze with heat she feared she'd spontaneously combust. With her voice on temporary hiatus, she did the only thing she could. She nodded her head, giving Randall carte blanche over her eager body.

Randall was one-hundred-ninety-five pounds of raw flesh. Damaged. Completely unworthy of the beauty that stood before him, but damn if that didn't stop him from taking what she was altruistically giving.

Palming the sides of her angelic face, Randall lowered his mouth over hers. The moment their lips touched, a surge of electricity arced, zipping down his spine, expanding, thrumming through him. And when Lana's lips parted on a sigh he ceased the opportunity, sweeping his tongue along hers. Answering the need that'd been stifled inside him for far too long.

Slowly he backed her into the hallway while their tongues tangled and tasted. He had every intention of taking her to his bed, but when his bare shoulder brushed against the cool surface of the wall the sheer craving he harbored for this woman halted him.

Turning slightly, he sandwiched Lana between his body and the wall, bracing his left hand against the smooth white plaster beside her head while his right began wandering. His calloused fingertips traced the contour of her shoulder, the outer curve of her round breast, finally coming to rest at her narrow waist. Her body was lean, but still soft and curvy in all the right places. She felt good pressed against him—and it was then he wondered what it would feel like to have her naked body mashed against his.

Tearing his lips from her luscious mouth he raised his head, gazing at her pretty face through hooded eyes. "Do you trust me, Sweetheart?"

"Yes", she whispered without pause.

Randall's heart thumped an extra beat, striking the center of his chest with a heavy thud. He didn't deserve her trust. Her unyielding faith in him was a priceless gift, one he knew she didn't readily give—at least not since that fateful day last May. He had no right to take what she'd so generously offered him, but damn if he was strong enough to resist the temptation hidden beneath the thin cotton of her dress.

"Put your hands above your head", he commanded gravelly. He waited while she complied with his demand, Lana's eyes never veering from his laser-like stare as her arms skidded along the wall, stretching toward the ceiling. Slowly, he gathered the hem of her dress in his fists, hauling the soft material up over her hips, past her waist, beyond her perfectly round breasts until the thin white cotton had cleared the bright red polish on her dainty fingertips.

Lana was paralyzed, her hands still positioned above her head. She flinched the moment the warm skin on her back pressed against the cool plaster behind her, but that was quickly forgotten when she realized she was standing in a pair of brown cowgirl boots, pale pink satin panties and a sage lace demi-bra. She ought to feel embarrassed—if she'd known earlier what she knew now, she'd have put more thought into matching her undergarments. But the hunger in Randall's eyes soon put her mind at ease.

She watched as two assessing gray eyes perused her body, his heated gaze searing her sensitive skin as it carved a perpetual path down the midline of her small frame.

*"Jesus...I've died and gone to heaven"*, she heard him mumble under his breath a second before his mouth landed against her lips again. Tongues collided: steadily tasting, exploring, grappling tenderly. And although technically this was only their third kiss, they found an easy, unhurried rhythm.

The backs of Lana's trembling hands gradually slid down the wall as the passion unfurled; unsure what to do with them while he seduced her mouth, she kept them pressed against the cool plaster on either side of her head.

This was so much more than a casual kiss—more than a simple means to an end. It conveyed something deep and powerful and aspiring. She'd never felt so precious. So desired. Warning bells sounded in her brain, but the utter pleasure mounting inside weakened her resistance.

*Don't think—don't worry—just feel—just enjoy…*

Torn between devouring her hungry kisses and exploring the hidden gems he'd unearthed minutes earlier, Randall peeled his lips away from her mouth once again, ready to delve into a sensual adventure he'd likely relive in his fantasies for years to come.

Lazily he tasted his way down her vanilla-scented neck, over the ridge of her collar bone until he reached the swell of her soft breasts. Without hesitation Randall tugged on the delicate cups until two hard pink nipples suddenly spilled over the lacey edges, just like he'd done countless times in his vividly-erotic fantasies.

The moment his hot, wet mouth settled over her left nipple she sucked in a shaky breath, arching her back in an effort to communicate how impossibly good it felt. Her entire body was ablaze and with every swipe of his slick tongue, every slight nip of his teeth, she surrendered to the exhilarating pleasure pulsing through her veins and pooling between her thighs.

*"Tell me what you like, Sweetheart"*, she heard him mumble against her breast before he sucked her nipple back into his hot mouth again.

Lana moaned, the back of her head aimlessly rolling over the wall behind her. "This", she uttered breathlessly. "I-I like this…" She felt his smile against her skin and then he was on the move again, paying homage to the other side before shifting lower. Her stomach quivered as his mouth skimmed down the center of her body.

Slow.

*Painfully slow.*

And when he reached her navel, a groan—deep and pure male—ricocheted off her tummy, causing a shiver to work its way over her feverish skin.

The discovery of her pierced belly button sent Randall's body in a tailspin. He could feel the grip on his self-control loosening, slipping through his fingers. He had an inherent hankering for using his brawniness to subdue the women he was intimate with. He wasn't hardcore—wasn't in to leather, whips, and torture devices; derived no pleasure from spanking. He wasn't a sadist, for heaven's sake! But he tended to use his male strength. Tended to be a bit rough.

And that's what frightened him.

Because the last thing he wanted was to hurt Lana.

It'd been a while for her—nearly ten months. He needed to stay calm.

*Go slow; she trusts you. Don't take her selfless gift for granted.*

Randall took a deep breath, kneeling in front of her, memories of his erotic fantasies flashing in his vision. His focus quickly darted to her face. She was breathing hard, trembling—

And she was watching him.

The grip on his restraint loosened slightly again. Knowing she was watching, studying, anticipating his next move made his cock ache to be inside her. But not yet, not until he had an opportunity to sample the sweet nectar veiled behind the thin sheet of pale pink satin.

His eyes trailed down her body as his fingertips hooked underneath the elastic along her hips, slowly drawing them down. Carefully, he helped her step out of them and when the thin barrier had been removed, he ran his hands up the backs of her thighs, tickling, teasing. "Spread your legs a little bit, Sweetheart."

He waited while she consented, dragging her boots along the wood floor until her feet were shoulder-width apart.

*Holy mother of God...*She was even more beautiful than he'd imagined—and lord knows, he'd imagined plenty over the last three months.

His eyes followed the narrow landing strip of dark hair, then eased downward where he found her slick with readiness. The dim, cave-like hallway was a mass of shadows, but even in the Cimmerian corridor he was able to discern how primed her body truly was.


Lana watched as Randall's tongue lightly brushed over her sensitive flesh, evoking a moan so carnal, so deep, she could no longer keep her eyes open. She unknowingly leaned her lower half into him while the backs of her shoulders pressed into the cool plaster, bracing her quivering frame against the sturdy structure to keep from melting into a helpless puddle of wanton woman. She reveled in the slick velvety texture of his lapping tongue, relished the sounds of his coarse groans as he steadily drove her toward the edge.

The unearthly end to her torturous pleasure was near.

So close—just beyond her reach.

He must have sensed how incredibly close she was, because the next thing she knew he was standing in front of her desperately tearing into a foil package with his teeth. Her body was humming, tingling, as he shoved his faded jeans down his hips. His sex sprang free a moment later, revealing his well-endowed dimensions.

Oh. My. God!


Randall knew she'd been mere moments from coming. He couldn't wait to taste the delicacy on his tongue.

And he would—but not yet. Because he wanted to feel her slick core pulsing around his aching cock, wanted Lana's eyes to be solely focused on his while her body gripped him.

"Hurry... *please*", she begged breathlessly.

His hands shook as he rolled the latex down his throbbing length, the sheer magnitude of how much he craved Lana's body clearly affecting his ordinarily cool disposition. Randall palmed her sweet ass with his lust-filled fingertips, lifting her, opening her up to him. Their noses touched as he pinned her against the wall with his powerful body. "Are you ready, Sweetheart?" He questioned with a voice so rough—so raw—it sounded as though he'd swallowed sandpaper.

"Yes", she breathed.

The affirmation had barely left Lana's sweet mouth when he lifted her higher, spearing her hot slippery core with his rigid cock. They moaned in unison as he buried himself to the hilt, her snug center sheathing him like a tightly-laced corset.

Bracing his left hand on the wall, he nuzzled her neck with the tip of his nose. "Jesus, Lana", he groaned, struggling to recover his restraint.

Submerged in wet, heated heaven he teetered on the edge of immoral and good. The raw intensity of lust pounding in his veins wanted release: hard, rough, carnal release. But his decent side—the side Lana so adamantly saw in him—wanted to go easy, slow.

He wanted to show her he was worthy of the gift she'd proffered, worthy of her body even though deep down he knew he wasn't. He just needed a few seconds to—

Lana squeezed her thighs, pressing them into his waist for leverage, then wriggled her bottom in a desperate attempt to garner friction, communicating what she needed, what she craved by way of her body language. Randall sucked in a breath through clenched teeth.

The woman was killing him.

*But oh, what a way to go...*

"How bad do you want it, Sweetheart, huh? Tell me", he urged gravelly. "I want to hear it."

"Please, I... I want..."

"Tell me."

"I-I need this. *I need you*", she whispered.

The last remnants of Randall's self-restraint slipped through his fingertips at her honest admission, eliciting bona fide masculine instinct to operate in its absence. Withdrawing from her tight heat, Randall slammed back into her body with a powerful thrust, then another. And another.

And another.

Their bodies collided, hearts pounded, and heavy breaths intermixed with moans, groans, and cries of pleasure.

But he wanted more.

Wanted to reign over her body, using the size and strength of his solid frame to his full advantage.

Sliding one of his arms between Lana and the wall, he held her snug against his chest, turning toward the master bedroom at the end of the hall.

Lana gripped his neck with her arms while her legs squeezed his waist. She wasn't entirely sure where he was going, only that Randall was hell-bent on taking her with him.

*Like there was somewhere else she'd rather be right now...*

Moments later they entered what appeared to be his bedroom. It smelled like him: a mixture of spicy cologne, coastal winds, and pure man. He turned on the small lamp next to his bed a second before she felt her back press against the soft mattress. There was no time to glance around at her surroundings, no time to probe into what the characteristics of the room said about the man hovering above her, because one look into his glazed-over gray eyes revealed a rabid man, ardently crazed.

For her.

The discovery raptured her breath. No one had ever looked at her like that before, like her body was a doubled-edged sword: a total cataclysmic breakdown of his control, and unclouded bliss, piled up into one irresistible package.

He was still buried to the hilt, hovering while his eyes roamed over her flushed skin. Aside from her lace bra, still askew from his oral reconnaissance in the hallway, and her brown cowgirl boots, she was completely nude. His attentive analysis suddenly allowed whispers of uncertainty to sneak up on her.

*What if he sees my imperfections? My flaws? What if—*

Randall's body slammed into hers again with such force—such passion—her body slid against the mattress toward the oak headboard. Lana cried out in pleasure, staring up at his captivating face.

He went still again. She could tell by the way his eyes

beamed an impassioned shade of steel-gray, the rapid rise and fall of his chest as he sucked air into his lungs, and by the way he tightly clenched his jaw that he was holding back. She didn't want that; didn't want him to curb his desire.

Because she wanted him—*all of him.*

Every inch, every ounce of what he was capable of. Digging the blunt heels of her boots into the mattress for leverage, she lifted her bottom, grinding her body against his, pleading for him to ease the ache between her thighs.

Breath hissed through his teeth as Lana seductively rolled her hips, rubbing her slippery core against him. "God, Lana", he growled, the sound of his voice utterly unrecognizable. What little bit of sanity he had left was blown to bits. Randall sat back on his knees and firmly gripped her hips, plunging into her with as much power as he could muster.

Lana's lusty cries urged him on. Every time he sank into her tight heat he became more delirious; thoroughly maddened by how beautiful she looked sprawled across his bed, completely aroused by how fucking amazing she felt speared on his cock.

Tension swirled low in his groin. He was close, but he refused to go there—not without Lana. Gripping her boots at her ankles, he positioned her legs against his shoulders, then leaned forward a bit, bracing his hands on either side of her head. "Open your eyes, Lana", he murmured. "I want to watch you when you come."

Their new position shifted the angle, allowing him to sink even deeper into her slick channel. He pounded into her body with powerful thrusts, each one meant to drive them higher, further, until they reached the crowning point.

"*Oh, God! Randall!*"

He held off until her inner walls clamped down on his dick, milking him, extracting three long months' worth of pent up infatuation. His arms gave way as Lana's legs slipped from his shoulders. Afraid he'd crush her, he braced his upper body with his elbows, loving the sensation of her soft breasts mashed against his solid chest.

"You feel amazing, you know that?" He murmured as he nuzzled her neck, spreading light kisses along her vanilla-scented skin. Her silence didn't necessarily bother him at first; any woman who'd come apart as passionately as she had would find speaking a rather difficult task. But when his lips brushed the sweet spot just below her ear, her quiet demeanor took on a whole new meaning.

She was crying. *Shit!*

# Chapter 16

"Lana…"

She quickly turned her head away from him in an attempt to hide her tears, but it was no use; he'd already seen them, tasted them. Randall rose onto all fours and nudged her chin, turning her head to face him. A steady flow of hot tears spilled over her lashes. *God, look what you've done—you shouldn't have been that rough!*

"Did I hurt you?" he questioned frantically.

Lana's head shook from side-to-side just as a sob broke free. "Damn it, Lana, talk to me!"

Like a caged animal she battled for freedom, squirming underneath him, flailing her arms and legs until she managed to break free. She scurried toward the doorway, the rapid click of her boots matching the pace of his fleeting pulse.

Randall leapt off the bed and lunged toward her, but in the midst of the hysteria he'd suddenly found himself in, he'd failed to remember he hadn't removed his pants. The top of his jeans lay bundled around his knees, thwarting his hasty effort to latch on to her. Falling forward with a heavy thud, he reached for her just as she disappeared into the hallway.

*You have to fix this, damn it! You have to make this right!*

Bracing his palms on the pine floor Randall pushed his solid frame upright, hauling his pants over his hips as he charged into the hallway after her. The bathroom door smacked against the frame, immediately followed by the clicking sound of the lock as she barricaded herself behind the wooden door.

"Lana!" He shouted as he skidded to a halt. He frantically rattled the knob, even though he already knew it was locked, then pounded on the wood with his fists. "Lana, please, open up!"

The panic in Randall's voice only caused her tears to fall faster. Lana covered her mouth with her hand and tightly clenched her eyes shut as sob after sob spilled out of her.

She'd desecrated her vows. Spat on the promise she'd made nearly seven years ago. Tainted her body with another man's hands...

She'd cheated on her husband—*with his best friend*!

"Lana, damn it!"

She winced as he pounded on the door, vibrating the walls with such fury she was surprised cracks hadn't emerged along the plaster's smooth surface. Deep down she knew the overwhelming sense of panic mounting inside her chest was partly unwarranted. Jimmy was dead, and no matter how much she wanted him to, he wasn't coming back. Being celibate for the rest of her life was an unrealistic vision.

Wasn't it?

"*Please*, Lana", he begged softly, despondently. "Will you just talk to me?"

It was his defeated tone that tugged her heart most. Even as confused and baffled as she was by her feelings and what they meant, she couldn't do this to him. Randall had been so good to her, so caring. And tonight she'd pushed and pushed until he revealed what he wanted. He'd warned her more than once, giving her ample opportunities to walk away.

But she'd stayed anyway. And she knew why, too.

She was falling for Randall Burns.

Cradling her head in her hands she sucked in a hefty liter of air, expelling it through her pursed lips, calming her rattled body from the inside out. She couldn't barricade herself inside Randall's bathroom indefinitely. She needed to face the music—*preferably with her panties on*.

\* \* \* \* \*

"I-I need my clothes."

"Lana—"

"Please, Randall… I promise we'll talk once I get dressed."

Randall glanced at the pink panties and white dress next to his feet and quickly snatched them off the floor. "Okay, I've got 'em. Open up."

"Wait…"

Randall sighed, trying to ignore the instinctive urge to break down the door. "This isn't gonna work, Sweetheart. Not unless you open the door", he uttered with a calmness he didn't feel.

"Promise me, you won't barge in here until I'm fully dressed."

"Lana, I've seen every inch of y—"

"Please", she uttered just above a whisper.

If it meant she would finally spill what'd caused her to run off like she had, and more importantly, what he'd done to make her cry, he'd do it. "I promise…"


The clicking sound of the lock disengaging was subsequently followed by the groaning door. Lana reached one of her delicate hands through the thin slit, waiting for Randall to deliver on his part of the deal. And when he did she quickly snatched them from his grasp and nudged the door closed behind her, removing the temptation of barging in on her by turning the lock.

With forethought, she maneuvered her satin panties over her boots, turned her dress right-side out, and then slipped the soft cotton garment over her head. She stole a quick glance in the mirror.

*You look terrible, girl!*

Black moisture settled just below her eyes then narrowed into two distinct streaks, marking the vertical path her tears had taken, and her long brown locks were tousled in an unmistakable sex-induced mass. A few passes with her fingertips easily erased the smudges and a quick finger-comb soon had her I-just-got-laid hair back in order.

With a fortifying breath she turned the lock and opened the door, not the least bit surprised to find Randall standing in front of her with his hands braced on either side of the frame.

Randall peeled his hands from the molding and stepped toward her. "Are you all right?" He questioned anxiously, palming the sides of her face, his gray eyes boring into her blue depths.

With a subtle nod Lana closed her eyes and whispered, "I'm sorry."

"Don't be." His arms wrapped around her small frame. She stiffened at first, but soon relaxed, practically melting into his embrace. "God, I'm the one who should be apologizing. The last thing I wanted was to hurt—"

"You didn't hurt me…"

Randall pulled back to look into her eyes. "So why the tears, then, huh? Talk to me."

Lana moistened her lips with her tongue, buying herself a few extra seconds. "Remember when you asked me earlier if I trusted you?" She watched as his head nodded, the concern in his eyes turning the steel hue a deeper, drearier shade of gray. "Well, do you trust *me*?"

"Absolutely", he answered without hesitation.

"Then please believe me when I say: you did nothing wrong. I just…need some time", she sighed. "I need to sit on this for a while before I can talk about it. Does that make any sense?"

Randall nudged a strand of hair from her eye. "Not really", he uttered with a hint of a smile. "But…if that's what you need, consider it done."

"Thank you", she whispered.


The panic and fear that'd been practically palpable upon the door opening moments ago dissolved, allowing Randall to draw in his first deep breath since she'd appeared at his doorstep earlier. He still didn't have the answers he wanted, but just knowing his sexual aggression hadn't harmed her was enough.

For now.

Because he *would* get to the bottom of it eventually.

Leaning forward he pressed his lips against her forehead, lingering a bit longer than he'd intended to. He fought the urge to taste her kiss again—fifteen minutes without her sweet mouth and he was already jonesing. "Can I at least walk you to your car?"

"I'd like that."

The weak smile Lana revealed was a small victory, he knew. But considering how swiftly she'd scrambled from his bed, concealing herself in his bathroom, it was a step in the right direction. He'd give her twenty-four hours to mull over the details of what'd happened between them tonight—what'd been slowly brewing since that night in his truck nearly three months ago.

And then Randall would start pressing for answers.

# Chapter 17

Sunday's at the fire station were notoriously calm. No training or drills, no toilets to scrub, no trucks to wash, no schedule whatsoever.

Well, that wasn't entirely true—a ritual of sorts had been bred many moons ago. It involved warm doughnuts from Anderson's Bakery and a rather competitive round of hoops to burn the plethora of fat and calories they'd inhaled at the start of the day.

Today was no different from any other Sunday in recent memory. Randall had wolfed down three key-lime-glazed doughnuts upon his arrival, and as usual, his team consisting of Grant, Ty, and Mark, were currently up by sixteen points.

Yep, just an ordinary Sunday…

Only, it wasn't.

Outwardly Randall looked the same, but on the inside underneath his tough façade, he was a changed man.

Last night he'd sunk his cock deep inside his dead best friend's wife. He'd broken cardinal rule number one, and yet that matter was only the tip of the iceberg. It was the fact he'd enjoyed every blessed moment of it—*that he couldn't wait to do it again*—that gnawed on his conscience.

The sun's rays pelted his bare back as he dribbled the ball near the make-shift three-point line. Randall's eyes scanned the court, noting the positions of both teammates and opponents, charting the course he'd likely take.

Bouncing the ball three more times for good measure he

exploded forward, zigzagging, charging ahead until he reached the rickety goal. Pushing off his left foot he leaped into the air, launching the ball toward the faded backboard with his right hand. The basketball bounced off the weathered wood a moment later, then swished through the net, rattling the rusted chains as it squeezed through.

"Hell yeah!" Grant shouted, raising his hand in front of him for a high-five.

Randall smacked his palm against Grant's, then walked to the edge of the pavement for his water bottle.

"What is that, three games in a row, now?" Grant jived to the opposing team.

"You got lucky", Tommy countered. Tipping his head a bit, he gestured to Randall, now walking toward them. "Burns cut out early last night. Otherwise, he'd have been too hung over today to—"

Without warning, Randall shoved Tommy with enough force to cause the man to take a step back in order to remain upright.

"What the hell was that for?"

"What're you tryin' to get at, Tommy? Huh? Are you sayin' I'm a drunk?" Randall stepped forward, adrenaline coursing through his veins, his fists clenched into two tight masses at his sides.

"No, man—c'mon, it was a joke!"

In the blink of an eye Grant and Ty had Randall by the shoulders, carting him away from temptation.

"C'mon, buddy, ease up", Ty warned. "He was just shit-talkin' you—the same damn thing I'd do if I'd gotten my ass handed to me on the court."

Randall's eyes skittered to his lieutenant before landing on Tommy again. Angrily shrugging free from Ty and Grant's grip he raised his hand, thrusting his index finger at Tommy for emphasis. "Keep your fucking hands off Lana", he uttered through clenched teeth, then turned and stalked inside, leaving everyone to wonder how their normally calm Sunday had suddenly turned awry.

\* \* \* \* \*

It was one of the warmest spring afternoons in what felt like eons, Lana acknowledged as she scanned the calm surf for Connor's whereabouts. After a slew of cold fronts, the Florida Panhandle was returning to temperate bliss. The cloudless sky was a vivid shade of blue, the sun directly above showering the earth with luminous love.

Lana's parents had delivered Connor to her doorstep just before noon; not wanting to waste the beautiful day indoors, she'd decided to pack a picnic lunch and head to the beach. Gulf temps were still a chilly sixty-eight degrees—too cold for her just yet, but apparently not for Connor. He was currently digging by the water's edge, tossing the soft wet sand back into the ocean.

Stuffing their trash into the small portable cooler, Lana reached for her Diet Coke. She watched as Kendall played with Tenley, now nearly four-months old. "She rolling over yet?"

"No, but she's come close a few times. She'll get on her side and kick her legs for momentum, then teeter a bit before falling on her back again."

"She'll do it when she's ready", Lana explained. "I was the same way with Connor—I was so excited about the next milestone, sometimes I'd forget to enjoy the here and now. Savor this time—when you can lay her down and walk away knowing she'll be exactly where you left her—because soon she's going to be into everything you don't want her to and be everywhere you'd rather she wasn't."

Kendall reached for her last onion ring and popped it in her mouth. "You may have a point", she said as she glanced at Tenley, still lying in the same spot since their arrival.

"Ty finish baby-proofing the house yet?" Olivia asked while wiping mayonnaise from the corner of her mouth.

"Are you kidding me? The man brainstorms everyday trying to figure out ways to make the house safer. In fact I wouldn't be surprised if every hard surface isn't covered in bubble wrap by the end of the summer!"

Lana and Olivia howled with laughter, because they both understood that if someone suggested the bubble wrap idea to Ty, it would be implemented in no time.

"Speaking of Ty, I got a very interesting call from him before I left the house to come here", Kendall shared.

"Ugh!" Olivia mouthed as she covered her ears. "If you say you had phone sex with my brother before you came here, I'm gonna lose my lunch."

"No, no phone sex—at least, *not this time...* Actually, it was about Lana."

Lana slapped her hand against her chest. "Me?" She questioned incredulously.

"Uh-huh, seems you were the heart of a scuffle this morning at the fire station."

Baffled, she asked, "What kind of scuffle?"

"Well according to Ty", Kendall began while preparing Tenley's bottle, "they were playing a round of basketball when Tommy made an innocent dig about the other team only winning because Randall wasn't hung over, incidentally implying he was a drunk, I guess. Apparently Randall didn't take it so well and charged at him."

"*What?*"

"I don't get it", Olivia cut in. "What does that have to do with Lana?"

"That's the mystery. Because when Ty and Grant hauled him away, Randall said to Tommy, and I quote, 'keep your fucking hands off Lana'."

Both Olivia and Kendall examined her closely. Her face suddenly felt hot—a symptom that had absolutely zero to do with the sun's warm rays and everything to do with the memory of Randall's rough hands gliding over her bare skin last night. "H-he said that?"

"Come to think of it, Grant mentioned something last night about Randall seeing red when you were dancin' with Tommy", Olivia divulged.

Lana fought the urge to squirm as two pairs of analytical eyes probed her guileful exterior. She picked the red polish from her left thumb before finally breaking the silence. "Oh, c'mon, I'm not sleeping with the guy." *Not Tommy, anyway...*

"You know that"—Kendall gestured to Lana—"and we know that. But you also know how the people in this town like to talk, or should I say *embellish.*"

Cradling her head in her hands, Lana released a groan of frustration. "I bet Jenny is fuming right about now. Gosh, if I'd known how out of hand all of this would've gotten, I'd have told him no when he asked me to dance last night." Lana's eyes skittered to the shore in search of Connor. He was oblivious to the drama unfurling as he shuffled his feet through the chilly Gulf water.

And she prayed he remained that way.

"Frankly, I felt sorry for the guy", she went on. "I was just trying to be polite, you know? He was a complete gentleman on the dance floor—never once tried to cop a feel or anything!"

"Jenny would have a lot of nerve bein' upset—she cheated on *him*, for heaven's sake!" Olivia stated. "Tommy dancin' with you is G-rated compared to what she did with John O'Reilly—"

"*Allegedly*", Kendall reminded the group, never one to encourage nasty gossip. "Anyway, I think Rand was just being overprotective, you know?—looking out for you. I wouldn't doubt he feels a responsibility to Jimmy to make sure—"

"Did anyone bring dessert?" Lana didn't miss the expression on both her friends' faces at her obvious attempt at changing the subject. Clearly the two were curious about Randall's outburst, but even more so about Lana's not-so-subtle attempt to ditch the topic. But one of the things she loved most about these two was their ability to sense when to pry and when to leave well enough alone.

Olivia and Kendall shared a quick glance before Olivia reached into her small basket. "How do doughnuts from Anderson's Bakery sound?" she asked as she opened the bag. Instantly they were accosted with the sweet aroma of succulent bliss as the popular delicacy merged with the salty breeze.

"I love you", Kendall stated flatly.

Olivia shrugged. "That's what friends are for."

Yes, Lana thought as she reached for a key-lime-glazed doughnut, good friends provided comfort in the form of support and glazed pastries. They gave advice when one needed it, and held their tongues when it wasn't. She was lucky to have these two in her life. Very lucky.

But their presence here today only magnified how profound her feelings had become for Randall. Because he'd comforted her in a different way last night, a way in which she hadn't thought she'd needed.

A method she longed to experience again.


Lana and Connor returned home just before dinner. She was exhausted—both physically and emotionally—and was thankful Connor had agreed to Chef Boyardee, exempting her from kitchen duty for the evening. But her son was a tricky little thing, using her lack of enthusiasm for slaving over a hot stove in exchange for a round of football in the backyard.

He was good, real good—maybe too good—for his own britches. It didn't take much coaxing on his end, just a little pout of his lower lip and she was putty in his tiny hands.

Connor devoured the can of cheese ravioli in record time, then raced into his room to change into the Florida State jersey her parents had given him for his birthday a few weeks ago, returning with his new football tucked under his arm. "C'mon, mommy, you can be my quarterback!"

Reluctantly she followed her son to the backyard, noting how the gulf breeze had gained momentum, rustling the trees. She'd play until dark, which judging by the sun's position, would be half an hour—tops.

Connor got into position beside her, knees bent, chest forward, ready to dash across the yard on her cue. "You have to pretend to hike the ball, Mommy, then throw it over there", he instructed, pointing toward the back corner of the fence. "This is a really big play; the whole team's countin' on you."

Lana scanned the yard. There's nothing like the pressure of upsetting an invisible team to motivate a quarterback... "Okay, ready?" she questioned.

"Yep."

"Go!"

Only he didn't. Connor straightened and put a hand on his hip. "Mommy, you're supposed to say *hut*, not *go*."

"Oh, okay... Hut!"

Connor dashed across the yard in a perfect line, then

darted to the right. Rearing her hand back, she launched the ball as hard as she could, wincing as she watched it wobble in the air, falling to the ground in the middle of the yard.

"That was horrible."

Lana turned at the sound, the voice both teasing and pure male.

"Randall!" Connor shouted, sprinting toward him in a frenzied rush, almost as if his eyes needed to prove to his mind that the image wasn't an optical illusion.

*Good to know she wasn't the only one*—because she'd spent the better part of the day studying the apparition of a man with thick black hair, two gray eyes swirling with desire, and a body corded with a mass of solid muscle.

"Hey, squirt—"

"Can you play quarterback? Mommy throws like a girl."

"Hey", Lana remarked, resting her hands on her hips. "I *am* a girl, encase you two haven't noticed."

"I noticed plenty, *trust me*", Randall uttered wryly.

Lana didn't miss that his wry comment was in reference to last night, when his mouth and hands had traversed her female form. A shiver of awareness zipped down her spine, settling low in her belly at the memory.

"I think it's time your mom got a throwing lesson, don't you?" Connor's little head bobbed up and down with excitement. "What do ya say, Lana?—you ready for this?"

His double entendre was unmistakable, she thought to herself. Because what he really wanted was truth. He wanted clear answers to chase the murkiness away, opacity she'd created when she'd scrambled from his bed and barricaded her panicked soul in his bathroom. She'd asked for some time and he'd been gracious enough to grant her some.

But now her time was up. She needed to form her feelings into words—difficult when she didn't quite understand them herself. "I'll try", she uttered just above a whisper. "But I'm not sure I'll be any good at this."

Randall gestured for Connor to fetch the football from the middle of the yard, catching it with ease when her son launched it toward him. Smiling, Randall slowly ambled toward her, stopping once he stood directly behind her. "I'm right here, Sweetheart. We'll do this together."

# Chapter 18

Randall swallowed a moan as he slowly reached one of his large hands around her middle, hauling her back against the hard plane of his solid chest. Her tummy quivered beneath his fingertips and the sound of her quickened breaths almost made him forget about the throwing lesson—and more importantly, that Connor was patiently waiting at the opposite side of the yard to catch the ball.

*Focus, Burns—now's not the time to reminisce about last night.*

Easier said than done. Because holding her made him want things, things he couldn't have.

"Lesson number one", he began, "is all in how you grip the ball. Line your fingers along the laces, like this." Taking her hand he spread her fingers over the laces, noting how they trembled. "One of the keys to a perfect spiral is to grip the ball with your fingertips—not your palm; palming the ball is a recipe for disaster."

Lana nodded, summarizing the lesson aloud. "Grip with fingertips—no palm. Got it."

"Keep your eyes downfield, but turn your body sideways", he uttered softly as his hands slid to her hips, rotating them until she was in the proper position. It wasn't necessary to the lesson, per se; she could've turned on her own. But, God, touching her...

"Place your other hand underneath the ball and bring it up toward your ear."

"Like this?" she questioned as she demonstrated.

"Yeah."

"You mean, I'm supposed to throw it with two hands?"

Chuckling under his breath, he answered, "No, this is for stability and control."

Lana turned her head to look at him. "Are you laughing at me, Randall Burns?"

"Wouldn't dream of it. Now, get back into position." He waited while she complied, then went on to explain the importance of proper footwork.

"This is a lot to take in", she admitted softly. "How does anybody remember all this, huh?" Lana turned, looking up at him with those beaming midnight orbs. "How does everyone make it look so easy?"

Somehow, Randall got the inkling they weren't talking about the mechanics of throwing a perfect spiral. A sudden gust of wind blew a strand of silky brown hair across her pretty face, and without a second thought Randall reached up and tucked it behind her right ear, loving how her eyes closed when his fingertips brushed her cheek. "Just takes practice. Soon it'll become almost second nature. You won't have to think about each of the steps, you just... do 'em."

Lana's eyes fluttered open a moment before Connor impatiently yelled across the yard to throw the ball. "Okay, here goes." Turning her attention downfield where Connor stood, she yelled, "Ready?"

"Yeah—don't forget to yell hut! It's the rules, right Randall?"

"Sure is, Squirt!"

"C'mon, Randall, is that really necessary?" asked Lana.

Randall took a step back, hands low on his hips. "You heard the man", he uttered softly as a smirk emerged. "It's in the rules."

"Fine." Lana drew in a deep breath while she lined her fingers along the laces, and after yelling "hut", she brought the ball to her ear, positioned her feet accordingly, aimed and released the ball, watching in amazement as it soared toward Connor in a nearly perfect spiral. "I did it!" she shouted, throwing her hands in the air in celebration.

Christ, she was beautiful when she smiled. Unable to resist, Randall stepped forward, lifting her up as though she'd thrown the winning pass at the championship game. He twirled her around in a circle, letting her laughter rain down on him, wishing—even if only for a moment—things could be different.

Because he couldn't overlook how right she felt in his arms, couldn't deny the way she made him feel.

It was more than physical, although it'd probably started that way that night in his truck three months ago. Lana Phillips had wriggled her way into his shattered being, painstakingly piecing his broken spirit back together again with her radiant smile and her kind, forgiving heart.

He came here tonight with noble intentions, came here to apologize for what'd happened last night; explain that he'd made a mistake—one that wouldn't happen again. But he couldn't follow through. Not when he tossed and turned every night thinking about her. When he now understood how amazing she felt, how delicious she tasted. Not when the simple sound of her laughter warmed him from the inside out.

Was he being selfish?

Absolutely.

He should be down on his knees begging for forgiveness for what he'd done, but instead he wanted something else: one irresistible, Lana Phillips.

*Heaven, help me...*


"I had to bribe him with a promise to get ice cream tomorrow after school to get him to close his eyes and go to bed", Lana shared as she sat down next to Randall on the back porch step. "Wish it worked for everything in life", she uttered quietly.

Randall nodded, not knowing what to say to that. He didn't want to complicate her life any more than he already had; being solely responsible for her husband's death was plenty complicated enough.

Leaning forward, he placed his forearms against his knees, releasing a puff of air from his chest. "So, about last night..."

"You sure don't waste any time, do you?"

Her tone was teasing, but underneath he sensed how ill-at-ease she truly was.

Typical. She was trying her damnedest to forge a brave smile, just one of the many things he admired about her. Shaking his head in response to her question, he waited a few beats, allowing his silence to indicate he was ready to listen.

"I, um..." Running her fingers through her hair, she sighed, "Gosh, where do I begin..."

"The beginning. The beginning is a good place to start."

"Right. Okay..." Drawing in another deep breath, she began, "After Jimmy died I felt broken, alone. He was...my *everything*. Guess you don't realize how much you depend on someone until they're gone. In the beginning I was overwhelmed: trying to establish a new sense of normal for Connor and myself, trying to just keep my head above water, you know?"

Randall nodded. He knew what that was like. Hell, he'd nearly drowned himself in whiskey over the summer in a desperate attempt to numb the guilt.

"And then you came back... I can't tell you how good it felt to have an ally—a partner—again. For the first time in ages I felt strong—like I finally had the strength to move on. I started... thinking about things. *Wanting* things."

"What kind of things?" he questioned gravelly.

Lana covered her eyes with her hands. "Gosh, this is so embarrassing."

Randall carefully peeled her palms away from her face. Holding her wrists steady, he gazed into her deep blue eyes. "Tell me", he urged. "Tell me what you wanted."

Swallowing hard, she gathered her courage. "I wanted to be kissed, touched, cherished. I-I wanted... I wanted *you*."

Resisting the urge to lean in, he kept his expression unreadable. Stone-like. Because her confession only generated more questions. He watched as she nervously nibbled on her bottom lip, so uncertain about his reaction, so insecure.

Didn't she know how beautiful she was? Couldn't she see what she did to him every time they were together? "Let's fast-forward to last night…"

"Last night was…" Lana closed her eyes, searching for the right word. A word that would encompass how truly amazing it'd been. "Life changing", she whispered. "Last night was life changing."

"Okaaay", he drawled. "Is that a good thing or a bad thing?"

"Good. *Definitely good.*"

Randall smiled for the first time since the conversation began. The heavy mass that'd been pressing down on his chest since last night eased a bit. But the biggest question of all still remained: Why had she fled? "So last night was good for you?"

"Yes", she breathed.

"Tell me what happened afterward. Why were you crying?"

"Because I… I've never been with anyone besides Jimmy. And for a moment I just… panicked, I guess. It sort of felt like I'd betrayed him."

*We did. Damn it, we both did.*

The fact didn't sit well with him—and clearly it hadn't with Lana, either. But it was almost as if they were powerless to do anything about it, like their attraction was too strong, the allure too spellbinding to resist. "And what about now, huh? How do you feel now?" he asked as he palmed the side of her face, his thumb gently brushing over her cheek.

"I still want you", she uttered just above a whisper. "God knows I shouldn't, but I do."

With a groan Randall gave in to temptation, pressing his mouth against her soft pink lips. He kissed her like he meant it—like she meant something to him.

Because she did.

Lana had become the single most important thing in his life. She was his beacon in the dark, his guiding light.

*You should stop. Do the right thing. Walk away.*

Lana released a breathy moan when their tongues collided. The sound went directly south to his groin, instantly silencing his conscience. Hauling her onto his lap, he gripped her hips, grinding her core against his already hard cock, allowing her to feel just how much he wanted her, too.

Lana tore her mouth away, gazing at him through hooded eyes. "How are we going to do this?"

"Any way you want, Sweetheart", he uttered, his voice low and gritty. "From behind. Against the wall—hell, right here." Randall placed his lips against the hollow of her throat, releasing a groan when she tilted her head back, allowing him better access.

"No—I meant us." Palming the sides of his face with both hands, she drew him away from her neck and looked into his eyes. "How do we do us? *Is there an us?*" She asked with uncertainty.

"There's definitely an us. Definitely..." Randall nipped her bottom lip with his teeth, then laved the succulent flesh with his tongue. Her half-moan/half-sigh threatened his self-control. He'd spent the better part of the last twenty-two hours replaying that sexy sound in his head, wondering if he'd ever be privileged enough to hear it again. It was even better than he remembered. The soft, breathy whimper signified that Lana was losing the battle against her self-restraint, too—that her mind and body were both in tune, coexisting in harmony, both focused on one common goal.

Him.

With a deep guttural groan, Randall swept his tongue between her lips as though her kiss was his only lifeline, desperately clinging to the safe haven her body provided. A sudden burst of hissing wind rushed past, vigorously thrashing the leaves on the oak canopy. Lana's long brown locks surrounded him like a veil of dark silk as bamboo wind chimes clanked and crickets serenaded.

It was then something strange took hold of him—an odd sensation, really. It was like a cold shiver, raising the hair on the back of his neck, followed by a kick of adrenaline. The fight or flight response caused his hands to shake, his heart to quicken.

And with good reason, too. Because the splintering crack of wood snapping, followed by a thunderous crash as the solid oak limb fell to the earth caused his already jittery body to jump.

"Omigod!" Lana gasped. "What was that?" Glancing over her shoulder, she quickly climbed off Randall's lap, covering her moistened mouth with her hands. "Omigod, Randall—Connor was standing underneath that tree a half-hour ago! What if... what if he'd—"

"Don't", Randall uttered as he stood, gathering her in his arms as much for her comfort as his own. "You can't think like that."

"I'm a mother—I have to think like that! If he'd been standing there, he would've... he could have..." Lana closed her eyes. "I can't lose someone else I love, Randall. I'm not strong enough."

Nuzzling his face in her hair, he squeezed her tight, breathing her in. "I'm off tomorrow. If you can push a permit through first thing tomorrow morning, I'll start cutting it down." Randall felt her subtle nod against his shoulder. If that's what it took to put her mind at ease he'd gladly do it.

He owed her that much.

Eyes tracking the mass of oak, overflowing with prosperous green leaves, Randall got that strange feeling again. He didn't believe in ghosts, but he was beginning to think maybe something—or rather, *someone*—was trying to send him a message.

*I'm sorry, Jimmy. So damn sorry...*

# Chapter 19

"Hey, stranger", Kendall greeted as she rounded the corner at aisle three, her three-inch heels tapping against the white-speckled linoleum floor.

*Shit. Busted...*

Turning his body, Randall eyed the woman he'd spent nearly two years of his life obsessing over. "Sorry, Ken, I was sort of in a hurry. Nothing personal."

"I can't believe you actually tried to sneak in here without sa—*Omigod, Randall!* What happened to your shoulder?"

"It's nothing. Just a little gash."

Kendall stepped closer, gently bracing her hands on his solid body. His white T-shirt was smeared with dirt and sweat, and the rather substantial red stain along the top of his sleeve clearly challenged his "little gash" tale.

"Honey, little gashes don't bleed like that! Why didn't you go to the hospital? You're most likely gonna need stitches."

Randall shook his head from side-to-side. "I'm fine—just need an antiseptic and some steri-strips."

"But—"

"No hospital, no stitches, all right?" He retorted, surely, harshly, noting how she flinched. The moment he'd uttered the words, he wanted them back. "I'm sorry."

"It's okay." Kendall reached for a bottle of Bactine, a package of steri-strips, gauze and tape, then turned to Randall. "Well if you're not gonna go to the hospital, at least let me help you clean up. Come with me; we can do this in my office."

Randall followed her down the aisle and behind the pharmacy counter, acknowledging her assistant, Marcus, with a firm nod. They ventured down one of the narrow passages that led to her office, various bottles of medication situated in perfect rows to his left and right. "Slow day?"

"Yeah, why?" She asked as she opened her office door.

Randall gestured to the shelves. "Looks like it was an OCD kind of day."

"Wipe that smirk off your face, Randall Wade Burns, because I'm about to get '*OCD*' on that little gash of yours", she lectured, clutching the various first aid items she'd snatched from aisle three moments ago against her chest. "Take your shirt off and have a seat."

Stepping into her modest-sized office, Randall gathered the hem of his white T-shirt and carefully drew it over his shoulder, wincing when he raised his left arm above his head. He then balled the cotton tee in his fists and took a seat.

"How on earth did this happen?" Inquired Kendall as she tore into the package of sterile gauze.

"Tree trimming." He still couldn't believe this'd happened. He'd been so careful balancing on a sturdy branch, slicing into a smaller limb positioned just above his head. The chainsaw ripped into the wood like a hot knife carving into butter. Easy. Effortlessly.

But mere moments before the saw severed the branch, the weight of the leaves at the other end caused the wood to snap prematurely. The segment he'd been cutting suddenly jerked upward, then swung down toward him with calculated vengeance. There was no time to react—no time to dodge the solid branch as it barreled toward him, slicing into his shoulder before finally falling to the ground. Thankfully he'd had enough sense to anchor his body to the trunk. A twenty-five foot fall would've undoubtedly caused a bigger injury than this.

"Tree trimming?" She asked incredulously. "Well, obviously the tree got its revenge."

Randall chuckled. "Yeah, I guess you could say th—*son of a bitch!*" He bellowed as sharp, fiery jolts of electricity surged down his arm toward his fingertips. Glancing over his shoulder, he eyed the bottle of Bactine Kendall held in her hand. "Thought that shit had Lidocaine in it?"

"It does."

Tilting his head back for a moment, he clenched his eyes shut and drew in a deep breath. "Damn, that hurt."

"I'm sorry. I just figured it'd be better if I just did it without warning you first." Leaning forward, Kendall pursed her lips and gently blew on the gaping wound. "Better yet?"

There was a time, not so long ago, when the sensation of her breath on his skin would have sent him into a reckless tailspin. He'd lusted after Kendall Porter for nearly two years, for heaven's sake! She'd been one of his best friends and had held the starring role in his fantasies every one of those seven-hundred-thirty nights.

Until roughly three and a half months ago.

Because a new woman had been cast in that role. A woman with midnight eyes, long brown hair, and vanilla-scented skin; a heavenly woman with an uncanny ability of ensnaring his highly-regarded self-control, transforming him into a living, breathing sex fiend.

A woman utterly clueless about the effect she had on him.

"Yeah, the Lidocaine must be kickin' in, now." Randall closed his eyes while Kendall gently wiped away the dried blood that'd settled around the wound.

"So whose tree should I send the bill to?" She teased as she tossed a red-stained gob of gauze into the nearby bio-hazard bin.

"Lana's."

"*Oh...*"

Head still leaning against the back of the chair, Randall opened one of his eyes at Kendall. "Okay, spill it. What's on your mind?"

"Nothing", she quickly countered. But she should've known better. Because suddenly she was the recipient of *The Look*: Randall's bullshit detector. A three inch gash in his shoulder and the man could still make her practically sing what was on her mind.

"Okay, so maybe it isn't *nothing...* I heard about what

happened yesterday at the fire station between you and Tommy."

"Your husband has a big mouth."

"So you're saying you didn't almost get into a fight with one of your good friends yesterday?"

"I don't want to talk about it, Babe."

Kendall opened the steri-strips and carefully placed them perpendicularly across the deep laceration, and when that was done, she covered the wound with a mound of four-inch gauze pads.

"Does Lana know?" He asked softly, finally breaking the awkward silence.

"Yeah."

*Great. Fucking great.*

He'd sort of hoped his outburst would've remained unnewsworthy. But this was Butler Island, after all; gossip in this town was as steady and reliable as the changing tides.

"What's going on with you, Rand? You used to tell me everything. But now…"

"Just…stuff, Babe. Stuff I can't get into right now." His answer seemed to satisfy her. For now. Because he knew she sensed something was going on with him—hell, aside from Jimmy, she was the one person that probably knew him best. And right now, she knew he was hiding something. "You done?"

Kendall added one last piece of tape to hold the gauze in place. "I am now."

Standing, Randall turned toward her, kissing her forehead. "Thanks for your help, Babe."

"Anytime", she whispered, gently wrapping her arms around his neck. "I worry about you, you know."

"Don't. I'm okay. *Really* okay."

And it was the truth. Because at that moment Randall suddenly realized he wasn't in love with Kendall Porter. That realization should've been welcoming news.

Trouble was he'd fallen for Lana. Hard. Fast.

And he was in way too deep to simply walk away, now.

\* \* \* \* \*

This is all my fault", said Lana as she stared at the gaping wound on Randall's upper arm, located just below the bony protuberance of his left shoulder. "I never should've agreed to let you climb up there today."

"That tree needed to be trimmed back after what happened last night, remember?"

"Yes, but I could've hired someone—a professional."

Randall took a seat on the wooden stool in front of the small vanity and glanced at her reflection in the mirror. "And you would've easily spent a couple grand, too."

"I don't care about the money, Randall. You could've..."

Died. She didn't say it aloud, but then again she didn't need to; it was written all over her pretty face. It hadn't occurred to him, until now, that his brush with danger earlier this afternoon could've spelled death. If that branch had sliced into his Jugular, it would've demolished Lana. Just thinking about how she would've reacted to the news made his chest ache.

"So what am I supposed to do?" She asked after carefully removing the saturated gauze he'd arrived with.

Snatching the bottle of Bactine off the counter, he handed it to her. "Pour this over the wound, then pat it dry with some gauze." Randall clenched his teeth, bracing his body for the fiery jolt that would soon race down his arm, igniting his nerves in an incandescent blaze until the numbing agent, Lidocaine, took effect. He groaned softly as the cool liquid collided against the three-inch groove.

"Omigod—I'm sorry!"

"It's fine", he managed feebly. "Just stings like hell at first."

Reaching for the pile of gauze on the vanity, Lana began gently patting the wound dry. "How did you manage to bandage this yourself?"

"I didn't—Kendall helped."

Lana stilled for a few long beats, catching Randall's gaze in the mirror, then quickly grabbed the tape off the counter, securing the dry gauze pads to his bare clean skin.

Randall carefully observed her reflection. She was desperately attempting to appear as though his running to

Kendall didn't bother her. But clearly it did.

"I know what you're thinking."

"Really?—Then you probably get how upset I am that you didn't go to the hosp—

"That isn't it. And you know it." Randall sighed, suddenly feeling guilty—like he needed to clarify how he'd ended up shirtless in Kendall's office today. "Look, I didn't purposely seek out Kendall today. I was—"

"You don't owe me any explanations, Randall ", she uttered softly as she concentrated on her nails, feverishly chipping away at her violet polish.

"Look at me." He waited until her head lifted, her eyes targeting his in the mirror's reflection. "I don't have feelings for Kendall anymore. Not like that. Not like I used to."

"That's... that's not what I was—"

Randall turned his body one-hundred-eighty degrees on the small wooden stool so that Lana now stood between his legs. He gently tugged on her waist, drawing her closer, then looked up into her pretty face. "Yeah, you were..."

One of his thumbs trailed across the hem of her thin tank top until he managed to slip underneath the green ribbed cotton. The moment his callused thumb caressed the soft skin of her stomach, she inhaled a quick breath as though the mere sensation of his gentle touch was beyond pleasurable.

Like she'd been aching for it all day.

Gathering the hem in his fists, he drew the material up further, revealing the jeweled navel ring he loved so much. He watched as her chest expanded, then retracted, rapidly, over and over, feverishly anticipating his next move. "You have no idea how beautiful you are, do you?"

"*Me?—beautiful?*"

"Yeah. *You.*" Unable to curb the overwhelming need mounting inside him, he bent his head forward, kissing her belly, slowly migrating upward until he reached the bottom curve of one of her breasts. Her hands were in his hair, gripping, holding him steady.

*Like there was somewhere else he'd rather be, right now.*

Nipping her pink nipple, he raked his teeth gently over the hard nub, drawing out the breathy moan that'd haunted him for nearly forty-eight hours, then sucked the delicacy in his mouth again. "Feel good, Sweetheart?—huh?" he graveled softly. "Does it make you wet? Does it make you want to sit on my cock, right now?"

"Y-yes."

With a low carnal groan Randall possessively palmed her sweet ass lifting her feet off the ground, settling Lana onto his lap so that her legs straddled his powerful thighs.

Careful not to bump his injured shoulder, Lana clung to him, likely both surprised and turned on by his sudden loss of control. Nose to nose, they paused for a moment, looking into one another's eyes, breathing the same air. And when the pull became too strong, their mouths met in an all-consuming kiss.

Lana palmed the sides of his unshaven face, tilting her head a bit to deepen the kiss while her hips slowly rocked, grinding her sex against his hard rod in an attempt to ease the pleasurable ache.

The sensual glide of her hips beneath his hands threatened his sound mind, which was pretty ironic considering his thoughts tended to be rather flawed and dirty where Lana was concerned. Tearing his mouth away from her lips he trailed hot, moist kisses over her chin, down the hollow of her throat, stopping occasionally to nip her vanilla-scented flesh with his teeth.

The tempo of her hips slowed as she added more pressure, rubbing her sex over him good and hard. "Christ, Lana", he growled against her neck.

Reaching down between them, he pulled her knit boxers and panties to the side with his fingers, then ran the pad of his callused thumb over her slippery, wet clit. The sweet sound of her soft whimpers urged him on as he rubbed the ache away in gentle, lazy circles.

His shoulder screamed with pain, but that didn't matter. Not now. Not when she was panting, whimpering. Not when her sweet honey coated his fingers. Not when he was so close to watching her come apart in his arms again. "Tell me what you want, Sweetheart. I want to hear you say it."

"I... please, I... Don't stop", she breathed.

"Tell me more", he growled, low and rough, increasing his

pace.

A soft carnal whimper fled her parted lips a moment before she uttered, "Make me come. *Please...*"

With his thumb still gliding over her sensitive nub he rotated his right hand a bit, allowing his fingers to delve between her slippery folds. Almost immediately he could feel her hot flesh drawing tighter around his fingers in preparation.

Then something unexpected happened. There was a steady pounding on the door, followed by, "*Mommy?*"

In an instant Lana's eyes flew open in panic, her feet landing on the tile floor in the blink of an eye. "Connor, you're supposed to be sleeping!" she uttered through the door, her voice trembling with both arousal and fear.

"I need a drink of water."

Lana quickly straightened her clothes, then carefully opened the door just enough to squeeze her body through. "C'mon, you can have a few sips, and then it's back to bed, okay?"

" 'kay."


Lana removed the Brita pitcher from the fridge, pouring just enough water into his favorite Spiderman cup to quench his thirst, and then handed it to her son. "Better?"

Connor nodded, then handed his mom the empty cup.

"C'mon, I'll tuck you back in." Retracing their steps back into the hallway, she followed behind her little boy, eyeing the bathroom as she continued to Connor's room. Her face flushed red at the memory of what'd taken place minutes ago behind that wood-paneled door.

Lana couldn't believe how quickly she'd lost control. She'd basically dry-humped Randall in her guest bathroom, then begged him to make her come after he'd pulled her panties to the side. What was it about Randall Burns that drove her normally-sane mind delirious?

*Piercing gray eyes, broad chest, chiseled abs.*

Pick one.

His perfectly sculpted body, the low timbre of his voice

while he urged her on, and those sinfully talented hands and mouth of his didn't help, either.

Nope, not one darn bit.

She drew the comforter back while Connor slipped back into bed, then hauled the covers over his little body, planting a kiss on his forehead before turning to leave.

It was becoming blatantly obvious to Lana that Randall Burns was soon becoming her Achilles heel. An incurable weakness. His touch, his kisses were lethal to her normally-subdued sensibility.

"He all right?" Randall questioned when Lana emerged from Connor's room.

Nodding feebly, Lana carefully closed the door behind her and motioned for Randall to follow her into the living room. "That can't happen again", she uttered quietly. "Do you know how close we were to Connor walking in on us?"

Randall ran his hands through his dark hair before resting them low on his hips. "I know. It was too close."

"We can't do this"—she gestured between them with her hands"—when he's here. It's too risky. I'm sorry."

Randall stepped forward, palming her face, tilting her head back a bit so he could look into her blues eyes. "We'll be more careful next time—there *is* a next time, right?"

Seductively nibbling her bottom lip, Lana smiled. "Are you kidding me? After the way you left me hanging a few minutes ago, you *owe* me a next time."

# Chapter 20

Mayor Cliffburg sat on his throne at the front of the small auditorium as eager residents filed into empty seats for the monthly city commission meeting. He liked to think he was a charismatic man—these mindless imbeciles had voted him into office for two terms, after all. Obviously they liked him.

Typically he could be found chatting up the residents on a night like this, mingling, laying the foundation for what would likely be another term in office come this November.

But not tonight.

Because at the moment he couldn't peel his eyes off the lovely Lana Phillips.

It wasn't an unusual phenomenon, really: watching her. But tonight there was something mysteriously peculiar about her. He couldn't quite put his finger on it yet, but he would. He had a keen sense, a God-given ability to read people—just one of the reasons why he was such a successful politician. He used these artful skills regularly, analyzing body language, interpreting the hidden meaning behind idle conversation. Hell, he knew what most of the feeble-minded people in the room tonight wanted before they did.

But something about Lana's calm, buoyant demeanor eluded him.

She seemed…different, somehow. Good different.

The average Joe here tonight probably hadn't noticed the change. At first glance she appeared normal, which was to say: simply beautiful. But his trained eyes saw something new—a brilliant spark, if you will.

The kind of radiance a woman exhibited when she was open to change.

Open to...*possibilities*...

Squirming in his leather executive chair, he tried to find a comfortable position that didn't expose the bulge growing behind the fly of his khaki Dockers. Eyeing the clock, he reached for the coveted gavel and gave the small square block a hard whack, transferring his sexual frustration to the wooden mallet.

The mayor cleared his throat before addressing the room. "Good evening, folks. We have a lot to cover tonight, so if you don't mind I'd like to get an early start."

His eyes targeted Lana's angelic face. He noted the confusion that'd briefly settled between her dark brows, and then his focus landed on the sway of her hips as she hurried to her seat, the rapid tempo of her black heels tapping against the floor conjuring up all sorts of inappropriate images in his mind. Reaching for the device she used to record the meeting in its entirety, she sunk into her chair, giving him a firm nod to proceed.

"Okay... For the record, today's date is April seventeenth, two-thousand-thirteen. And let the record also reflect that Commissioner Anthony and Commissioner Rhodes are both present, as well. The first topic on our lengthy agenda this evening touches on the scheduled repaving of Main Street. Commissioner Rhodes", he uttered into the mic as he turned his head slightly to the right, "can you give us an update about that project?"

"Certainly, Mayor Cliffburg. The proposed repaving of Main Street is..."

With the crowd's attention focused on Commissioner Rhodes, the mayor's eyes veered to the brunette sitting in the front row to his left. The hem of her pale yellow skirt had risen to mid-thigh, exposing her bare, lean legs. She'd crossed them like the lady she was, her top foot subtly swinging.

Up. Down. Up. Down.

The back of her shoe slipped off her heel, and she balanced the black stiletto on the tips of her toes.

The mayor swallowed a groan.

He'd waited long enough. It was time.

She was finally ready to take the next step in her life—he sensed that, now. And if he had anything to say about it, that next step was going to be with him. He was the most powerful man on the island—what woman didn't want a powerful man hovering above her in bed?

Just then Lana glanced up from her notepad, meeting his gaze with a breath-taking smile.

Yes, it was definitely time to make his move. And he knew just what to do...

Eyeing her watch, Lana sat in a booth at the local diner, drawing the smell of grease and fresh-baked apple pie into her lungs while eagerly awaiting the arrival of her lunch date.

"Sorry I'm late", Kendall explained as she slid into the seat across from Lana. "Chatty Debbie dropped by to pick up her prescription and somehow managed to steer the topic to waxing."

"Waxing? You mean, like hair—"

Kendall thrust her palm forward. "Trust me—you don't even want to know."

Lana laughed despite her best effort not to; she could only imagine how graphic and uncomfortable that conversation was. The woman was an open book, if you will—not the least bit concerned about airing personal subject matter to anyone within earshot.

"You order yet?"

"Yeah, told the waitress you were joining me; she went ahead and put your order in, too. Wasn't sure how late you'd be and I still have a ton of transcribing left from the city commission meeting the other night."

"I'm sorry", Kendall uttered genuinely. "If I'd known you were so busy, I wouldn't have asked you to lunch today."

Lana swept her hand in the air, waiving the suggestion aside. "It's fine, really. After spending most of the morning staring at my monitor, I kind of needed the break." Reaching for the glass of sweet tea to her left, she asked, "How've you been?"

"Well, it's allergy season. So the pharmacy's been a busy place this month."

"And Tenley?"

Kendall beamed at the mention of her daughter. "Rollin' all over the place—which is driving Ty bonkers. She rolls off the area rug and you'd think she was jumpin' off the roof the way he swoops down to rescue her!"

Laughing, Lana placed her tea on the table in front of her. "You have to admit, Kendall: that's pretty sweet."

"Yeah", she uttered wistfully, "I guess it sort of is." Kendall peered into space for a few long beats before emerging from her sappy trance. "All right, I have a confession."

"Okaaay", she drawled.

"Aside from the fact that we haven't had an opportunity to catch up in a few weeks, I had another motive for asking you to lunch today."

"Oh?" Reaching for her glass again, she took another sip.

Kendall nodded. "It's about Randall, actually. Have you noticed he's been acting sort of *strange* lately?"

Caught by surprise, Lana coughed, choking on her sweet tea. Pounding her fist against her chest, she regained her composure. "Strange? How do you mean?"

"I don't know—like he's hiding something, I guess. Remember last month when he sliced his shoulder open?" Lana nodded feebly. "Well, when I cleaned the wound I got this... weird vibe", Kendall shared, tucking a strand of inky-black hair behind her ear. "I asked him what was goin' on, but the only thing I managed to drag out of him was 'just stuff.'"

Moving her hands under the table, Lana began picking the coral polish from her thumb nails. "Maybe he's still not over you, Ken. I'm sure the idea of you and Ty still bothers him a little."

"That's what I thought at first, too. But my gut says differently..." Kendall placed her elbows on the table, resting her chin on her fists. "You see him a lot these days. Does he seem different to you?"

Swallowing hard, she glanced down at her pitiful-looking

manicure, scrambling to find her voice. Because she knew Randall's secret: it was the same one she'd been carrying around for the last month, as well. "Um, what do you mean?"

Kendall shrugged. "I don't know... Is he seeing anyone?"

"Wh-what makes you say that?"

The waitress chose that particular moment to approach the table, *thank goodness*, balancing their meals on a large circular tray. In a frenzy to accommodate the growing lunch crowd, she quickly lobbed their plates down on the table, then stole the ketchup from the small table behind them, striking the butt of the glass bottle against the tabletop with a thunderous whack. *"Sorry"*, she mouthed silently before dashing across the room to take care of another customer.

"Poor thing" Lana murmured. "Looks like she doesn't have any help at all today."

"We'll leave her a good tip, then." Kendall assured her. After removing the lid from the ketchup bottle she gave it a few good shakes. "So, back to our conversation..."

Crud. She'd sort of hoped the perfectly-timed interruption moments ago, coupled with the aroma of Kendall's favorite meal, had short-circuited her good friend's brain, giving Lana an out. But apparently that wasn't going to happen. "What were we talkin' about again?" Because if she couldn't dodge the subject completely, she could at least buy herself a moment or two to prep.

"Randall."

"Oh, yeah. Right."

"Has he confided in you about what's goin' on in his life?"

*You drive me crazy, Lana. I want to do things to you. Dirty things...*

"Um, yeah, I guess you could say that."

Kendall gently set the ketchup bottle on the table. Folding her hands in her lap, she gave a weak smile. "Good. I'm... I'm glad he's talking to you. I was really worried he was keeping it all in."

Lana didn't miss the hurt in Kendall's eyes: Randall hadn't come to her. The dynamic of their friendship had changed. And whether the alterations were permanent or temporary, the effect it had on Kendall was just the same.

"Look, Kendall—"

"It's okay. I knew the choices I made last year were going to affect our friendship... I miss him—I really do—but if I had to do it all over again, I'd have done the exact same thing. Even knowing how much I hurt him, I would." Kendall winced. "Gosh, that came out completely wrong—I sound like a cold-hearted bitch!"

"No, you don't", Lana countered as she stabbed a lettuce leaf with her fork. "You sound like a woman confident about the choices you made. And judging by how deliriously happy both you and Ty are, I'd say it was the right one."

"Thanks, I appreciate that. It's just... I want Randall to find what I have with Ty, you know? I want him to find the woman he's meant to be with." Kendall dipped an onion ring in ketchup, then popped it in her mouth. "I won't ask you to repeat what he shared with you, but can I ask you something else?"

*Oh, God.* "Yeah. Sure."

"Do you think he's close to finding her?"

A jolt of something that felt an awful lot like jealousy knocked against the inside of Lana's chest. Because the mere thought of Randall doing dirty things to another woman didn't sit right with her. "I don't know, Ken. I'd like to think he is. I really would..."

A low rumble unfurled from Lana's stomach as she situated herself in front of her computer just after lunch. She'd only managed to eat a few slivers of iceberg lettuce from her Cobb salad before her stomach protested. Funny how uncomfortable conversation could do that to a person: utterly suppress their ravenous appetite. And the subject matter over lunch with Kendall had managed to do just that.

And now she was paying the price, because her stomach was practically gnawing on her backbone. Thankfully she'd had enough sense to ask for a to-go container; she'd transcribe for a bit then take an early break, maybe even sit outside in the small courtyard for some fresh air. Yeah, that sounded like a good plan.

But it was incredibly hard to concentrate on her unfinished tasks when her mind kept drifting to Randall.

It'd been a month since he'd stripped her down to her bra and cowgirl boots in his hallway, twenty-seven days, to be exact, since he'd pressed her back against his mattress. And after Connor had nearly walked in on them several days after that, they'd agreed to err on the side of caution.

And it was killing her.

Oh, they still managed to steal a kiss here and there; "accidently" brush against the other in passing. Quite frankly, the last twenty-seven days could be summed up as one very long bout of foreplay.

But their dry spell would end this weekend when her parents took Connor for the night.

She'd be lying if she said she wasn't having doubts. Last time had been… well, phenomenal, but it'd also been entirely spontaneous. The only mission she'd had upon arriving at his place that night was to coerce him in to telling her why he'd barreled out of The Saloon without so much as a goodbye.

He'd told her, all right—right before he'd claimed her mouth and backed her into the hall.

Lana shivered at the memory.

This time she knew what she was getting into, and as exciting as that notion was, she was sort of nervous about doing it again. Her anxiety had absolutely nothing to do with Randall—at least, not directly.

Make no mistake: she wanted him. The desire she harbored for Randall Burns was deep. Bone-deep. So imbedded in her body she feared she'd never rid herself of the overwhelming need his touch inspired.

So what was causing this sudden bout of hesitation, one might ask?

Simple: Jimmy.

She'd already betrayed him once. Could she do it a second time? A third? A fourth?

*It's been nearly a year, Lana. It's not like you jumped in the sac with the guy immediately; wasn't as if you didn't spend countless nights awake trying to refute your attraction to his best friend.*

Placing the small headphones attached to the voice recorder over her ears, she pushed the worry aside and opened the Word document she'd saved just before lunch. Her stomach read her the riot act again at the mere thought of food, groaning its disapproval over her decision to return to work.

Her finger hovered over the PLAY button on the recorder when Mayor Cliffburg's deep voice wafted from his open door. "Lana, can I see you in my office for a minute?"

"Be right there, sir", she called out. Quickly removing her headphones, she pushed to her feet, stepping into the mayor's office with a cautious gait.

"Close the door and have a seat", he requested, poring over a pile of papers scattered about on his desk.

Picking at her nail polish—or rather, what was left of it— Lana nudged the door closed and slowly lowered her rear end into one of the burgundy winged-back chairs in front of his desk. Suddenly feeling as though she needed to explain why she was behind on loading Tuesday night's meeting minutes to the town website, she cleared her throat and lunged into an explanation. "If this is about the website, I can assure you everything will be uploaded by the time I leave today. There was just so much discussed at the meeting, I—"

The mayor placed his pen on his desk and leaned back in his chair. With his elbows resting comfortably on the arm rests, he tented his fingertips into a point just below his chin. "Good to know. But that's not why I asked you in here."

"Oh."

"I actually had an idea I wanted to run by you. I want your opinion."

"*My* opinion?" She questioned dubiously, slapping her palm against her chest. The mayor nodded. "I'm not sure if I'm qualified enough to—"

"I have a proposition."

"What kind of proposition?" She uttered, baffled.

The mayor studied her for a moment, his eyes softening. "I've been thinking... Memorial Day's coming up in a few weeks."

Lana fidgeted uncomfortably in her seat. She didn't need

Mayor Cliffburg to remind her of that; the holiday didn't mean the same thing to her anymore. Memorial Day wasn't an excuse to stay home from work and barbeque like it'd been in years' past. Its significance was personal, now. Tragically personal.

"Like I said—I've been thinking, and I'd really like to start a new tradition this year; get the entire town involved. How would you feel about conducting a charity event following the boat parade in Jimmy's honor?

"We could do a silent auction, have residents and businesses on the island donate various items for the cause, and the proceeds would benefit the Public Service Society—which, as you already know, lends support to injured public service workers and their families."

Lana sat motionless—speechless—as the clock on the mayor's desk ticked-off the seconds.

Tick. Tock. Tick. Tock.

*What did she think?* Well, Jimmy was a simple man. A modest man. His motivation for doing good deeds had zero to do with notoriety. A fundraiser in his honor was probably the last thing he'd want, but...

But she believed in the charity's mission, knew firsthand the kind of good the organization was capable of. "I-I don't know what to say... I'd..." Lana glanced at her lap while she found her voice, finally settling her gaze back on the Mayor. "I'd appreciate that. Very much."

Mayor Cliffburg smiled. "Then it's settled: The island's first annual Jimmy Phillips, Jr. Charity Silent Auction." Shifting his weight forward, he braced his forearms on the desktop. "With that established, we need to focus our attention on planning the event. Maybe you could load something on the website, advertising the affair."

"Of course—no problem—"

"And we need to hit the pavement, requesting donations from local businesses and residents."

"Consider it done."

"This is going to take some time to organize. You think you can make yourself available after regular office hours for the next few weeks?"

Lana nudged a strand of hair that'd fallen in her field of vision. "It shouldn't be a problem. I can make this happen—I *want* to make this happen."

"I have faith in you, Lana. You never cease to amaze me."

# Chapter 21

A cool, sharp breeze swept over the boardwalk as the sun slumped below the horizon. Seagulls squawked overhead searching for an easy meal, no doubt, and the occasional pelican observed the growing crowd, perched on wood pillars along the pier railing. Randall drew the crisp salty air into his lungs as the soles of his shoes knocked against the wood.

Clap. Clap. Clap. Clap.

His shift had ended roughly half an hour ago. He'd quickly gone home to shower before falling into his Saturday night ritual. The promise of two dollar domestic drafts at The Saloon beckoned him week after week without fail. Exercising his skills on the billiard table, sipping cold frothy beer from a frosted mug, fraternizing with the guys, had lured him to the smoke-filled bar once again. But for the first time in recent memory he wasn't the least bit thrilled about being here.

Shoving the heavy wood door aside Randall slipped into the dim lounge, weaving through the growing crowd toward the billiard area at the back of the establishment. Beams of colored light highlighted the smoky haze on the dance floor, flickering in time with the beat of Jason Aldean's *Dirt Road Anthem*. The dance floor was swarming with people—mostly women—yet through the congestion of swaying bodies it'd still only taken mere seconds to zero in on Lana.

Vivid hues of pink and blue light flashed across her silken skin. Long brown hair fell around her pretty face in soft waves, his fingers practically twitching at the thought of running them through it. Arms in the air, her hips moved with the kind of fluidity that made a man take notice. Visions of Lana straddling his lap while rolling those flexible hips over his cock crept into his mind...

And that's when he suddenly became aware that his feet were no longer in motion. He wasn't sure how long he'd been standing there enjoying the show, how long he'd been practically drooling at the sight of her, but he did know for certain he'd draw unwanted attention to his involuntary reaction if he didn't get moving again.

Tearing his eyes away from the sweet spectacle, he willed his feet to move toward the pool table in the back corner where Grant already awaited him.

"What took you so long, Burns?" Granted greeted, slapping his palm against Randall's before pulling him in for a shoulder bump. "Thought you were gonna stand me up."

"Stopped at home to take a shower."

"You got a hot date or somethin'?"

Randall snatched a cue stick from the wall display, then sidled up to the pool table. "A date with a cue stick and a boatload of beer."

Grant chuckled. "Easy there, buddy—wouldn't want anyone to accuse you of moving too fast on the first date."

Randall's gaze averted to the brunette leaving the dance floor, heading his way. Those deep-blue eyes locked onto his, the hint of a smile playing across her soft pink lips.

"Hard to go slow when something tastes so good." And Randall should know—because the anticipation of tasting Lana again tonight after a month of slow torture was wreaking havoc on his head. Both of them.

"Womack", Lana called out over the music. "Where's your wife? She was supposed to be here almost an hour ago."

Grant smiled, shaking his head. "I talked to her earlier this afternoon. She said she was headed to Ty's to work in the dark room for a bit." Swallowing a mouthful of beer, he set his mug on a nearby high-bar table, freeing his hands so he could begin racking the billiard balls. "I swear the woman loses all sense of time when she's in there. You want me to give her a call?"

Lana waived the offer aside. "She probably got caught up playing with Tenley and talkin' to Kendall."

Randall braced the edge of the pool table with his hands, digging his fingers into the green felt to keep from reaching for her—his grip so tight the skin covering his knuckles paled. Across the crowded room she'd been gorgeous, but up close she was damn near irresistible.

His grip tightened when she turned to him and smiled—not an *I'm-trying-to-be-polite* kind of smile, but rather *I'm-secretly-picturing-all-the-naughty-things-I'm-going-to-do-to-you-later-tonight* kind of smile. Randall swallowed a groan. Fuck, how the hell was he going to make it the next few hours without touching her?

"Good to see you, Randall", she uttered skillfully, the mere tone of her voice resembling something more like a purr.

"Same goes."

She studied him for an extra beat, nibbling on that bottom lip as though she was holding back what she really wanted to say. "Well, I'll let you boys get back to your game, then." With a deliberate sway to her hips, Lana returned to the dance floor, squeezing her way through the sea of bodies to a less crowded segment of the dance arena.

*Just take a deep breath, Burns. You've waited a month to be with her again—what's three more hours?*

Three more hours of pretending not to notice the way she looked in that orange mini dress would likely be his cause of death. The sweater material caressed her silhouette much in the same way a Ferrari hugs a winding road. And don't even get him started on those brown fuck-me cowgirl boots...

The waitress appeared through the thick haze balancing a tray of various cold beverages. She carefully handed Randall a frosted mugful of Miller Lite.

"Keep 'em comin', darlin'", he told her a moment before catching the rim of the glass between his lips. Because he had a feeling it was going to be a long night.

A very long night indeed.


Stalking the perimeter of the pool table, Randall contemplated his options. All that remained in order to win this round against Grant was the solid green number six, and the black eight-ball. Problem was they were practically rubbing elbows, and the last thing he wanted to do was slip up and knock the eight-ball in prematurely.

He did another quick lap around the perimeter, finally accepting that his best shot would require him to lie across the length of the table to sink number six into the opposite corner pocket.

Randall got into position, adjusting the angle with which he held the cue stick until the chalked-tip was perfectly aligned with his mark. He eased the stick back and forth over his left thumb a few times before he committed to it, then with a deep breath slowly drew the stick back again. The tip was a whisper away from colliding against the white cue when a glimpse of orange entered his peripheral. And in that split-second—when the success of the shot depended on his undivided attention—his concentration lifted from the table.

Vital mistake: number one.

"What the fuck was that?" Ty ribbed beside him.

The white cue rolled to the left at a snail's pace, finally coming to a halt about a foot away. Damn!

"Either I'm getting' better, or you're havin' one hell of a bad night, Burns", Granted boasted, exposing the signature GQ grin the women on the island still went gaga over.

Needless to say, it had no effect on Randall.

"The latter", Ty announced wryly. "Definitely the latter."

Rising from the green felt-covered table, Randall stood and reached for his beer, draining the remainder in one swift gulp.

Chrissakes, the woman got under his skin. And judging by the way she was looking at him right now, midnight eyes ablaze with need, he was getting to her too.

After stealing a quick glance at his watch, Randall slapped Mark on the back, shoving the length of the cue stick against the guy's chest. "Play this round for me; I'm sittin' this one out."

"But I suck at pool."

"Couldn't be any worse than me tonight." Randall turned

toward the dance floor, closing the distance between him and the woman in orange.

"Hey", he greeted, coming to a halt in front of her.

"Hey."

Electricity crackled around them. He shoved his hands in his front pockets in an attempt to control them. "Where's your two sidekicks?" He asked, referring to Olivia and Kendall.

"Bathroom. You know us women: we always do bathroom breaks in pairs."

"So", he uttered, shifting his weight, "you're all alone out here, then?"

"Why, are you offering to keep me company?" Lana smiled, then caught her bottom lip between her teeth.

*Holy mother of God!*

He couldn't do this anymore, couldn't be in the same room with this woman and pretend he didn't want her. Couldn't pretend to give a shit about playing pool with the guys when what he really wanted was to strip her out of her orange number and home in on the treasures beneath.

"C'mon, we're dancing", he announced, taking her hand. Not a request, but rather a *command*. Dodging bodies in motion, he led her through the crowd to the other side of the dance floor, wrapping her in his strong arms. The lights dimmed blue and the once upbeat tempo suddenly slowed as Sugarland wafted from the speakers.

The slow ballad gave him an excuse to hold her closer, to feel her soft body press against his.

Vital mistake: number two.

Because just like that he was caught in her spell.

Bowing his head a bit he breathed her in, amazed that even through the thick cloud of nicotine haze he still caught a whiff of vanilla. "You pick that dress out tonight to torture me?" He uttered.

Smiling innocently, she answered, "Why, you like?"

"Very much. In fact, I think orange is my new favorite color."

"You mean: peach."

Raising his head he looked down at her pretty face, currently a subtle shade of blue from the overhead lights.

"What is it with you women: always referring to colors as food. Suddenly purple's eggplant or grape, green's lime or avocado, and orange can be anything from salmon to carrot to—"

"Peach", she interrupted.

"Yeah, *peach*."

Lana's lips lifted into a smile. "You have something against peach, now?"

He thought back to the night he'd argued that sippin' pink wine put a man's masculinity into question. The night of their first kiss. "No, I happen to like peaches. So sweet. So juicy…"

Randall wet his lips, satisfied when Lana's gaze moved to his mouth. Her lips parted slightly in anticipation, her eyes aflame with wantonness and blazing need. "You keep lookin' at me like that, Sweetheart, and I'm liable to throw you over my shoulder and take you home", he warned.

"And how am I looking at you?"

"You're undressing me with your eyes."

"Am not!" But when Randall gave her his bullshit detector glare, she quickly changed her answer. "Okay, so maybe I am. A little."

Their eyes met and held. Electricity snapped around them again, sizzling, popping as their chemistry ignited. Without thinking Randall swept a strand of hair from her face, noting how her eyes closed, relishing his touch.

Vital mistake: number three.

*Control yourself, Burns. People are watching.*

As the song wound to an end, he bowed his head, his mouth inches from her ear. "I want you to go home, now. Strip down and wait for me…"

Lana gasped softly. "Strip?"

With a wry grin, Randall nodded. "Everything except for the boots; I do have a weakness for those boots."

"Come with me", she murmured, the sound of her voice a little more breathless than she'd intended.

The corners of his mouth rose in unison this time. He was getting to her. And when the assessment sunk in and took hold, his expression turned serious—as in seriously hot. "As much as you want my rod, right now—as much as I want to give it to you—we can't leave together. It'll look suspicious—

*especially* if my truck's spotted in your driveway all night."

*And the fact that the two of you are still pressed against one another while the rest of the crowd's moving and twirling to a hasty beat isn't suspicious?*

Point taken.

Peeling his hands from the small of her back, Randall reached for her hand, entwining their fingers before hauling her off the dance floor.

*All night*, she recalled him saying a moment ago.

*All night!*

Lana shivered. Her body just involuntarily reacted to him. The tenor of his low gritty voice, the feel of his big hands gliding over her skin, the sight of broad sinewy muscle bulging beneath his T-shirt unified, stirring a deep yearning. The combination practically liquefied her bones, leaving a weak, wanton woman in its wake. She tried to talk herself down, tried to reason with her limbs, but her body rebelled.

Bad, bad body.

Because she'd been so caught up in Randall Burns, so unhinged by his close proximity, she'd nearly forgotten they were still on the crowded dance floor surrounded by women that believed gossiping was a competitive, full-contact sport.

Randall gave her hand a firm squeeze before loosening his grip. The moment his fingers slipped from her grasp she already missed them. "How much longer are you going to be?"

"Long enough to play one more round", he answered, shoving his hands in his pockets again.

"*Hurry.*"

The neediness in her voice caused a grin to spread across his lips. "What's in it for me?"

"Oh, don't worry—I'll make it worth your while."

And just like that, his smile disappeared. "An hour—tops."

# Chapter 22

The cadence of Lana's rapid heartbeat drummed in her ears as she stared at her reflection. Ten minutes. She only had ten minutes until he arrived.

And she was freaking out!

She'd spent the last month fantasizing about tonight, methodically planning how she'd seduce the socks off Randall Burns. And now that the time had arrived she feared her courage would fizzle.

She was new at this seduction thing. Last time with Randall had been so spontaneous—*so hot*—there'd been no time to be nervous, no time to second guess.

This time was different.

Anticipation had been building for a month—one very long month. What if she didn't live up to his expectations? What if tonight proved to Randall she hadn't been worth the four-week wait?

Lana ran a brush through her long brown locks, pondering her last thought. It was her own insecurity, she knew. She'd lost her virginity at seventeen to Jimmy, and although they'd had an active sex-life, that by no means qualified her as an "expert" on the subject.

*Randall's not looking for an expert. He wants you.*

A shiver worked its way down her spine at that realization. He wanted her.

Randall Burns wanted *her...*

Lana's heart thumped against her chest. She wanted to be

bold, wanted Randall to understand how she ached for his touch. Steeling her spine, she vowed to follow through with her carefully-calculated plan. No regrets.

The sound of the front door closing drew her from her contemplative trance. This was it, the moment they'd both been waiting for.

"*Lana?*" She heard him call out from the living room.

Giving herself a last minute once-over, she drew in a fortifying breath. Tonight was a new beginning. Because if the last year had taught her anything, it was that life was precious and utterly unpredictable.

It was past time for her to take a risk.

It was time to start living again.


Using the key she'd given him a few months back, Randall unlocked the front door and stepped into the dimly lit living room. His eyes immediately homed in on the lone kitchen chair in the middle of the room, or more importantly, the hand-written note that read "SIT HERE", propped along the ladder back.

*What is she up to?*

Following directions, he lowered his large frame onto the wooden chair, then called out to her. He'd done everything he could to cover his tracks tonight, beginning with the deliberate loss he'd incurred back at The Saloon. Everyone knew he hated losing—at pool, at anything, really—which gave him an excuse to pay his tab and cut out early. He'd gone home, parked his truck in the driveway, then made the four-street trek to Lana's by foot. And the nosy onlookers were none the wiser.

Just the way he and Lana wanted it.

He heard the soft click of Lana's boots before he actually saw her. And when she finally emerged from the hall wearing a barely there, see-through white tank top, a pair of white lacey panties, and those fuck-me cowgirl boots, he went instantly hard. "Thought I told you to strip down—everything off except the boots."

"You did. But seeing how you enjoyed watching me dance

tonight, I figured I'd"—Lana drew in a shaky breath—"give you a private show."

Randall interlocked his fingers behind his head. "You have my undivided attention, Sweetheart."

*You can do this. Be brave,* she silently chanted. Reaching for the remote she turned on the stereo and slowly walked forward, beginning her seductive performance as Whitesnake washed over them. Her hands trembled at first, her knees weak, but Randall's attentive gaze, coupled with the sound of the popular eighty's band soothed her rattled nerves.

She stood in front of him just out of reach, her body flowing gracefully, effortlessly. Gathering the hem of her thin white tank, she teased him with a glimpse of her pierced navel. He groaned softly in appreciation, and suddenly she wasn't afraid. Suddenly she felt like the most beautiful woman in the world.

Suddenly she felt powerful.

With a renewed sense of courage, she stepped in between the V of his legs and raised the hem higher, higher still. She barely managed to get her top off before he reached for her breasts. Swatting his hand away, she flashed a wicked grin. "Huh-uh, I'm not done yet."

He humored her for another minute or two, but when she turned away from him and sat on his lap, wriggling her sweet ass against his fly, his self-control snapped. He reached around, cupping her breasts while spreading soft kisses over her bare back.

Lana gave in to the pleasure for a few beats, then abruptly stood to warn him he wasn't playing by the rules.

Only he followed her up and came at her with eyes blazing.

She took off running down the hall, squealing when she glanced over her shoulder, discovering he was one step behind her. When he finally caught up to Lana in her bedroom, he reached for her arm and gave it a tug, twirling her around to face him. Without a word, he placed the palm of her hand against the rock hard bulge behind his fly.

"See what you do to me?" He graveled, slowly backing her further into the dimly lit master bedroom.

The moment she felt the duvet against the backs of her legs she sat, the palm of her hand still rubbing the fly of his faded blue jeans. "You're overdressed, Mr. Burns."

With a wry grin, Randall reached over his shoulder and yanked the light blue tee over his head, his hooded eyes glued to hers. They stared at one another for a beat or two before Lana lowered her gaze to his broad, bare chest, down over the ridges and valleys of his six-pack abs, to the dark trail of hair that disappeared behind the denim.

She watched in amazement as his muscles bunched and bulged, loving the way his abs tightened as her fingers worked to unbutton his jeans. The moment his sex sprang free she gripped him, running her tongue along the length of his hard shaft she sampled the bead of hot liquid that'd collected along the tip.

A deep moan vibrated from his chest a moment before he palmed the sides of her face; tilting her head back he looked into her eyes. "Lie back", he ordered softly, sternly.

Randall tore into a foil package, quickly rolling the latex down his length before losing his pants. And when he was gloriously naked, save from the thin layer of latex sheathing his large shaft, he carefully hauled her white panties down her thighs, over her fuck-me boots.

Lana stared up at him as his eyes raked over her bare skin. His slow perusal heightened the ache between her legs. He had this way of looking at her, a way of making her feel cherished and beautiful. She loved that about him. Loved how riveted he was at the mere sight of her unclad body.

"Spread your legs for me, Sweetheart", he uttered just above a whisper. He waited while she complied, observing the slow movements of her knees as they gradually opened. "Christ, you're beautiful." Climbing onto the bed he pushed her knees further apart with his hands.

She should feel embarrassed, humiliated, bashful. But the carnal look in his gray eyes seemed to fan the flame burning inside her. The moisture between her legs blossomed as he hovered above, his strong hands holding her knees apart while he looked his fill.

"This is what you do to me", she whispered seconds before

his mouth came down on her.

The first slick lap of his tongue had Lana panting, and when he added a finger to the mix, and then another, she reached down, grabbed a fistful of his hair and rode the wave of pleasure pulsing deep inside. Her orgasm swiftly slithered through her writhing body, catching her by surprise. She'd been wound so tight—had been waiting for this moment for four long weeks—that nearly thirty seconds into his oral escapade, she'd detonated.

At some point she became aware that his hair was still lodged in her firm grip. "S-sorry", she said releasing the thick black strands.

"Don't be", he mumbled against her hip, spreading soft kisses up her body. "I love it when you lose control." His lips brushed over her stomach near her piercing, steadily continuing north until he reached the swell of her breasts. He briefly paid homage to her nipples, sucking each hard nub into his mouth, reigniting her desire almost instantly. "Please", Lana moaned, feeling the throbbing ache return between her legs. She had to have him.

Now.

Needed to feel this powerful man fill her with purpose and pleasure and... love.

Answering her plea Randall's weight came down on her, chest to chest. Skin to skin. Spreading open-mouth kisses along the hollow of her throat, he wrapped his arms around her and rolled to his back, which inevitably shifted her body above him.

And then he kissed her, an all-consuming, deep kiss that told her he was right there with her—teetering on the edge of control.

"I like this vantage point", Randall murmured when she broke the kiss and sat upright, her legs astride his hips. Lana smiled, her long brown locks falling around her pretty face. His hands slowly migrated up her smooth thighs until they reached the moist, succulent folds between. And when the pad of his thumb gently brushed over the sensitive nub where his tongue had been minutes ago, her smile faded on a gasp.

"Now, please", she begged in a voice she barely recognized

as her own.

Planting one of her palms against his broad, solid chest Lana lifted her bottom, then guided the tip of his sex into position with her other hand. Inch by glorious inch, she lowered herself onto him, giving in to the pleasure-pain as her tight flesh stretched to accommodate his thick shaft.

"Christ, Lana." With Lana now fully seated on his cock, he dug his fingers into her hips to hold her steady. "Hold on, Sweetheart. I just"—Randall blew a puff of air from his lungs—"need a sec."

Feeling generous she gave him exactly two seconds before she wriggled her bottom, garnering enough friction to cause a whimper to flee her lips. She was burning up inside, smoldering when she looked down at him again. Because something about his unsteady breaths, his tightly clenched jaw, and the salacious haze in his hooded eyes hinted that he was barely clinging to his self-control. Randall Burns was an alpha male through and through. He was the commander in his previous relationships—always the one to lead—always dominating. The ringmaster.

And he was giving that up. Giving her carte blanche over *him*.

This was her show, now. She was the director.

She was in charge.

Gazing into the depths of her blue eyes he eased his grip, giving Lana the signal she'd been waiting for.

Planting both palms on his solid chest for leverage, she lifted her bottom, rising onto her knees until the tip of his cock brushed the gateway to her core. And when Randall drew in a breath through clenched teeth with a hiss, she slid back down his thick rod until she was fully seated again.

Lana quickened the pace to her unbridled ride, feeling powerful and unbelievably sexy. The expression on his face, the passion in his eyes, fueled her. Knowing she had this effect on him brought her closer to the pinnacle of pleasure. His roughened voice urged her on until finally she shattered, throwing her head back, chanting his name, practically melting into him, never wanting the riveting sensation to end.

With a few choice obscenities, Randall gripped her hips

steady and thrust into her from below, his body flexing under her fingertips as he followed her over the edge.

Moments later Lana leaned forward, pressing her weary, sweat-slickened body against his. There was a stretch of comfortable silence as they both worked to draw air into their lungs.

Still buried deep in her tight heat Randall swaddled his arms around her, needing to get closer. Nuzzling her neck, he swept his lips along her salty-vanilla skin. "I have an idea."

"I'm all ears", Lana sighed contentedly, feeling him smile against her neck.

"Let's hit the shower. I'll wash your back, you wash mine."

"Feeling dirty again, are you?"

Randall chuckled softly against her ear. "Something like that."

"Good. I like it when you're dirty."

With a sudden renewed spark Randall gripped her ass and stood, making his way into the master bath, letting Lana's sweet laughter wash over him.

# Chapter 23

It was well after three in the morning before they fell into bed again—to sleep, that is—because after they'd lathered one another in the shower (a bout of foreplay Randall wasn't likely to ever forget), he'd plunged into her body twice more.

His eyes scanned the room. Repetitive rows of bright light traversed the lavender walls as the sun's splendor permeated the blinds. Overhead, the ceiling fan pirouetted unsteadily, causing a rhythmic click as the seconds ticked by. It hadn't been his intention to stay the night, but holding Lana as she drifted to sleep, hearing the cadence of her soft, even breaths, had been hard to walk away from.

And wasn't that the crux of it. Because last night he caught a glimpse of what a lifetime with Lana might look like: losing himself in her heavenly body, kissing, laughing, their sated souls finally falling into bed together with exhaustion after hours of loving. A deep ache unfurled in his chest. He wanted this with her, wanted to make a go of it, but that couldn't happen.

Not now, maybe not ever.

Staring up at the whirling fan blades he pondered that. He'd really made a mess of things. Steering clear of Lana Phillips was the right thing to do, but even knowing this he just... *couldn't.* He tried to tell himself it was because of the promise he'd made to Jimmy on the brittle forest floor back in Tate's Hell last year, but then he'd be lying. His presence in Lana and Connor's life may've started out that way, but it was more than that, now.

Being here didn't feel like an obligation anymore. In fact, he couldn't remember the last time guilt lured him to this address. He liked the person he was with Lana, liked that she saw him as someone worthy, important.

*Of all the women in your life, why did you have to fall for her?*

Nothing good could come from loving his best friend's wife, that much he did know. Because just the mere thought of the emptiness she'd leave behind when this thing was through warped his weary mind. Randall pinched the bridge of his nose and clenched his eyes shut, searching his brain for his next move. The right move.

He'd been so caught up in Lana Phillips' spell he'd almost believed that this thing between them was real. It wasn't, at least not philosophically speaking. Because there was no denying the realness of their combustible chemistry. But believing there could be more, that he could play the leading male role in her life, was just about the most moronic idea he'd ever cooked up. And Lord knew how many of those he'd had over the course of his thirty years.

"You do that every morning?"

Randall's head snapped to the gorgeous brunette lying beside him, hair a bit disheveled from sex and sleep. "Good morning. How long have you been lying there awake?"

Lana turned to her side and propped her hand against her temple. "Long enough to witness the deliberations goin' on inside that head of yours."

"Which head are we talkin' about?" He teased, but one look into her probing blue eyes assured him she wasn't buying his witticism this morning.

"You know what I meant", she uttered softly. "Does this"—she gestured between them with her free hand—"feel weird to you? I mean, being here, in this house—in this bed— with *me.*"

Rolling on his side to face her, he raked an unruly strand of hair from her face with his fingertips. "It should, but for the life of me I can't figure out why it doesn't. Because right now", he mumbled against her jaw, "there's nowhere else I'd rather be."

And that was the God's honest truth—no matter how sick or twisted it was, this was exactly want he wanted.

In the next instant he rolled her beneath his hard body, kissing her long and deep. His fingertips traipsed across her bare skin, gradually making their way to the succulent folds at the apex of her thighs.

"Mmm, you're so wet", he murmured against her ear, his finger disappearing into her body.

"I dreamt about you", she breathed.

"Yeah? Tell me about it. What did I do to you?"

"I...y-you did...we...we were—*Omigod, Randall!*" She screamed when he sucked her nipple into his mouth.

"What's wrong, Sweetheart—having trouble multi-tasking? Huh?" To make his point, he added a second finger while his thumb worked over the responsive bundle of nerves at the juncture of her thighs, his mouth simultaneously suckling her sensitive nipples, causing her to cry out in pleasure. "Can't think past how good I make you feel?"

Lana's nails bit into his shoulders as her lithe body squirmed beneath his. "Randall", she whimpered. "I want you—that's all I've got, right now."

"Tell me more, Sweetheart; I need to hear you say it. What do you want?"

"You—inside me. *Please...*"

The neediness in her voice startled her for a beat, but she didn't waver. And when he withdrew his fingers from her body, she quickly reached for the lone condom lying on the nightstand beside her and rolled it down his engorged shaft.

His weight came down on her again, but instead of pushing into her he took his time, caressing her skin with his hands and mouth. Lana's hips bucked in frustration, desperately seeking friction to ease the pulsing ache between her legs.

"Huh-uh", he whispered against her jaw. "This time we're going slow."

"Are you trying to kill me?"

Randall chuckled under his breath. "No, but what a way to go." He nibbled the delicate skin along her collarbone for another minute or so, then finally ended the torturous foreplay by sliding into her wet sex.

Randall filled her completely—physically, emotionally. His slow, methodical thrusts, his masterful touch and endearing kisses released something inside her, threading the final stitch in her broken heart. This incredibly giving man had managed to close the gaping hole, his strong presence mending the unfathomable.

And she loved him for it.

"Don't hide", he groaned softly. "Look at me."

Those skillful fingers reached down between them again, gliding over her wet flesh in soft, lazy circles, drawing the tension tighter.

"Come for me, Sweetheart. I want to watch you."

Meeting his piercing gaze she tumbled over the peak, raking her nails over his back, her sensual whimpers echoing off the walls of the room.

"God, Lana", he growled through clenched teeth as her body pulsed around him, milking his shaft as he spilled into the latex barrier.

They'd barely recovered when the sound of her mother's voice echoed from the living room. *"Lana...?"*

Sharing a quick holy-shit expression, they scrambled out of bed in search of cover. Randall snatched his jeans, then dashed into the bathroom, his broad shoulders crashing into the door jamb before shutting the door behind him.

*"Lana!"* Her mother called again.

"Be right out!" She fed her arms through a white terrycloth robe, cinched the sash around her waist, and opened the door, desperately taming her wild mane with her fingertips as she journeyed to the living room.

She was mortified to find Connor sitting on the couch sucking on a Blow Pop, her mother righting the kitchen chair that'd been knocked over the night before when Randall had charged at her during her strip tease. But that wasn't the worst of it, because when the chair was finally upright, her mother bent to pick up the note Lana scribbled last night, directing Randall into position.

This was awkward.

"Hi, Sweetheart", Lana said to her son. "Did you have fun?"

Connor popped the purple sucker from his mouth and nodded. "Want some?"

"No, thanks." Lana turned to her mother. "I, um... I thought you were bringing him by around noon."

"It *is* noon."

"Oh. I didn't realize, I guess."

Her mother's accusing eyes narrowed a bit as if to say: *obviously not, considering you were preoccupied.*

"Connor, why don't you finish your sucker in the kitchen? I'll be there in a few minutes to clean your sticky hands. I need to speak to Nana about something." Connor leapt off the couch with a buoyant step. "Don't bite down on the candy, all right? Don't want you to choke."

"I won't", he hollered back a second before a loud crunch sounded from the entrance to the kitchen.

Lana blew a slow, steady stream of air from her lungs, both from frustration of her son's disobedience and the uncomfortable conversation she was moments away from having with her mother.

Lauren Crawford waited until her grandson was out of earshot, then launched into her investigation. "Who's here?"

"Nobody—"

"Lana Kay, a woman doesn't make sounds like that when she's alone."

"It's the twenty-first century, Mom—you'd be surprised."

Her mother crossed her arms as surprise swept over her face. "I'm going to pretend I didn't hear that", she finally uttered on a sigh.

"Sorry."

Her mother's laser-like stare assessed her again. "I take it he's someone I know?—Someone Jimmy knew?" Lana nodded feebly. "Oh, honey, what are you doing? Do you have any idea what this'll do to your reputation?—How your carelessness might affect Connor?"

Lana felt anger boil inside her. "So what am I supposed to do, Mom? Spend the rest of my life alone? Give up hope of ever being happy again?"

"No, that's not what I'm saying—"

"Then what am I supposed to do? Since you think you're suddenly an expert on the subject, you tell me."

"I never claimed to be an expert, Lana. I just don't want you to do anything rash without first thinking about the possible outcome." Her mother stepped closer, placing her hands on Lana's shoulders, softening her tone. "Maybe this is the right thing for you. I don't have a crystal ball, honey; I can't see what tomorrow will bring. But you have to take into consideration there's also a possibility this whole thing could backfire. Are you prepared for that?" she asked worriedly. "Because no matter how much time has passed, the people loyal to Jimmy aren't going to like the idea of you moving on."

*She's right—especially when they discover who you've been moving on with.*

"Just promise me you'll give this relationship some thought and prepare yourself for what happens if things go—"

"Hey, Randall", Connor yelled excitedly after popping the sucker from his mouth. "Wanna see my tongue?"

Lana's eyes darted away from her mother's, quickly landing on the broad silhouette lurking in the shadows of the hallway.

"You've got a purple tongue, Squirt." She heard the shadow say.

Lana winced as her mother slowly turned her heard to glance over her shoulder.

*This is bad—really bad!*

But Lauren Crawford made no mention of the man eavesdropping in Lana's hallway. Instead, she pulled her daughter in for a hug before reaching for her purse on the end table. "I put a casserole in your fridge. It's a new recipe. Give me a call after dinner and let me know whatcha think."

And then she was gone, leaving Lana to pore over her mother's prudent plea.

# Chapter 24

Lana spent the remainder of April and most of May gearing up for the first annual charity auction in her late husband's honor. A myriad of details had immediately demanded her attention once the venue site had been chosen. She had to take into consideration crowd size, refreshments, auctioneer fee, etcetera, etcetera, etcetera.

After speaking with much of the island it was determined that nearly all eleven-hundred residents were planning to attend, which had made offering refreshments a bit of a problem. Luckily the local Senior Committee offered to provide lemonade and bottled water, and Chief Handler had volunteered the fire department to serve hotdogs to hungry bidders, leaving the city only responsible for the cost incurred by the auctioneer.

Day after day, Lana had marched into local businesses asking for donations for the upcoming auction. She'd already managed to collect a wide range of interesting items from the businesses located on the island, but it still wasn't enough. She wanted the charity event to be a tremendous success; couldn't wait to present the Public Service Society with a sizable check. Just thinking about all the good the organization could do with that money made her heart sing with pride.

Lana eyed the clock, noting she still had nearly forty-five minutes until her normal workday ended. She'd planned to venture to the mainland after work and convince more businesses to support the Public Service Society by donating items and services to the charity auction, but seeing how her inbox was completely empty at the moment she figured maybe she could get a head start.

Rising from her desk she peered through the mayor's opened door. "Got a minute?"

Mayor Cliffburg glanced from the document he'd been poring over since lunch and smiled. "For you, always. My eyes could actually use the break." He gestured to the twin winged-back chairs positioned in front of his desk and waited for her to take a seat. "Everything all right?"

"Um, yeah, everything's great."

He eyed her curiously for a stretch, almost as if he was trying to solve a riddle. "Good. Glad to hear it. And how're the donations coming along for the auction?"

"Well, that's actually why I wanted to talk to you."

The mayor leaned his back against the expensive leather, bracing his cheek with one of his manicured hands. "All right, let's hear it."

"Frankly, I've managed to get donations from just about every business within city limits—a whole range of items and services, actually. But I know we can do better. I was thinking of involving businesses on the mainland. It'd be an opportunity for them to show support for a local charity and draw new customers to their businesses—an invaluable marketing strategy, if you ask me."

A smile splayed across his lips. "I think it's brilliant. You really have a knack for this kind of work, Lana. I really mean that."

"Thanks", she uttered quietly. "It's a great cause and—"

"Yes, but it's more than that. You have this way about you—an innocence... It speaks to people."

"Thank you, sir."

"You're welcome...So, you headed to the mainland tonight?"

"Well since things are kind of slow at the moment, I was hoping to get a head start. Maybe drive to Apalachicola right now?"

"I don't think that'll be a problem. In fact"—he leaned

forward—"why don't I accompany you this evening? Teaming up with the mayor could entice more donations."

Lana tucked a lock of hair behind her ear. "Um, yeah, sure."

"Excellent", he announced cheerfully as he rose from his chair. "How 'bout I drive—we can pound the pavement, grab a bite to eat, then I'll swing you back by afterward to get your car."

A brisk, eerie chill swept over her spine, raising the hair on the back of her neck. She shivered slightly, recalling having felt the frigid bite once or twice before.

Stress. That's likely what it'd stemmed from.

She'd been cast into a highly strenuous role. And as thankful as she was for the opportunity to raise funds for the organization, bestowing a heroic legacy upon Jimmy's name, she couldn't deny the task had caused many sleepless nights.

Of course, Randall had been partly to blame for that as well.

"Lana?"

"Yes?"

"You ready?"

"Yeah, I'll get my purse."


"The auction will benefit the Public Service Society, a non-profit organization aimed at helping injured public service workers, like firemen and police officers, and their families. And..." Lana steeled her spine with a deep breath. "If the worker dies as a result of his injuries, the organization lends support to the widow."

"That sounds real nice, ma'am", said the owner of Jetson's Jingles, a small gift store in Apalachicola specializing in homemade jewelry. "I'd like to help—really, I would—but business is pretty slow these days. Tourism's down, which directly affects my bottom line."

Lana tucked a lock of hair behind her ear and smiled. "Mr. Jetson—"

"Please, call me David."

"Okay, David, I understand business has been slow. And

helping a complete stranger seems impractical when you're struggling to make ends meet too..." Clearing her throat, she continued, "The proceeds for this auction will help people like me, David. My husband was killed last year from injuries he sustained in the Tate's Hell brush fire."

David reached for his chest in surprise. "That was *your* husband?" Lana nodded feebly. "I'm... I'm so sorry for your loss."

"Thank you. I can't tell you how shocked I was to find the fire department chief and my husband's best friend at my door step that evening. Even more shocking was the sudden realization that my husband wasn't coming home. Frankly the first week or two after the accident was... a blur. But once the new bill cycle regenerated, I realized I had a whole new set of problems..."

Mayor Cliffburg was in awe. Lana was slowly reeling David in, inch by inch. The owner seemed kind enough—a law abiding citizen, turning his talent for making jewelry into profit. The recession had affected Florida tourism. Snow birds from up north, majority of whom lived on fixed incomes, hadn't migrated to the mild Gulf Coast last winter, and Jetson's Jingles, like many other businesses along the Panhandle, had surely suffered.

He knew, deep down, David wanted to help. He just needed to be convinced there was something in it for him.

"So you see, David, donating several pieces not only benefits families like mine, it also benefits you. Because not only will bidders see your beautiful creations, they'll also be made aware of your generosity. And you may not know this", she uttered quietly as she leaned over the jewelry counter for emphasis, cupping her hand around her mouth, "but word travels fast on Butler Island. And you know what they say: word-of-mouth is one of the most credible forms of advertising—not to mention, it's virtually free."

That assessment definitely seemed to intrigue the owner. David chewed on the information for several beats, tapping his fingertips against the glass jewelry display. Knowing she likely had David exactly where she wanted him, Lana remained silent, allowing her powerful argument to take root.

The woman was a born negotiator. She knew how to play her cards—when to push, and when to bite her tongue. And not for the first time that evening, Mayor Cliffburg wondered if she was like that in the bedroom. Did she give as good as she got? Was she a wildly fearless lover, disguised in an innocently beautiful package? He intended to find out.

"Well, you make a valid point, young lady. I could sure use a boost in sales. Guess it doesn't make a difference whether business is local or tourist-driven as long as it is business. Know what I mean?"

"Yes, I do."

David eyed them for another stretch then reached his hand over the jewelry display. "All right, I guess I can donate a few pieces for the auction."

Lana placed her dainty hand in David's and gave it a firm shake. "Thank you so much! I promise, you won't regret this decision."

Crimson stained David's cheek at her praise. The man was putty in Lana's small, delicate hands. No surprise there. She'd turned on the charm, related her personal experience with the organization, put a face on the difference the association could make in one's life as a result of selfless people like him.

Brilliant.

"Wait right here while I get everything ready."

David retreated to the back of the store, leaving Lana and Mayor Cliffburg alone. As soon as the owner disappeared behind a curtain of hand-threaded beads her bravado deflated, her shoulders sagging noticeably lower than they had been mere moments ago. "That was close", she uttered under her breath. "For a moment there, I thought no amount of convincing would sway him."

"Want to know what I think?" He asked, nudging an unruly lock of milk chocolate hair from her eye. "I think you don't give yourself enough credit. You're a force to be reckoned with, Lana Phillips. Frankly, the man didn't stand a chance."

Lana chuckled softly and smiled. "I suppose not." Then

her smile slowly faded as if she were recalling a long forgotten memory. "Jimmy used to say I could talk a person into just about anything as long as I could find an ounce of logic behind it."

Yes, he could see that. He could also see his usual tactics weren't going to woo Lana Phillips into his bed. Nope, she was far too sharp to fall for that. What he needed was finesse—get her talking about her late husband, get her to briefly revisit the utter despair she'd suffered. And when she suddenly needed someone to console her, she'd turn to him.

Mayor Cliffburg stole a peek at his silver Burberry watch, noting the time: six-o-eight. This was it. Tonight he'd finally make his move. "Listen, why don't we grab a bite to eat? I spotted an Italian restaurant across the street. I can head over and grab us a table while you wait for Mr. Jetson's donations."

There was a long stretch of silence, made all the longer by the way she chewed on her bottom lip. "Okay", she said finally. "A quick bite, then I have to get back to my car and head home."

"Of course."

He resisted the urge to pump his fist in the air once or twice in victory as he pushed through the glass door of Jetson's Jingles. He'd managed to get over the first hurdle: getting her to agree to have dinner with him. But Lana wasn't the type of woman he could simply wine and dine—at least, not entirely. It was time to set his well-thought ploy into action.

"Good evening, sir. One?" The young hostess asked as he approached the black podium in the lobby of Leo's Italiano.

The mayor shook his head and gestured with his fingers. "Two, and we'd like your most private, romantic table, please."

"Certainly. Right this way…"

# Chapter 25

It'd only taken another five minutes for Mr. Jetson to appear behind the jewelry display again. The items he'd selected for the auction were simply beautiful, three necklaces and two brooches, varying from classically elegant to glamorously ornate. After thanking him profusely for his generosity, Lana set her sights on Leo's Italiano, trying to ignore the uneasiness settling in the pit of her gut.

She'd been experiencing that feeling a lot lately—sort of like a sixth sense. Apprehension and awareness would trickle down her spine and burrow deep in the hollow of her stomach. Immediately she'd become alert, only she wasn't quite sure what she was supposed to be looking for.

"Hi, I'm meeting someone—"

The hostess glanced from the seating chart splayed across the podium's surface and smiled. "Tall, attractive in an *I'm-intelligent-and-important* kind of way?" The young woman inquired.

"Um, well, I—"

The girl smiled again, turning her back on Lana in mid-sentence. "Right this way."

She followed the hostess into the dimly lit dining room, weaving through a slew of near empty tables before entering a long, narrow corridor. The sounds of dishes clanking together, the low rumble of boiling pasta, and the organized chaos of chefs busily preparing authentic, gourmet cuisine greeted her on the other side as they passed through the kitchen, finally coming to a halt at a private corner booth.

"Anything I can get you?" Lana heard the young college girl ask.

"Already been taken care of, Meagan", the mayor replied.

Lana sank into the booth, dropping her purse down on the seat beside her, noting how Meagan nearly melted at hearing her name on the Mayor's lips. Mayor Cliffburg didn't seem to notice the effect he had on the poor girl. Good, considering he was nearly twice her age.

"That was quick", he stated.

"Yeah, and we even managed to get two additional pieces: two brooches. Guess he really took my generosity spiel to heart."

"That's because you're a hard woman to say no to."

There it was again—that cold, odd zing. Fidgeting uncomfortably in her seat, she reached for her glass of ice water and took a sip.

"Here you are, sir", the waiter announced after placing two wine goblets on the white-clothed tabletop. "Our finest Cabernet Sauvignon." He presented the bottle to the mayor, allowing him to read the label, then worked the corkscrew into position.

"I wish you hadn't done that", she said, gesturing toward the now open wine bottle. "I'm fine with just drinking water."

"You can't just drink water on a night like tonight."

"A night like tonight." she slowly echoed, baffled. "What's tonight?"

"Tonight's the night we celebrate all the hard work you've put into making the very first *Jimmy Phillips, Jr. Charity Auction* a success."

"Isn't that a little presumptuous? I mean, talking Mr. Jetson into donating a handful of one-of-a-kind accessories is only half the battle; we still need people to bid on them."

"Of which I have no doubt they will." Mayor Cliffburg gently nudged the wine goblet toward her. "Besides, does there really need to be a reason to enjoy a delicious glass of red wine at the end of a busy day?"

Maybe she was overreacting a bit. After all he'd kindly accompanied her this evening, lending his stature and support to a cause very near and dear to her heart. In fact, none of this would've even been possible if not for him. It was no secret the city of Butler Island was still in the midst of a budget crisis, which left funding for events, like the one they were currently planning, very limited.

And yet he'd suggested it anyway, honoring her late husband's selfless sacrifice. Lana reluctantly reached for the goblet, completely perplexed by the crescendo of mistrust creeping up spine. "I guess one glass couldn't hurt."

"Atta girl..."

Everything was going according to plan, he acknowledged as he topped her glass off again. His clever imagination really astounded him sometimes. Sure it'd taken a little convincing on his part to get Lana to agree to the wine, but he wasn't below playing dirty in order to get what he wanted.

All it'd taken was a few sips of robust cabernet to loosen her up a bit, and a feigned interest into the man her late husband was, and he was swiftly back on track. He'd engaged her mind, distracting her lovely, deep-blue eyes away from his hustling hands—hands artfully refilling her glass in steady increments.

Currently, she was babbling on about her son, Cody... Carson... Hell, did it really matter what his name was? The kid was a spitting image of his good-for-nothing dad and a little hellion to boot.

He hated kids.

Snotty noses, temper tantrums, whining, always demanding attention...

Needless to say, pursuing a single mom wasn't his usual M. O. I mean, what man in his right mind wanted to share a woman with a bratty kid that wasn't even his?

But there was just something about Lana Phillips— something that grabbed him by the balls and made him take notice. For seven long years he'd wanted her. Oh, he tried to move past his bone-deep attraction, using various women over the years to ease the yearning.

But it'd never worked, of course; there's no substitution for perfection.

"And what about *you*."

"Me?" Lana asked, palming her chest.

"Yes. How are you handling things? I'm sure the anniversary of Jimmy's passing isn't going to be easy."

"No", she uttered almost inaudibly. "It's not."

*Time to go in for the kill.* "You know"—he reached for her hand, reassuringly caressing her silk-like skin with the pad of his thumb—"you're not alone. It's going to be a hard day for a lot of people—me included... I can't tell you how many sleepless nights I've spent going over that day in my mind; how differently things may've turned out if only I'd have contacted Chief Handler—asked him to stand down."

Lana slid closer in the corner booth, narrowing the twelve-inch gap between them. "What happened to Jimmy wasn't your fault, Mayor Cliffburg. And we both know you had no authority to reject the fire department from responding to that brush fire."

His eyes bored into hers for a stretch. "Michael", he finally said.

"What?"

"Call me, Michael. You've been my secretary for the past seven years, Lana. Think we're far beyond formalities by now, don't you? And about Jimmy's death being my fault: logically, I know it isn't. But I can't help but feel indirectly responsible in some way."

Candlelight flickered across her pretty face, making her eye's gleam. Concern swam in their blue depths. Okay, so admittedly he usually wasn't one for pity-fucks—never had to resort to that kind of ploy before. But he liked where this was going. Maybe he'd been going on about this all wrong. Maybe the key to getting Lana Phillips naked wasn't his ability to console her. No, it was about her comforting *him*.

"You're not responsible—no one is..."

Unable to resist, he let his gaze lower to her luscious lips. He wanted to taste them, nibble on them—

"Wow, you certainly move fast, don't you?" Jenny Carson stood before them, gripping a white bus tub, her auburn hair pulled back into a high ponytail. "First, Tommy; now the

Mayor."

"Excuse me?" Lana asked incredulously. "I never—"

"Let me guess: you never slept with my husband, right? Well you know what?—doesn't really make a damn bit of difference. Half the town saw the two of you cuttin' up the dance floor that night. They settled on a conclusion. And they couldn't wait to run back and share it with me."

Mayor Cliffburg sensed some serious animosity between the two women. Serious animosity.

"You know, Jenny, we've been friends for a long time— good friends. And to think you'd believe a bar full of loose-lipped instigators over the word of a good friend, shows how very little you must actually think of me."

The two women were silent for a stretch. The Mayor's eyes cautiously darted back and forth between them. The air was thick with tension.

"You don't even want to know what I think of you at the moment", Jenny seethed through clenched teeth. "I'll spare you the expletives since you're on a date."

Lana gestured between her and the mayor. "This isn't a date, it's a business—"

Jenny stepped forward, resting the bus tub on the edge of the table. "Sittin' in a private, romantic corner booth away from prying eyes, candlelight, wine, the two of you practically holding hands... How do you expect me to believe a word that comes out of your mouth when you can't even fess up to what this—"she swept her hand in the air—"really is?" Sensing she'd successfully made her point, Jenny picked up the large, white bus tub and disappeared into the kitchen.

"I'm really sorry about that", Lana offered quietly.

"No apology necessary. Really." He looked her over for a few beats, noting how her brows drew together, how her hands trembled. "I sense there's a story behind what just happened." Lana nodded feebly. "You all right?"

"Yeah, it's just..." She paused for a moment, running her fingers through her milk chocolate hair. "I'm sorry, can you just...take me back to my car, now? I'd really like to just go home."

"Yeah, sure. Whatever you want." Mayor Cliffburg caught

the waiter's attention and asked for the check. As predicted, Lana reached into her purse for her wallet the moment the waiter placed the black leather check presenter on the tabletop. "Don't even think about it. Tonight's on me."

"But—"

"No 'buts'. Tell you what: I'll let you buy next time." Because there *would* be a next time. He'd see to it.

With a weak nod she let go of her purse, quietly waiting for the waiter to return with the receipt. Mayor Cliffburg hurriedly scribbled his name, then gestured toward the back exit with his chin. "Ready?"

Nodding, she slid to the edge of the booth, rising unsteadily to her feet, quickly gripping the edge of the table for balance.

"Whoa, you all right?"

"Yeah, I..." Pursing her lips, she slowly released a stream of air. "Wow, I guess the wine decided to pick this moment to kick in."

"Between that and the fact you barely touched your food, I'd say so."

Lana tucked a wayward strand of hair behind her ear and closed her eyes. "Gosh, this is so embarrassing", she uttered on a sigh. "What kind of person gets drunk in front of their boss?"

The mayor sidled up beside her. "I'm more than just your boss, Lana. At the very least, I'd like to think we're friends." And then it happened. Lana opened her eyes, turning those deep-blue peepers on him and smiled.

"We are. And I hope you believe me when I say I don't normally get like this—drunk, that is."

Smiling, Mayor Cliffburg offered to escort her back to his car. "C'mon, I'll drive you home. You're in no condition to get behind the wheel of your car at the moment."

# Chapter 26

Neither of them spoke much during the ten minute drive back to Butler Island. Lana had nestled her gorgeous body against the cream leather of his 1966 Ford T-bird, resting her head against the seat back while the wind twirled wisps of caramel hair around her pretty face.

Her navy skirt had climbed several inches upon sitting, revealing the smooth flawless skin along her lean thighs. His mouth watered at the thought of kissing his way up those silky legs...

Swallowing a rousing groan he squirmed in his seat, suddenly aware of the cramped conditions in the crotch of his gray Dockers. "You're not going to pass out on me, are you?"

The back of her skull still resting against the seat, she turned her head and gave him one of those tantalizing smiles he'd become so fond of. "Don't think I'm that far gone, Michael."

*Michael...* Hearing his name on her lips delivered a sharp jolt of lust to his groin again. Unknowingly he increased the pressure on the accelerator, eager to get her home and make his move.

He noted the black Mini Cooper parked along the edge of the street as he maneuvered his car into the drive. It belonged to Olivia Everitt—now Womack: the wild woman whose three-hour Jet-ski joyride as a teenager became the stuff of legends around these parts. She was a brilliant photographer—pretty, too—but her free-spirited, gutsy attitude and sassy mouth did nothing for him.

Nada.

Shoving the car into PARK, he drew in a deep breath.

"Thanks for the ride", she murmured softly. "The food, the wine—everything... It was really sweet." Flashing him a grateful grin, she reached for the door handle.

"W-wait!" He stammered, reaching for her arm in a desperate attempt to keep her from leaving the car. "There's... there's something I've been meaning to talk to you about."

"Okaaay", she drawled, puzzled, leaning back into her seat again.

Swallowing hard he forged ahead. "It's about us. Look, I know you've spent the last year trying to piece your life back together again. I won't pretend to know what that's like, because I don't." He palmed the side of her face with his left hand, subtly stroking her cheek with the pad of his thumb. "Your strength and courage over the last year... Well, it was a fascinating thing to watch."

"Um, I—"

"We have a connection, you and I. I've felt it for a really long time, and tonight I think you felt it too."

"I think—"

"C'mon, Lana", he mumbled, leaning in to her. "Don't fight it." He was halfway to her luscious mouth when the palms of her hands pressed against his chest, her eyes wide with panic.

"I-I'm sorry, but...I think you've got this all wrong, Mayor Cliffburg."

Pulling back, he leaned his shoulder against the leather seat. "*Mayor Cliffburg*... Are we back to formalities again?"

"I'm sorry. It's just..." Lana took in a liter of air and slowly blew it through her pursed pink lips. "This is sort of sudden."

"Not for me, it isn't... I'm... I'm in lo—"

Lana's eyes slid closed. "Please, don't. Just...*don't*."

He eyed her for a stretch, completely baffled. How had he misread her signals? He just didn't understand it. "Okay... I have to admit, Lana, this isn't how I pictured tonight ending."

"How did you picture it? You know what?—on second thought, don't answer that."

"So, tonight: bad timing?" He asked drumming the steering wheel lightly with the side of his thumb.

Hugging her purse close to her chest, she cleared her throat. "Something like that, yes. Listen, I've gotta go. Olivia's had Connor since he got out of school, and I'm sure she's ready to head home."

Mayor Cliffburg nodded sharply. "Of course." She reached for the handle and gave the heavy door a firm push. He gave her smooth legs a parting peruse as she maneuvered out of the car. "Hey, Lana", he called when she finally stood.

"Yes."

"I hope you won't hold tonight against me."

Closing the door, Lana bent her knees and peered through the open window. "Same goes."

And then she was gone. He idled in her driveway until she was safely inside her home. Tonight hadn't gone like he'd expected. If it had, she'd be halfway to naked right now. Backing out of her drive, he continued down her street until he reached the stop sign, and then took a left.

He wasn't giving up on Lana Phillips. She just needed more time to get used to the idea.

What he needed was a new tactic—a new ploy. It would take some time to formulate a fool-proof plan, but then again he had plenty of that, didn't he? And if his first date with the lovely Lana Phillips tonight proved anything, it was that she was well worth the torturous wait.


"Hey! How'd it go tonight?" Olivia greeted at the sound of the front door opening. "You get more donations for the— Sweet baby Jesus, you all right?"

Lana leaned her back against the door, nudging it closed with her body. "Connor sleeping?"

"Yeah, I took him home with me after school to play Frisbee with Dexter on the beach. We came back around seven and he conked out just before eight. What's goin' on?"

Dexter was Grant and Olivia's chocolate lab. Connor was an active kid with droves of energy—didn't usually tire easily. Lana made a mental note to use Dexter in the future when her son needed an energy drain. "Something happened tonight."

"Well, obviously. Spill it."

"The mayor just tried to kiss me."

"What! When?"

"Just now, in his car."

"What were you doing in his car?—wait", Olivia interrupted, placing her palms in front of her. "Before you answer that, you sit down. I'll get us a glass of wine." She returned less than a minute later, handing Lana a glass of white zinfandel before plopping down on the couch next to her. "Okay, I wanna know everything; don't you dare leave anything out."

Lana explained how innocently the evening began, how Mayor Cliffburg came to accompany her, and how she'd finally ended up tipsy, idling in the passenger seat of his car in her driveway mere minutes ago.

"Wow... You see", Olivia began, pointing her finger at Lana, "this is why I became a freelance photographer: no creepy bosses to worry about. What're you gonna do?"

"What do you mean, what am I gonna do? I need this job, Liv; I'm not exactly in a position financially to quit, right now."

Olivia propped her elbow on the back of the couch, resting the side of her head against her hand. "Think he'll treat you any differently from now on?"

Lana shook her head, tracing the lip of her wine glass with her fingertip. "No, I don't think so. He was very nice about the whole rejection thing."

"Well, of course he was. Most politicians are bred to be well-mannered and courteous—which makes the inevitable retaliation all the more surprisin'. Because kindhearted, optimistic people like you never see it comin'."

"He's not a bad person, Liv."

"Don't let your friendship with the mayor shroud your good judgment, sugar. Because at the end of the day, a wolf in sheep's clothing is still a wolf... Just promise me you'll be careful, all right?"

Lana flashed a weak smile. "I will."

\* \* \* \* \*

The slivered moon was a sight to behold in the cloudless, night sky tonight, made all the more striking by the array of twinkling stars embedded in its dark vastness. And if Randall listened closely he was certain he could even hear the calm Gulf as it gently lapped the sandy shore.

The residents of Butler Island were a fairly predictable bunch, rarely swaying from their humdrum routines. On any given weeknight most everyone was nestled in their cozy homes by nightfall, lights out by ten o'clock; which was precisely why Randall had waited until eleven P.M. on the dot to throw on some basketball shorts, a tee, and a pair of running shoes. His course varied every night, but the destination always remained the same: Lana's house.

Tonight his weary body ached as his feet struck the pavement, jarring his raw, painful joints, pulverizing the bones in his knees to fine dust. He'd spent his days off during the previous month laboring on his Boston Whaler. Truthfully the vessel should've been refinished months ago, but needless to say he'd been preoccupied with more… important things.

Randall rounded the corner onto Third Street, sucking salty air into his lungs. The moment he spotted the familiar gray and white house he was revived, the bone-deep ache he'd experienced moments ago replaced with an inherent yearning.

A deep-seated urge to burn the midnight oil loving on Lana's unclad body took hold, pushing his body forward. Climbing the front porch steps he let himself in with the key he'd been given a few months ago, surprised to see light spilling from the kitchen.

But even more surprising was the discovery of Lana sitting on the counter, her legs dangling over the edge, her head resting against the maple cabinetry. Her deep-blue eyes were staring at the ceiling as if the secret to life was hidden in the roughened texture.

"A penny for your thoughts…"

Startled, Lana's head swiftly turned, following the low tenor of his voice. "I didn't hear you come in."

"Yeah, I see that." Moving into the kitchen he stepped in

front of her, bracing his large hands on the counter. "Rough day?"

"I think it's getting better, now."

"Yeah?"

Lana smiled. "Yeah."

Her thin pink nightshirt was slightly askew, invariably revealing one of her bare shoulders. Unable to resist he dipped his head, spreading soft kisses along her smooth, vanilla-scented skin.

"Yeah", she sighed. "Definitely better."

His mouth traveled to the crook of her neck, tasting, nibbling. "Let's continue this in your bedroom, shall we?" He graveled, lifting her body from the counter. It took every ounce of control he possessed to set her feet on the ground. Hell, he'd have taken her right there on the kitchen counter if not for the fact that Connor was sleeping down the hall.

Yes, they'd certainly upped the risk by having sex in the house with her son home—but somehow keeping their hands off one another the last month had seemed... riskier. They did take precautions: he arrived by foot at eleven-fifteen, they locked her bedroom door, they were quiet. And when their bodies were sated, he'd slip from her bed and return home, counting down the hours until he could do it again.

Following her down the hall they made a left into the dark master bedroom. Quietly nudging the door closed behind him Randall turned the lock. The air was thick with sexual energy and the hypnotizing scent of vanilla, a potent combination that sent an electric jolt of lust to his groin.

"Where were we?" Lana asked, her voice soft and eager. "Randall?"

Wrapping his arms around her small frame, he hauled her close, catching her bottom lip between his teeth. "Right here, Sweetheart. Right here."


Randall had been lying next to Lana for over an hour, listening to the slow easy rhythm of her breaths. He shouldn't be here; it was just after five in the morning. He should be home—in his own bed—catching up on some much-needed shut-eye. But somehow the thought of leaving this bed—this woman—paralyzed him. His heart kicked against his chest.

He was in love with her...

And that terrified him.

They couldn't keep doing this—sneaking around, night after night. He'd been fooling himself to think there could ever be a future with Lana. He wanted one, though—God, he wanted one. But he'd been living in a fabled state, where pleasure ruled and love prevailed. A place where criticism ceased to exist. A safe-haven where consciences were clean of greed and guilt.

Cautiously untangling his limbs, Randall eased from the bed and reached for his clothes. He glanced over his shoulder one last time before he stepped into the hallway, knowing it'd probably be the last time he'd see her like this: content, peaceful.

"It has to be this way, Sweetheart", he whispered softly. "I'm sorry."

Moments later he slipped into the stillness of pre-dawn, directing his tired legs forward. And although he wanted to, he didn't look back.

# Chapter 27

Mayor Cliffburg awoke to the sound of nails repeatedly scratching at his bedroom door. He opened his eyes; the room was still dark. God, he was so tired. After spending much of the night pacing back and forth, trying to formulate a foolproof scheme to woo Lana Phillips into his bed, he'd collapsed into a heap of exhaustion. And he still had no plan in place.

The scratching happened again.

Moaning, he rolled over and pushed his body upright. His Shih Tzu, Scotch, was the culprit responsible for the noise, and if he didn't get the fur ball outside, and quickly, he'd have a hell of a horrid mess to clean up. Reluctantly rising from bed, he slipped on a pair of Adidas pants, a plain white tee, and some leather flops, scooping the mutt off the ground with one hand.

"You're becoming a pain in the ass, you know that?" He mumbled. The dog produced a pathetic-excuse-for-a-bark before licking Michael's roughened chin, not the least bit concerned that the sun was still nearly two hours from rising.

He didn't even really like the damn mutt, but the long white hair and cute little face had never failed to get him lucky over the last year. Women were suckers for men with adorable lap dogs—men pushing baby carriages, too—but that was taking it a bit too far. He hadn't been that desperate to get laid.

Shuffling into the living room, he snatched the leash from

the foyer and clipped it to Scotch's blue collar. "Let's make it snappy this time."

Yeah, right. Snappy.

Michael roamed the empty streets of Butler Island for nearly twenty minutes before the damn dog decided on a spot, but it'd been well worth it once the fur ball kicked grass with his hind legs and prissily trotted away. He just didn't understand it—how a dog barely weighing in at twelve pounds produced two pounds of shit.

A gust of soggy wind surged out of the south. The mayor checked his watch: barely five A.M. and he could already tell it was going to be unbearably humid today. Not that it was any surprise. Florida, even here, along the Panhandle Coast, could be summed in two words: excruciatingly hot.

Enjoying the moderately muggy temps—the word "enjoying" used rather loosely—he headed toward Third Street. It was a bit out of his way, maybe adding an extra ten minutes to his early morning stroll, but that was fine by him. He was already up, Scotch seemed to like the idea, and besides, it gave him an excuse to coast by Lana's.

He'd just rounded the corner when he caught movement up ahead on the right. The door to the gray and white bungalow opened slowly, but it wasn't Lana that emerged from the small dwelling.

No, it was Randall-fucking-Burns!

Dodging behind Mr. Humphrey's beloved rose hedges as not to be seen, Michael peered through the fragrant shrubs as Randall took off in the other direction, noting the man's shirt was inside-out.

*I'm sorry, but...I think you've got this all wrong, Mayor Cliffburg.*

*This is sort of sudden.*

*So, tonight: bad timing?* He'd asked.

*Something like that, yes.*

His hands shook with rage. "Lying whore", he muttered under his breath. No one made of fool of him.

No one.

Lana—his sweet, beautiful Lana—was living a double life: the town's sweetheart by day, cold-hearted, conniving tramp by night.

With Randall out of sight Michael straightened, retracing his steps back home. Scotch's little legs worked overtime to keep up with his fleeting pace, huffing and puffing during the four-block trek. They made it back in half the time it'd taken Scotch to select his dumping ground, the furry mutt collapsing into a heaping mound of panting white hair just inside the front door.

Mayor Cliffburg ran his hands through his dark hair in frustration, pacing back and forth while the idea of Lana and Randall sunk in and took root. Damn, he still couldn't believe it, couldn't believe he hadn't seen the signs until now.

Lana Phillips was fucking her husband's best friend...

His vision narrowed, his heart galloping to a hasty beat. He'd done so much for her. This charity auction idea was all for her. Celebrating the life of a man he loathed was a sacrifice he'd been willing to make.

All for her.

Her gratitude and admiration was all part of his carefully calculated plan. Suddenly she'd see him—not as her boss, but as a man. A man she would be forever indebted to. And when it came time to collect, he'd finally claim her body, finally acquire what he'd been lusting after for seven long years.

But that was over now. Everything was ruined!

She was going to pay for this—pay for humiliating him like she had. He'd nearly confessed his love for her last night, for Chrissakes! She'd probably gone inside and had a good laugh with Olivia at his expense.

Nobody made a fool of Michael Cliffburg.

Lana Phillips was definitely going to pay...


With only three days remaining until the town gathered for the charity auction, Lana's mind was overwhelmed. Last minute details required her attention, and she still needed to tweak the order in which some of the items were presented. She wanted to ensure they were building interest and momentum throughout the affair, the value of each item increasing until they reached the grand finale: a fifty-five inch flat screen T.V.

And to make matters worse, the first named tropical storm of the season was brewing in the warm waters of the Gulf of Mexico, the local weatherman predicting landfall some time during the early evening hours on Memorial Day.

She'd gone to the mayor earlier, inquiring about postponing the auction until after the storm, but he'd been completely against it.

*"We'll move the boat parade and the auction up an hour to give the breakdown volunteers time to clear everything before the storm arrives",* he'd suggested. A minor change that required a ton of work on her end, because now she had to notify everyone of the last minute change.

But that was only a fraction of the static currently wreaking havoc on her weary mind.

Jimmy had been gone one year. One year...

There wasn't a day that went by that she didn't think of him. Sometimes she'd still catch herself calling out his name—like he was just in the other room. Like he wasn't buried beneath six-feet of sodden dirt in the Apalachicola Cemetery.

Those first six months without him had been hellish, and there were still moments when she panicked—when something as simple as drawing air into her lungs seemed laborious, impossible. That feeling would never go away entirely, she knew. She'd never rid herself of it completely, but she could live with that.

She could live with that because she'd found a solid source of strength, a new passion for life. It was sort of like stepping into color after living in a world of black and white.

The life she'd come to know had suddenly looked different—scary, even, at first. Thrust into a new, vivid reality, she'd just been going through the motions, simply surviving.

Until Randall.

Those assessing gray eyes saw right through her tranquil veneer; the deep timbre of his voice soothed her battered soul, enveloping her in a harmonious cocoon. He'd guided her into this new, colorful world... and she loved him for that.

She loved him.

This, of course, was the core of her dilemma, because she feared Randall didn't feel the same way about her.

He'd been a no-show for two nights running. And when she'd phoned to find out what'd happened he'd brushed her off with an I've-got-a-lot-of-things-going-on-right-now.

Which was true—they both did. But...

But something just... didn't feel right.

Shaking her head a bit, she returned her attention to the lengthy list of donations she'd accumulated over the last month. There were several items she still needed to enter: A three-course dinner for two at Bruno's Italian Diner, and the beautifully-crafted necklaces and brooches David Jetson had kindly donated several nights ago.

Lana's fingertips rapidly tapped the keyboard, almost as if they had a mind of their own. She thought about that night— the night Mayor Cliffburg had accompanied her—the night he'd almost kissed her. She was relieved to find the air between them the following day had been rather... normal. There'd been no awkwardness—no signs whatsoever that he was harboring a grudge. And for that she was grateful.

The mayor's door swung open just then, diverting Lana's attention to the tall figure that halted in front of her desk. "Can I get you anything?" She offered.

Bracing his hands on the edge of her desk, Mayor Cliffburg smiled. "How 'bout I buy you lunch? I'm starved."

"Thanks for the offer, but"—she gestured to the explosion of papers and files scattered along her desk—"I've a ton of things still left to do. I brought some fruit. I'll probably just eat at my desk today."

"All right, suit yourself", he uttered as he pushed off her desk. "I'll be back in about an hour. Call me on my cell if you need me."

And then he was gone, leaving Lana alone with a myriad of scribbled notes, and a distinct, eerie chill.

# Chapter 28

Mayor Cliffburg had been sitting at the shoddy little bar three doors down from Leo's Italiano for nearly twenty-five minutes. The place was downright filthy, and the smell... A mixture of nicotine, sweat, and stale beer was...

Well, needless to say his suit was ruined.

The place was small, dark, the ceilings abnormally low—sort of reminded him of a dungeon. The walls, most likely once white, were dingy, yellowed by layers of cigarette smoke. He wanted to get this meeting over with, wanted to get the hell out of this run-down joint before his health suffered irreparable damage.

The bell attached to the front door jingled as it slid open, spilling bright light into the cave-like room. Moments later a scorned woman with auburn hair and creamy skin settled onto the stool beside him.

"You're late."

Jenny Carson flashed a humorless grin. "Look, you may run the city of Butler Island, but if you think your *my-time-is-more-important-than-yours* routine is gonna work on me, you're wrong. So let's cut to the chase, shall we?"

"All right, fair enough... I have some information I think the town of Butler Island would be very interested in knowing."

Jenny snatched the whiskey tumbler from the bar and took a sip, wincing slightly as liquid heat trickled down her throat. ""So have your girlfriend put it on next month's city commission agenda."

The mayor chuckled under his breath. "You're a firecracker, Mrs. Carson; I like that in a woman."

"Flattery will get you nowhere, Mr. Mayor."

"Only when it's delivered under false pretenses. I could use someone like you on my side, someone with top-notch people-reading skills. A mayor is only as good as his staff."

She eyed him suspiciously for a stretch. "You're offering me a job—in your office? What's the catch?"

"Now, what makes you think there's a catch, Mrs. Carson?"

"Because you're a politician—you don't do anything unless there's something in it for you, too."

Michael's dark eyes narrowed, his jaw clenched. If he didn't need her help, he'd have smacked that gloating grin clear off her face. He was the fucking mayor, for Chrissakes! He deserved respect!

But he did need her help. Couldn't pull this off without Jenny—at least, not if he wanted to remain the town's savior for the next four years. A scandal like this would ruin him.

That couldn't happen.

So he begrudgingly relaxed his jaw and forced the corners of his mouth skyward. "Another straightforward assessment", he agreed. "All right, there is a catch... It's regarding your B.F.F, Lana Phillips—"

"She's not my—"

Michael stuck his palm out, interrupting her midsentence. "Let's just say I've stumbled upon a rather... *interesting* secret she's been keeping, something I think many folks in town would be fascinated to learn about her."

"Oh no!" Jenny cried sarcastically, placing her palms over her cheeks like Macaulay Culkin in *Home Alone*. "Trouble in paradise already?"

Leaning forward, he lowered his voice for emphasis. "She humiliated you in front of everyone at The Saloon a few months back, correct?" The amplified, boastful grin disappeared almost instantly. She didn't utter a word—just stared back at him as if he'd slapped her across the face.

Time to go in for the kill.

"Just when you thought there was a chance of you and Tommy patching things up, Lana swoops in and shows him a good time on the dance floor—shows him the kind of woman he ought to be spending his time with. Remember that, Jenny? Do you remember the way it felt to be humiliated like that—by someone who claimed to be one of your friends? Huh?"

"What do you want?" She mumbled.

A devious smile splayed across his lips. "Simple, really: During the charity auction on Monday, when the town is focused on their beloved sweetheart, you're gonna stand up and unearth some disturbing news." The mayor leaned closer. "She's going to be publicly humiliated, Mrs. Carson; she's going to suffer karma's ugly wrath. And you"—he gestured with his finger—"are going to have a front row seat."

Jenny chewed on the offer for a few long beats, then drew in a deep breath. "Didn't you mention something about a job? Because bussing tables doesn't exactly pay well."

"For your well-timed public outburst, you will be rewarded with a position as my new secretary. With elections just around the corner, I'm afraid the scandal involving my current secretary will taint my upcoming campaign. I mean, what would the good residents of Butler Island think of me if I didn't cut ties with the subject of a scandal of this magnitude?"

"When do you need an answer?" she asked nervously, chewing on her lip.

Rising from his stool he reached into his back pocket and laid a crisp twenty on the bar, then handed Jenny his business card. "Auction's in three days, Mrs. Carson. My offer is good until five P.M. today or all bets are off. Call me on my cell if you're interested in the position."

Mayor Cliffburg pivoted, heading for the exit with an extra bounce in his step. It was a risky plan, yes, but high risks tended to yield the biggest rewards. Pushing the door open, he stepped into the hot, merciless sun, inhaling his first clean breath in nearly forty-five minutes. After sliding into his T-bird he loosened his tie, then removed it. He needed to get out of these clothes—fast. Turning around, he headed back to the Mainland Bridge, the wind blowing his dark hair, hammering the wretched stench from his clothes. He'd stop at home to change before returning to the office; he didn't want to have to explain to Lana why he reeked of cigarettes and stale beer.

Michael had just maneuvered his car into his driveway when his cell phone rang. "Hello?"

"Okay... I'll do it."

Dark, angry clouds lingered above the island, stretching its somber arms south toward the approaching tropical storm. The wind was steady at ten miles per hour with gusts nearing twenty. Choppy conditions had made for an interesting boat parade, the normally calm Gulf reminding onlookers that beneath its serene surface lay robust power and strength.

Lana stood on the pier along with Kendall and Olivia as boats decorated in red, white, and blue traveled in single file, drivers carefully maneuvering their vessels through the tumultuous Gulf while judges scored their decorative creativity.

Randall's Boston Whaler was toward the end of the pack, she knew this because she'd checked the order that morning. Swags of patriotic colors lined the edge of the boat, an American flag attached to the back flapped furiously in the wind. The moment she clapped eyes on him her heart kicked an extra beat. His black hair blew in the steady breeze, his strong hands gripping the wheel tight, causing the corded muscles in his forearms to bulge.

She had no idea what was happening between them. Last night marked the fifth night in a row Randall had been absent from her bed. She told herself it didn't mean anything. They'd both been terribly busy the last week in preparation for today, and after laboring on his boat in the hot sun all day, he'd probably been too tired to toil with her beneath the sheets.

And yet...

She still had an inkling there was more to it than that. Tonight, after the stress of the previous month was finally behind them, they needed to talk. She needed to know where they stood—if there even was a "them" anymore.

"Oh, there he is", Kendall uttered excitedly, pointing at Randall. She nudged Olivia with her elbow. "I hope you're getting some good close ups."

Olivia's Nikon clicked repeatedly as she twisted the long lens. "Well, if you stop clobberin' me with your elbow, I might be able to!"

"Sorry", she murmured, retracting her arms close to her body. "It just...I'm so excited for him! He's wanted that boat for years."

Lana's gaze landed on Randall again. Dark shades covered his eyes, but she didn't need to see his steel-gray orbs to know they were looking at her. She could almost feel them whispering over her skin. And then the corners of his mouth lifted. It was subtle—no one on the crowded pier probably caught it—but Lana knew that smile was meant just for her.

It was exactly what she'd needed at that moment. She'd been riding a rollercoaster of emotions all day, dizzy with highs and lows, but somehow just the mere sight of him calmed her turbulent mind.

"All right, ladies, I'd love to stick around for the rest of the parade, but I have to meet the auctioneer in front of the stage at eleven-thirty."

"You want us to come with you?" Olivia asked.

A wave of emotion took hold of her. Her friends sensed the struggle she'd been grappling with all morning, sensed she was teetering on a slippery slope of sadness. Lana swallowed the lump that'd suddenly lodged in her throat, shaking her head. "No, I... I'll be fine. You guys stay here, finish watching the parade. I'll catch up with you after the auction."

"You sure?" Kendall asked. "We really don't mind."

"Positive." Lana backed away from the railing, forcing her trembling lips into a smile.

*Pull yourself together, Lana.*

Pivoting, she burrowed through the crowd with her head down, knowing just one sympathetic look from a concerned bystander would undermine her frail facade. Because when that first teardrop fell, she knew she'd be powerless to stop the avalanche of tears that followed.

Utterly powerless.

With most of the town settled into a semi-circle in front of the small, modular platform, Lana shuffled forward on wobbly legs, halting when she reached the podium at center stage. A prickle of awareness crept down her spine, the same cold, eerie sensation she'd felt before—only sharper, stronger. The unyielding sensation intensified as she adjusted the microphone closer to her mouth with quivering hands.

Her heart beat roared like rolling thunder.

Boom. Boom. Boom. Boom.

Faster and faster.

Ba-boom. Ba-boom. Ba-boom.

Lana worked the muscles in her throat, trying to swallow, trying to find her voice.

Her knees wobbled again—they'd buckle if she didn't clutch onto something sturdy.

She palmed the edges of the small podium in front of her for stability while her eyes scanned the crowd, searching for the one person she knew would settle the panic threatening to consume her. But there were so many people.

"You all right, darlin'?" Someone yelled from the crowd.

"Y-yes, yes I'm... I'm fine", she answered feebly. "I'm just... overwhelmed. Really, I... I can't tell you want it means to me that you're all here. And I know Jimmy would—"

"Oh for heaven's sake, stop the grieving widow routine, already, will ya?" said a voice from the front row.

Lana's eyes homed in on said voice, but somehow her brain was having difficulty believing her eyes.

Jenny stood now, auburn hair whipping in the wind, arms crossed, satisfaction practically seeping from her pores. "Jimmy's casket was barely lowered into the ground before you started whoring around."

"What?—Th-that's not true!"

"You mean, all those late nights at the office, secret romantic dinners with the mayor were—"

"My late nights at the office were spent catching up on

work!" she shouted breathlessly, gripping the podium tighter.

Jenny stroked her chin sarcastically. "Is that what they're calling it these days?"

"I... I never... You know how much I loved Jimmy."

"Of course, you loved him. I'm just merely pointing out to everyone how quickly you managed to get over—"

"How. Dare. You", she seethed. "My relationship with Mayor Cliffburg is completely platonic!"

Blood roared in her ears.

Ba-boom. Ba-boom. Ba-boom.

Moisture clouded her vision, although not enough to obscure the shocked expressions worn by the audience. Cold sweat trickled down her neck. She shivered.

"What about Randall Burns?" Jenny asked, her ice-cold eyes narrowing.

"What about me?"

The crowd gasped as Randall and Tommy suddenly appeared from the edge of the crowd. Lana's eyes darted to Randall as if pleading for him to do something. But with so many people huddled around the makeshift stage, crowd-surfing was likely his only hope in getting to Jenny in time.

Jenny's vengeful gaze never left Lana's. In fact, a hint of a crooked smile splayed across her lips. "Your relationship strictly platonic"—she emphasized with air quotes—"with him? Huh?"

Silence settled over the crowd, waiting for Lana to deny the accusation. She opened her mouth to speak, then abruptly closed it.

What could she say?—Jenny was right. Her relationship with Randall was anything but platonic.

Just then Lana caught a glimpse of her mother and her son. Her mother's hands were resting on Connor's tiny shoulders while his head turned from side-to-side, his six-year-old mind desperately trying to figure out why everyone looked so angry.

Desperately trying to grasp why everyone was so mad at his mommy...

"Yeah", Jenny jived, "didn't think so."

Vision blurred, breaths quick and shallow, Lana backed

away from the podium.

*Oh, God. Oh, God!*

A sob escaped her trembling lips.

*Run!*

Palm covering her mouth, Lana bolted from the stage, fleeing the chaos and confusion spreading through the crowd. She ran as fast as her shuddering legs would allow.

"Lana!"

*Don't stop. Must get out of here!*

Her car finally in sight, Lana snatched the keys from her pocket.

"Damn it, Lana—wait!"

*Can't. Must go!*

Lana turned the ignition, the distant sound of tires squealing behind her. She just needed to make it home. And then she could fall to pieces.

# Chapter 29

Randall sprinted to his truck, his wheels cloning the path taken by the small Corolla moments ago.

His mind was still frantically trying to piece together what'd just happened. After the boat parade he'd loaded his Boston Whaler onto the trailer, securing the vessel before hauling it from the choppy Gulf with the intention of storing it in Mr. Morgan's boat warehouse during the storm. He'd then driven to the beach, expecting to find the charity auction already in full swing.

Instead he'd stumbled upon his biggest fear: a malicious and frankly, unwarranted attack on Lana's character.

Turning onto Third Street he stomped on the accelerator after spotting her Corolla up ahead, whipping his Ford F150 recklessly into her narrow drive as she bounded from her car. "Damn it, Lana, quit running from me!" Leaping from his truck he raced across the yard, hurdling up the steps after her.

He finally caught up with her in the hallway, colliding into her body from behind, trapping her against his solid frame and the wall. "It's okay, Sweetheart. It's me", he murmured softly. "It's me…"

Lana stilled the moment his breath whispered over her ear, his low, soothing voice weakening her defenses. Scared and vulnerable and frail, a powerful sob worked its way up her trembling body, rising, gaining momentum until it inevitably fled her lips. Her body shook with it, her knees buckling as grief rippled through her small frame, but Randall was right there to catch her.

He held her like that, her back against his front, while she wept, whispering words of encouragement, supporting her languid body until the volume of her cries softened.

"I-I just don't un-understand", she uttered just above a whisper, turning in his arms to face him. "Why would sh-she do that?—in front of the whole t-town—*in front of m-my son?*"

"I don't know."

"I mean, I knew she was up-upset with me, but—"

Randall palmed her face, needing to feel her soft skin beneath his rough fingertips, needing her to listen to reason. "She's bitter, Lana. Morally bankrupt. Angry about her marriage ending and looking for anyone to shoulder the blame instead of accepting responsibility for her actions."

Sweeping his thumb across her sodden cheek, he wiped away the dark lines marring her pretty face. The wind howled as he pinned her with his gaze. Lana's deep blue eyes were dull and listless, her long lashes matted together with mascara and fresh tears. And those full pink lips—lips he'd tirelessly tasted and nibbled—quivered with grief.

"We were friends", she whispered. "Good friends..." Lana clenched her eyes shut, then opened them again. "How'd she find out about us? How'd she—"

"I don't know", he answered truthfully, because he honestly didn't have a clue. They'd been so careful—dotted every $i$, crossed every $t$. "It was either a lucky guess or—"

"She saw us", she finished.

The back of Lana's head thumped against the wall, exposing her slender neck. He wanted to dip his head, run his tongue along her smooth skin, breathe in the arousing scent of vanilla and wanton woman.

What did that say about him? What kind of person could think about sex at a time like this?

A low, pathetic, soulless man, that's who.

The urge to touch her, kiss her, *love her* was on a cellular level, deeply embedded in his make-up. He craved her every minute—every second—every day, which made what he knew he had to do all the more difficult to execute.

How did one begin to purge an essential part of themselves?—a part tightly knitted around every fiber, tainting every cell?

*You could start by taking your hands off her pretty face.*

Randall brushed the pad of his thumb over her cheek one last time, committing the silky texture to memory before placing his hands down by his sides.

"I can't believe this is happening", she muttered. "God, the look on Connor's face... What am I supposed to tell him when he asks me what happened?"

"I...I don't know."

"Tell me what you do know, then."

Running quivering fingers through his thick black hair, Randall met her gaze and uttered the words he prayed he'd never have to say aloud. "This was a mistake."

"This?" she questioned, her brows drawing together in confusion.

Randall shifted his weight, nodding feebly. "Us." Damn it, why was this so hard?

*Because you're going to hurt her.*

Because although it was the morally correct thing to say, it wasn't how he really felt at all. Not even close. "The night you followed me home, I... I crossed the line, Lana. I should've..."

"Should have what?"

Randall blew a puff of air from his lungs and leaned his back against the opposite wall, the howling wind nearly muffled by the sound of his raging pulse. "I should've asked you to leave."

His words had delivered a heavy, callous blow; he could tell by the way her breath hitched, by the way her body jerked. Her reaction was that of a woman that'd been slapped. Utterly stunned. And given the choice, he knew she'd have preferred physical pain over the emotional sting he'd just inflicted.

Sometimes words *did* hurt.

Because bruises would heal, fade, but acrid remarks stayed with you, eroding your insides, leaving scars too heavy and broad to heal. Sometimes cutting words were unforgivable. Unforgettable.

"When did you come to that conclusion, huh?"

"Does it really matter?"

"Matters to me", she uttered softly.

Randall forced the words over his throat, steeling his spine for the pain he would inflict again. "I knew the moment I opened the door and found you on my front porch that night."

"And yet you pursued this"—she gestured between them—"anyway. Not once, not twice, but over and over again..."

"I'm no saint, Lana—you of all people should know that."

"You're wrong", she whispered.

"Am I? Think about everything's that happened in the last year, Lana. I'm the common denominator", he explained, placing his palm over his chest. "I'm responsible for everything bad that's happened to you since—"

Lana shook her head. "No. What happened to Jimmy... it wasn't your fault!"

Randall's mouth stretched into a faint smile. "One of the things I admire most about you is your ability to see the good in people. You have every right to be jaded, empty, and yet you're not. Don't ever lose that."

"I-I don't understand, I—"

"I'm trying to do the right thing, here, Sweetheart", he disclosed, wiping his palm down his face.

"Which is?"

His gaze lowered to her trembling hands, feverishly scraping the red polish from her nails. He hated himself for doing this, hated himself for dealing blow after agonizing blow. She deserved better. Lana deserved a worthy man. She deserved happiness—not misery and despair. He'd tried for months to become that man, and for a while he'd even convinced himself he was.

But that was nothing more than wishful thinking.

He loved her deep and hard, fierce and absolute. Christ, he wished things were different, wished he could right all the wrongs, undo all the damage he'd caused. Because standing in front of her now, he realized the truth.

He wasn't worthy.

He never would be.

"End this. Walk away."

A single tear trickled down her cheek as she inhaled a shaky breath. "So everything... the past two months... they meant nothing to you?"

"I don't regret one minute I spent with you, Lana—just the parts that led up to it. The outcome."

"So you're just going to walk away?"

"It's better this way", he managed in a voice he barely recognized. Randall pushed off the wall, pointing his feet toward the front door. He didn't need to look over his shoulder to know she was following him.

"Better for whom?"

"You. Connor. Everyone."

Lana latched onto his elbow several paces from the door, digging her heels into the wood floor. "Please, Randall, don't do this!" she pleaded desperately. "I've l-lost everything—I can't lose y-you, too!"

Randall turned to face her, swallowing hard. This was it. He had to sever ties—before he lost his nerve. "Losing me is the best thing that's ever happened to you, Sweetheart. In time, you'll see." Peeling her from his body he took a step back, watching as her small frame melted into a puddle of hopelessness.

"I Love you! Please, d-don't leave m-me!"

Randall glanced over his shoulder, one foot already out the door. Lana sat on the floor, her legs tucked under her, a steady river of tears cascading down her angelic face. He'd lain awake many nights wondering what it'd be like to hear Lana utter those three simple words.

*She loved him.*

Part of him wanted to turn around, scoop her grieving body off the floor and show her just how much he loved her too.

But he didn't deserve to be loved—especially by Lana Phillips.

"That's impossible, Sweetheart; the person you think you fell in love with doesn't exist—at least, not anymore."

The screaming wind mixed with the sound of weeping woman as Randall hustled to his truck. Turning the ignition, he squealed out of her driveway in a mad dash to make it home before the heavens opened up.

Because he couldn't be here.

He wasn't sure where he was headed just yet—Steinhatchee, Jacksonville—hell, did it really matter? Where ever he ended up he'd still be the man solely responsible for destroying the best thing that'd ever happened to him.

Randall left the engine running while he went inside to pack an overnight bag. He'd be back in time for his shift on Wednesday, but in the mean time he'd seek shelter from the storm.

The one brewing over the Gulf of Mexico, as well as the imminent metaphorical one, likely spreading across the island at this very moment.

# Chapter 30

"You were brilliant", Mayor Cliffburg praised as the breakdown crew disassembled the small stage behind him. "Did you see the shock on the crowd's faces?—the repulsion?"

"No, I—"

"If not for the approaching storm they'd have probably burned her at the stake!"

A deranged smile spread across the mayor's lips. He was practically foaming at the mouth over Lana's degradation. And while Jenny had taken great pleasure in her vengeful outburst at the time, the euphoria had quickly fizzled.

"What happened between the two of you, huh? What happened to make you hate her so much?" Jenny pressed, her long auburn locks whirling in the growing breeze. The mayor's expression suddenly turned cold, intense. A shiver worked its way up her spine, causing the hair on the back of her neck to rise.

"She deceived me", he answered through clenched teeth, stepping so close to Jenny she had to tilt her head back. "You'd be wise to remember that, Mrs. Carson."

Jenny nodded feebly. What had she gotten herself into this time?

"Listen, I need you to lie low for a few days, all right?—allow the domino effect to continue. I'll be in touch."

And just like that he was gone, leaving Jenny alone with an uncomfortable bout of remorse. She hadn't seen the crowd's expressions, but she had seen Lana's. Jenny feared she'd never be able to expunge the disturbing image from her mind.

Ever.

Turning on her heels, she hauled her purse over her shoulder and shuffled to her car. Particles of sand pelted her creamy skin, making the porcelain hue appear red and raw.

*Jimmy's casket was barely lowered into the ground when you started whoring around.*

*What?—th-that's not true! You know how much I loved Jimmy!*

Sliding into the driver's seat she closed her eyes. "God, Jenny", she muttered, "what have you done...?"


Pine needles writhed in the growing wind, synchronously thrashing and swaying, whispering and sighing a heavy warning. A storm, tropical and fierce, was quickly approaching.

Around these parts hurricane season was a double-edged sword, signifying the end to Florida's treacherous dry season and the birth of atmospheric violence. Hot sultry days and clear blue skies transformed into something wild and feared. The possessed heavens turned angry and black like clockwork as fiery beams of jagged light leaped from dismal clouds, landing with a thunderous roar. Thunderstorms: as tried-and-true as the changing tides.

But tropical systems were different. Unpredictable.

Powerful winds demolished.

Unrelenting rain pummeled.

The swollen ocean devoured.

Here, along the Gulf Coast, it wasn't a matter of *if* a tropical system would hit, but rather *when*. And when the demonic clouds cleared the cleanup would begin and soon the named storm would become nothing more than a distant memory...

But the debacle that'd just unfolded a short time ago on stage—the one that'd publicly outed Randall's relationship with Lana, humiliating her in front of the entire town—wouldn't be so lucky.

The shockwave of destruction would linger long after the powerful wind calmed, long after the heavy rain subsided.

Lana's entire world was in shambles. Her character and reputation reduced to a heaping pile of tangled rubbish. Needless to say, the clean up efforts would take far longer than the physical damage left behind by the first tropical system of the season.

Merging onto the desolate, two-lane road that led to I-10, Randall turned on his wipers. Conditions were quickly deteriorating. Guess his last minute decision to flee the chaos back home had been a little... rash. But there'd been a method to his madness. Skipping town for a day or two would allow the dust to settle; give everyone time to digest the news.

As predicted, it hadn't taken long for the backlash to unfurl. Randall had already received more than a dozen calls from Kendall and the guys he worked with. He hadn't answered, of course. Navigating the slick asphalt in this weather required two hands, and besides, he didn't need anyone to tell him what a worthless, despicable lowlife he was—*that* he already knew.

The winding road carved a path through the colossal forest, Longleaf and Slash Pines rising above droves of bushy Saw Palmettos. The canopies warped in the wind, swaying, thrashing, transporting Randall back in time to that fateful day one year ago.

He couldn't help but wonder the course his life would have taken if he'd only paid attention to his environment that day. Maybe if he had he would've seen the definitive signs, maybe he could've steered everyone away from the arms of doom. Hell, Chief Handler had drilled the importance of constant assessment into his brain since day one: use your senses, never lose focus, analyze the clues in your surroundings, predict what might happen next...

He failed his fellow brothers that day. Failed his best friend.

But that'd only been the beginning.

A hearty gust of air slammed into the side of his truck. Randall gripped the wheel, fighting the groaning wind. He'd disappeared for five months, leaving Lana to fend for herself.

Sure, she'd had friends, her parents, but that wasn't the same. She'd needed him. And he'd failed her.

Randall had made it his mission to make up for his absence upon his return last fall, stepping in as the interim patriarch of the Phillips household. After five months of feverishly working to fill the void left behind by Jimmy's death with eighty-proof whiskey, he'd welcomed the challenge. Amazingly, his presence seemed to lighten the load Lana carried, he'd even seen an improvement in Connor's filthy mouth. Things were looking up...

Until the night he'd driven Lana home from The Saloon. That night had changed everything.

That night he'd seen Lana differently—not as his best friend's grieving widow, but rather a beautiful woman. That night he'd set the stage for the ultimate betrayal, failing Jimmy yet again.

Failure seemed to be his mantra these days, seemed to be the only thing he was any good at.

Squeezing the steering wheel, Randall rounded a curve as the howling wind and pounding rain intensified, obscuring his visibility. The blanket of water falling from the heavens was nearly horizontal now. Squinting, Randall gently pressed on the brake, gradually reducing his speed to prevent his tires from skidding off the slick, narrow road.

Randall hadn't overlooked the irony: this wasn't the first time he'd skipped town, leaving Lana desperate, pleading, and alone. He could still remember the shrill of her cries as he'd bounded from his seat during Jimmy's funeral. She'd been hysterical, inconsolable. Hopeless.

Randall pressed on the brake until his wheels rolled to a stop, then ran his hands through his thick black hair. "Fuck", he sighed, the back of his head thumping against the headrest in defeat.

He sat still for a stretch, watching as the slanting sheet of water pummeled the earth. He'd left her again. Left her to fend for herself, left her hopeless and broken on her living room floor, pleading for his love and support.

And he'd fucking left her!

*"I've lost everything—I can't lose you, too! I Love you!*

*Please, don't leave me!"*

Chaos ensued around him: the growing wind roared, torrential rain hammered the roof of his truck. Mother Nature was exposing her almighty power. And yet in the midst of all the commotion and turbulence surrounding him, a whisper of calmness settled over his body...

He had to go back.

He wasn't quite sure what the future held for the two of them, but there was one thing he was sure of: This time Lana wouldn't be alone.

This time they would face the fury together.

Randall gently nudged the accelerator with the toe of his boot and yanked the wheel to the left, aiming his truck toward the coast. It was just after three o'clock when he began his journey home, although the emerging storm made the afternoon feel more like dusk.

It was slow-going now. Rain maliciously pelted his truck, resembling the sound of hail. It wasn't, of course; hail rarely accompanied tropical systems. The robust wind bellowed as it collided into the side of his Ford, attempting to shove the two-ton pick-up over the double yellow lines painted on the middle of the winding road.

There was good reason why emergency officials drilled the importance of staying off the roads when wind gusts tipped the forty mile per hour mark. It was unsafe—which probably explained why he hadn't seen another car since he'd crossed the Mainland Bridge roughly forty-five minutes ago.

Seems he was the only idiot crazy enough to impulsively leave town in the midst of a tropical cyclone. What was that old saying? Stupid is as stupid does...?

Lord knows he'd done his share of stupid things over the last year. And although getting involved with his best friend's widow topped the list, he didn't regret one minute of it. Lana made him feel things he'd never felt, made him want things he'd never wanted before.

Sure, there'd been a time when he'd wanted Kendall, too, but that'd been different. Back then he hadn't been able to see past the physicality of their relationship—which explained why they would've never worked. He could see that, now.

But with Lana it was different. Don't get him wrong—the physical part of their relationship was wild, hot.

Recklessly addicting.

He loved to watch her midnight eyes glaze over, feel her soft body writhing beneath his as she surrendered to sweet ecstasy, hear her choppy breaths and pleasure-filled whimpers as he drove her closer to the pinnacle of release.

But it was more than that.

Because for the first time in all his thirty years, Randall wanted the whole package. A beautiful wife, a white picket fence, and two-point-five kids...

Which was crazy-stupid considering who he was. Who she was. But damn if he didn't want it anyway. He allowed his mind to wander for a stretch, fantasizing about what his life might look like if the reverie were real. He visualized coming home from a long shift at the firehouse to the smell of a delicious home-cooked meal, kissing Lana's lips before roughhousing with Connor in the backyard. He pictured tucking the little guy into bed around nine o'clock—so he could spend the remainder of his evening taking his new wife to bed.

Completely absorbed by the blissful images flashing in his mind, Randall had unknowingly increased his speed. And when a particularly powerful gust of wind T-boned the driver's side of his pick-up, he suddenly snapped to attention. Startled from his musing trance, he overcorrected, yanking the wheel hard-left. The moment his back end swung to the right he knew he'd fucked up.

Randall quickly jerked the wheel to the right in an attempt to regain control, but it was no use; with so much water coating the slickened asphalt his tires had nothing to cling on to. The truck bed veered further to the right until the length of the two-ton pick-up became perpendicular to the road. Unable to sustain forward motion in its current position, the truck lurched and rolled.

The sound of crushing metal filled his ears as he tumbled down the deserted two-lane highway. No longer able to control the vehicle, he held on for dear life, gripping the wheel with every ounce of strength he could conjure while his body thrashed about inside the cab. The violent turbulence seemed to last an eternity, but likely only spanned five seconds. And when the ruthless churning eased and the first wave of pain rippled through his limp body, a specter of light crept into his vision, taking the shape of a man he hadn't laid eyes on since Memorial Day of last year.

Jimmy's brown eyes bored into his.

And then...

Darkness.

The windows rattled as a steady stream of harsh, tropical air clashed against the glass pane, adding to the orchestra of sounds already entertaining Lana as she lay on the couch in her dim living room alone. The power had gone out roughly forty-five minutes ago when the eye of the storm had washed ashore, forcing her to fetch the hurricane survival kit she kept in the pantry in utter darkness. And after stubbing her little toe on a kitchen chair, she'd lit the oil lamp, snatched a small metal flashlight, and returned to the couch.

Lana had seen a lot of tropical systems in her twenty-seven years having lived on the Gulf Coast her whole life. Didn't matter how many, though; hunkering down in the dark while Mother Nature disfigured the earth was still terrifying. Night storms were always the worst. And this time was no different.

She was completely alone, now. Her mother had phoned earlier informing Lana that she was keeping Connor for the night. They both agreed it was probably in his best interest, although that didn't mean she had to like it. Lying on the couch, she watched light and shadows dance across the ceiling, fluttering in time with the flickering flame. Her eyes burned from the friction of her tears, her lids gritty like coarse sandpaper. Her life was beginning to look an awful lot like a bad *Jerry Springer* episode: the ones where the audience practically chanted for the two-timin' hussy's blood.

Her tender heart ached, a myriad of emotions all fighting for dominance.

Betrayal, sorrow, guilt and despair.

Embarrassment and humiliation.

Worry.

Love.

She was in love with Randall Burns. She hadn't planned it—God knows she'd spent many nights denying her attraction to him in the beginning, but the magnetism and allure had been too powerful.

None of that mattered much now, though. Thanks to Jenny's ill-timed outburst, the entire town had condemned Lana before her feet had left the stage. Well, maybe not the entire town—Olivia had left a very kind message on her machine earlier. Seems Lana still had one ally...

Inhaling a shaky breath, Lana rose from the couch and reached for the small frame that housed a picture of Jimmy and Randall, taken two summers ago at the annual Oyster Festival. Behind the thin sheet of glass lay the two men that'd stolen her heart. They were as different as night and day— probably why they'd made such good friends.

And she loved them both.

She'd always cherish the years she'd spent with Jimmy. Always. He'd given her eleven amazing years and a son she adored beyond words. And she'd love him till her last breath for that.

But it was time to move on, time to stop living in the past and forge a future for herself and her son. More than anything she wanted it to be with Randall. He was trying to do the honorable thing, she knew, but Lana didn't need his noble gestures—she just needed his love.

Returning the small metal frame to the mantel, she shuffled to the window, shoving the drapes aside to watch the storm's fury. She expected to see high winds and pounding rain—maybe even a bit of debris—but what she hadn't counted on was Chief Handler and Grant Womack.

Snatching her hand from the curtain, Lana quickly moved to the door, tugging it open as the two men bounded up the porch steps. Her gaze darted between the two forms before her, one tall and broad, one short and round.

Both wearing wet clothes and stone-like expressions.

"Sorry to drop in like this", Chief Handler began. "But we

couldn't reach you by phone."

"I...I turned it off earlier."

Chief nodded firmly once, then shifted his weight, removing his hat. Lana stared in disbelief, feeling as though she was reliving that fateful night one year ago.

"It's Randall, Lana... There's... there's been an accident."

# Chapter 31

A fist hurdled toward Randall at lightning speed, striking his face with an almost supernatural-like power. A shockwave of pain exploded behind his right eye as his head snapped back from the brutal blow. Instinctively, he palmed the tender skin, feeling it swell beneath his bloody fingertips. His body felt heavy, weak. Pressing the heel of his hand against his throbbing eye he waited for his vision to clear.

Only he wasn't quite prepared to find his dead best friend kneeling in front of him.

"Long time no see, Brother", Jimmy seethed. "What's it been, one year?"

Randall stared skeptically for a stretch. "Yeah", he finally managed.

"Well, I would ask what you've been up to these days, but then, I already know..." Standing, Jimmy snatched him up by his shirt and slammed him against the side of his mangled truck. "I just want to know why... Of all the women, why did it have to be *her?*"

Randall stared into the eyes of a man he'd grown up with, two brown eyes raw with misery and strain. "You think I haven't asked myself that same question every night?" Relaxing the grip on Randall's shirt, Jimmy turned away, running his hands through his dark blond hair. "Doesn't matter now, anyway—it's over."

Jimmy turned, resting his hands low on his hips, his expression a mixture of rage, disbelief, and... appreciation?

"Why's that?"

"Well, I'm talking to you, right? If I'm seeing dead people, that must mean I'm..."

"Dead?" Jimmy finished, smiling.

Lana paced the hall outside Randall's hospital room, waiting for the nurse to give her the green light to rush in. Details were still a bit fuzzy, but it seemed as though he'd skipped town after leaving her earlier this afternoon. His mangled Ford had been found by a county sheriff deputy on a routine patrol just before seven 'o clock. It'd taken some time for the Franklin County Fire Department to respond—even longer to pry Randall's battered and unconscious body from the wreckage.

According to Chief Handler Randall had been wedged in the cab of his truck pretty good, and had likely lingered in that state for several hours before the deputy stumbled upon the crushed pick-up. She cringed every time she thought about him lying helplessly and injured on the side of the road, while blasting wind and unrelenting rain besieged his limp, crippled body.

Dr. Conrad hadn't given them much to go on; only that Randall had been slipping in and out of consciousness upon his arrival.

"Here", Olivia offered, shoving a small Styrofoam cup at her. "It's gonna be a long night, sugar. Might as well start loadin' up on the caffeine." Lana took the cup and swallowed a sip. "Any news yet?"

Shaking her head, she lowered the cup of sludge the cafeteria tried to pass off as coffee. "The nurse is in with him now. She told me I can pop in to see him for a few minutes after she has him settled."

"He awake now?"

"No, still fading in and out, last I heard."

Olivia nodded, leaning her shoulder against the wall. "What about you? How're you holdin' up?"

"I'm... I'm"—Lana quickly wiped a fleeing tear with her free hand and flashed a weak smile—"managing. Or, at least, trying to… Thank you for being here—it means a lot to—"

"Okay", Kendall interrupted as she and Ty stepped from the elevator. "I brought my entire collection of nail polish with me—not nearly as extensive as yours, I might add—but I'm sure we can still find a shade you'll like."

"Nail polish?" Lana asked, puzzled.

"That's right", Olivia added, nudging a damp lock of brown hair from Lana's face. "Instead of wearin' a hole in the floor in front of this room, you're gonna sit down while we paint your nails."

"Paint my nails?" Her response sounded more like a statement than a question, like she was testing the words in her mouth.

"So you can pick off the polish, of course", Kendall explained.

This time Lana wasn't able to stifle the sob that'd worked its way up the back of her throat. She slapped her free hand over her mouth, but the sound escaped anyway. In the blink of an eye, her two friends rushed forward, wrapping their arms around her as though they were lending her their strength.

Maybe her luck was finally turning around.

Just Maybe…


"Relax", Jimmy uttered. "You're not dead—just unconscious."

The tense muscles in Randall's shoulders eased a bit.

He wasn't dead…

There'd been a time not so long ago he'd have been disappointed at the news. The guilt over his best friend's death had ruled his worthless life in such a way that he'd come to terms with his own demise. But now… now he had something—*someone*—to live for. "Where is she?"

Jimmy sighed, then jerked his head toward the door. "She's in the waiting room."

"In the waiting room?" he asked, confused.

"Look around, Brother. You're at the hospital."

His eyes scanned the room. Peach pastel wallpaper,

beeping machines, and the unmistakable smell of antiseptic. Yep, he was definitely at Mainland Hospital. "I don't understand... How'd I get here?"

"By ambulance, of course." Jimmy sat down next to Randall, leaning his elbows against his lap as he leaned forward. "Look, I don't have a lot of time. So I'm gonna do the talkin' and you're gonna listen." He waited for Randall to nod before he continued. "I want to hate you, want to make you feel the pain I felt when I saw you makin' moves on Lana... But I can't.

"I love that woman more than you'll ever know. And I had to watch her mourn me—crumble, day after day after day— for months, last year. If I hadn't already been dead, it would've killed me again—"

"Jimmy, I—"

Jimmy held his palm in front of him, stopping Randall mid-sentence. "Let me finish. I'm not gonna lie, Randall; seeing you and Lana together... Well, no man should have to witness something like that. But", he sighed, "you make her happy. You walk into the room and her entire aura just lights up... That's... that's why I had to do it."

Randall's brows drew together in confusion again. "Had to do what?"

"I had to save you."


"Mrs. Phillips", the elderly nurse called out as she stepped into the waiting room.

Lana quickly jumped to her feet. "Yes?"

"You can see him, now, but only for a few minutes."

"Okay. Thank you." Lana glanced at Olivia and Kendall before following the nurse into the abandoned hallway. It was almost eleven, now. The bulk of the tropical storm had already passed, leaving intermittent squalls of heavy rain in its wake.

Slowly, guys from the department had trickled in to show their support for one of their own. The expressions on their faces revealed they were none too happy about the idea of Lana and Randall. But it meant a lot to her that they were still here. The Butler Island Fire Department were a dysfunctional bunch, yes, but they still stuck together. She loved that about these guys. In time, she hoped they would come to understand the choices she and Randall had made.

"Go on in, honey. I'll swing back by to getcha in about five minutes."

"Thanks", she uttered feebly. With a fortifying breath, she turned the knob and pressed the heavy door open.

Nothing could've prepared Lana for that first glimpse, though. Her body froze mid-step. Her breath hitched.

His left leg was splinted, wrapped with myriad layers of gauze and Ace Bandages. On his arms were legions of cuts and scrapes, likely from shattered glass. Her eyes slowly traveled up the length of his body until she came upon the nasty, swollen bruise that'd formed around his right eye.

Shuffling forward, she covered her mouth to muffle her sobs, collapsing into the chair at his bedside. Her eyes skittered to the monitors. She didn't know what half the information meant, but the jagged line steadily moving across one of them, coupled with a repetitive beep, assured her he was very much alive. Reaching for his hand she brought it to her lips, pressing a gentle kiss to one of the small cuts along the back of it.

*Could have lost him...*

The suddenness of that possibility rushed over her as she stared at his motionless body, the expanding ache pressing in on her lungs.

She could have lost him.

Lana interlocked their fingers, giving his hand a light squeeze. She needed to feel his warmth, needed the constant reminder that he was alive. Through a steady stream of tears she studied the even movement of his chest as he breathed.

Life was precious. Life was often unpredictable. Losing Jimmy had taught her that. The dirty looks and malicious whispers weren't going to deter her. She wanted a life—a future—with Randall.

But first, she had to say goodbye to a piece of her past.

"All right, time's up, Mrs. Phillips."

Lana head snapped toward the nurse, then back to

Randall. "I love you", she uttered softly. Brushing her lips over the back of his hand one last time, she gently placed it back on the bed, then stood, following the nurse into the abandoned hallway.

"When can I see him again?" She inquired as the nurse led her to the waiting area.

"Probably not until after his surgery tomorrow—"

"Surgery?"

"Just his ankle, honey. A few screws and he'll be as good as new."

Lana halted. "What about the rest of his injuries?"

The kind, elderly nurse stopped just outside the door that led to the waiting room. Hugging a stack of charts against her chest, she turned, eyeing Lana for a stretch before answering. "You know, I'm not really supposed to be discussing any of this with you. But... He's gonna be just fine. Aside from the ankle, he has a few broken ribs, lacerations from the shattered glass, and one heck of a nasty bruise on his handsome face. Rollover crashes don't always have happy endings, you know. So I'd say he was pretty darn lucky. Must've had an angel watching over him."

Lana smiled as a lone tear slid down her cheek. "Yeah, I think he did."

# Chapter 32

Vigorous whispers faded to uncomfortable silence as Lana reentered the small, packed waiting room. More than a dozen pairs of eyes settled on her, the weight of their gazes stimulating her fight or flight mechanism.

*Stay. Hold your ground.*

*Fight.*

"How is he?" Grant probed. "He awake yet?"

"No, but the nurse says he's gonna be fine." Lana explained the depth of his injuries, including the surgery required to realign the displaced bones in his ankle. The room fell quiet again, tense air swirling, suffocating.

*Stay. Hold your ground.*

*Fight.*

It was time to address the elephant in the room, time for everyone to know where her head and heart were at. Sucking air into her starved lungs, Lana forced the words over her dry throat.

"I love him—Randall. I know you all probably think it's crazy, sudden, *wrong*… But I do."

Tucking a damp strand of hair behind her ear with quivering hands, she continued. "I've learned a lot about life over the last year. I've learned that careful plans and good intentions can sometimes spell disaster. I've learned that life is meant to be valued and treasured. And I've learned that every bad outcome garners a silver lining… Randall is my silver lining", she reiterated, placing her palm over her heart.

Lana scanned the room, allowing her gaze to land on every face as she spoke. "Some of you are angry—I get that. Jimmy meant something to everyone in this room. We can sit here all night and play the *what-would-you-do* game, but until you've walked a day in my shoes, you don't get to judge me or the choices I've made.

"I watched Jimmy's casket while it was lowered into the ground", she uttered softly, wiping the river of tears now cascading down her sodden cheeks. "I watched every hope— every dream—slowly fade away... For me, that was rock bottom. That was the moment when everything inside me broke into a million little pieces.

"I'll never be whole again. There will always be a missing piece. Always. But, Randall... Well, he's the glue that put me back together... *He rescued me...*"

Randall ran his hand through his dark hair. "*You* saved me?"

"For the second time, yes—but who's counting?" Jimmy remarked sarcastically. Leaning back in his chair he smirked, his hands coming to rest behind his head.

Randall felt a smile spread across his lips too. Jimmy had always been a comedian of sorts. It was good to know his sense of humor was still intact. Good to know that after everything that'd happened over the last year, he wasn't jaded. Much.

After all, the man had thoroughly enjoyed ramming his fist into Randall's eye.

Jimmy's easy expression suddenly turned serious, his brows drawing together. "You love her."

Not a question—a statement. Because Jimmy's brilliant gaze could see through the bumps and bruises and broken bones, penetrating the layer of fibrous tissue surrounding Randall's scarred heart.

"Yes."

Jimmy sighed. Leaning forward, he propped his elbows against his lap. "Then tell her", he advised. "She needs to hear it. She *deserves* to hear it... God knows she didn't hear it from me as often as she should have."

"You make it sound so... simple."

"It is", Jimmy conceded, rising to his feet. "Living beings tend to overcomplicate things. Doesn't have to be that way, though. The secret to life really is simple. It all comes down to love: the love you give and the love others give you." His silhouette flickered a few times, warning his time was almost up. "Promise me something?"

Randall's throat suddenly felt tight. "Anything."

"Take care of Lana and Connor. Be the husband and the father I wasn't."

The backs of Randall's eyes burned as moisture spilled over his lashes. "I... I will, man. I promise."

"Oh, and uh, you might wanna ask the nurse for an icepack." Gesturing toward Randall's eye, Jimmy's mouth spread into a wide grin. "Guess I can still pack one hell of a punch."

The apparition faded then, just as quickly as it'd suddenly appeared. Muffled whispers echoed in Randall's head, swirling into a crescendo of nearly perceptible chatter. His chest hurt, every breath bitter and strained. The voices became louder—one male, one female. Sharp pain traveled up his left leg, so intense his lids fluttered open.

"Welcome back, Mr. Burns."


The beaming sun climbed the cloudless blue sky, its earnest rays warming the flesh on Lana's bare arms. The atmosphere looked completely different today: calm, bright, tranquil. Small twigs and scattered leaves appeared to be the only evidence left behind by yesterday's tropical storm. Chirping birds harmonized in the distance, filling the dead silence with whispers of life.

The air was thick and muggy and still as she navigated through the small cemetery, her hazy memory guiding her apprehensive gait. The soles of her sandals pressed into the spongy earth as she stepped off the winding brick path, her eyes scanning the row of headstones until her gaze landed on the third slab of granite from the end.

Clutching the small bouquet of blue perennials she'd clipped from the backyard, Lana willed her jittery legs to persevere, each step exponentially harder than the one before. Within moments she was close enough to read the engraved stone.

*James Phillips, Jr.*
*September 1, 1982 – May 28, 2012*
*Loving husband, father, and hero*

Falling to her knees six-feet above her husband's remains, she gently set the flowers on the ground as the first wave of agony and sadness rippled through her. Somehow seeing Jimmy's life reduced to three simple lines carved into sleek stone made the tears fall faster. Resting her head against the smooth granite, she ran her fingertips over the etched surface.

One year. Three-hundred-sixty-five sunrises and sunsets.

Jimmy had been gone one year...

"God, I miss you", she whispered, wiping the moisture from her cheeks. Lana drew in a shaky breath, forcing the air through her pursed lips as she exhaled.

"Sorry it's taken me so long to visit. I wanted to, but...I was afraid.... I guess I thought if I stayed away, I wouldn't have to accept that you're really gone. Crazy, huh...?

"Connor's getting big—grew nearly three inches in the span of a few months. He's playing football this fall. I'm scared to death, but... I know you'll keep him safe." Her palm muffled a fleeing sob.

Losing Jimmy hurt. But the thought of Connor growing up, never fully grasping the kind, loving man that created him, hurt far worse.

Lana tilted her face skyward for a few beats, letting the sun shower her with warmth. "I have a confession to make", she began again, returning her gaze to the etched granite. "I...I've been seeing someone. He's a good man, Jimmy; I know this because you admired him, too. In fact, you cared about him so much you didn't think twice before shoving him from the path of that falling limb.

"I know the fact that it's Randall is probably maddening. Sort of took me by surprise, too, if I'm being honest. But..." Lana clenched her eyes shut. She wasn't entirely sure why, but what she was about to say somehow seemed easier that way. *"I-I love him..."*

She paused for a stretch, waiting for lightening to leap from the clear blue sky, the earth to rattle and shake, or the ground beneath her to open up and swallow her whole. But all remained still and quiet.

And she wasn't quite sure what to think about that either. Because in order to move forward, she needed to make peace with her past.

"Please don't hate me, Jimmy", she whispered. "Please don't—"

Lana opened her eyes and sat motionless, paralyzed, her blurry gaze focusing on the butterfly perched on the top of Jimmy's headstone. Its brilliant blue wings fluttered a few times, almost as if it was trying to snag her attention. Completely transfixed on its vivid beauty, a lick of awareness whispered over her skin, and although the sultry air was thick and muggy, she shivered.

The butterfly lodged on its perch while Lana wept, watching as grief, sorrow, and guilt spilled from her lashes. And when the small creature fluttered its wings a few minutes later to take flight, a mysterious wave of harmony and peace swaddled her body.

She couldn't explain it—lord knows, it didn't make a lick of sense—but for the first time since that fateful day one year ago, Lana felt her equilibrium return.

Jimmy was sending her a sign.

*It's okay. It's time to move on.*

*It's time to let me go...*

# Chapter 33

"We need to talk."

The tip of Mayor Cliffburg's pen stilled as his eyes lifted toward the female voice. "What're you doing here? I thought I was pretty clear about you lying low for a few days."

"I needed more details."

"Then you should've called", he ground out, dropping his pen. "Anybody see you come in here?"

Jenny gently nudged the door closed behind her. "Relax. The building is nearly empty this morning."

"Yes, but the Public Services Department is—"

"The Public Services Department is buzzing with post-storm clean up coordination. Trust me", she claimed, stepping further into the mayor's office, "No one saw me."

Michael released an anxious breath, then placed his elbows against his desk, tenting his hands into a point under his chin. "You shouldn't be here. It's too risky."

"Then I'll get right to the point. You promised me a job in exchange for my performance yesterday. I'm here to collect."

Michael chuckled under his breath.

*Dimwitted bitch.*

Guess this is what he got for involving the redheaded broad in his crafty scheme. Recruiting an amateur for a role as crucially important as this one had been wasn't his usual M.O., but the opportunity had been too perfect to pass up. Tension had been mounting between Lana and Jenny for months: a clear-cut motive. That, coupled with the fact that there was no evidence linking he and Jenny together, made the woman an easy and obvious choice for the job.

But the permanent stain on Lana's "good girl image" didn't mean a damn thing if suspicious minds stumbled upon a connection. And every minute Jenny spent in this office with him threatened to do just that. "Well, *obviously* I need some time to make good on my end of the deal. Everything has to appear convincing, Jenny. Timing is key."

"That bit of information might've been helpful last week when you first came to me with your 'brilliant' plan", she emphasized with air quotes. "I already gave my two-weeks at Leo's."

*Was she mocking him? Mocking his superior intelligence?*

Placing his palms on the desk he rose from his leather chair, moving around the mahogany furniture until he stood directly in front of her. He could tell by the way her breath hitched, by the way her pupils dilated, that she was afraid of him.

Good. She should be.

He wasn't a violent man, per se, but he knew people that were. Having friends in low places was like an insurance fund: you pay them in a predetermined manner (in this case, turning a blind eye to their criminal activity) and if a situation should arise, you simply made a claim.

Tempting as it was to reach for the phone, it wasn't necessary; he could handle this bitch in his sleep. "A little rash, don't you think, Mrs. Carson?"

Jenny swallowed hard, the sound practically echoing off the plaque-filled walls. "We had a deal. If you can't uphold your end, then I'll—"

Cupping her chin with his hand, he squeezed. Hard. "You threatening me?"

"No, I just—"

"Because the humiliation Lana suffered yesterday is a drop in the bucket compared to what I'd do to you if you double-cross me. You got that?" He seethed, his face inches from hers. He loosened his grip when Jenny gave a weak nod, then shoved his hands in his front pockets. "Good. Now get the hell out of my office before someone sees you. I'll be in touch."

* * * * *

Jenny didn't need to be asked twice. She'd turned toward the door so fast she nearly made herself dizzy.

Damn, and to think she'd voted for the guy four years ago...

No doubt the man was a wolf in sheep's clothing, which only served to reiterate that she'd done the right thing. The blazing mid-morning sun nearly blinded her as she exited city hall, her porcelain skin branded by the singeing rays. Sinking into the driver's seat of her Civic, she drew in a deep breath, wiping her sweaty palms on the front of her denim skirt.

*The humiliation Lana suffered yesterday is a drop in the bucket compared to what I'd do to you if you double-cross me. You got that?*

Yeah. She got it, all right. Maneuvering out of her parking space Jenny set her sights on her next stop: Mainland Hospital.

"Where is she?" Randall whispered hoarsely. His throat felt raw, like he'd swallowed a bucketful of rusted nails. That was only the tip of the iceberg, though. Because there didn't seem to be a place on his body that didn't ache. And although his strong frame appeared battered and broken, it was his heart that garnered the most pain.

The nurse studied one of the monitors behind him and then scribbled the information in his chart. "You mean the cute brunette that's been wearing a hole in the linoleum in front of the nurse's station?"

"That'd be the one."

Setting his chart on the edge of the bed, she snatched the stethoscope from her neck and carefully inserted the earpieces. She listened to his lungs for a stretch, instructing him to breathe deeply, then normal.

Randall knew to keep quiet while she listened. As a paramedic, he couldn't count the number of times he'd arrived at the scene of an emergency, the kind where every precious second counted, only to be mistaken for a damn counselor.

Staring death in the eyeballs tended to do that to a person: make them spill their secrets, voice their regrets. He was trained to tune out the rising chaos, to concentrate solely on the patient's needs. Didn't make his job easier, though.

Plucking the stethoscope from her ears, the nurse hung it around her neck and reached for his chart once more. "Your stomach may feel a little queasy for a bit; that's normal after general anesthesia. I'm going to get you some crackers and juice. If you do well with that, I'll let you pick something from the menu for dinner."

"And could you—"

"Yes", she interrupted, "I'll send her in."

"Thanks", he managed hoarsely.

Fingers of sunbeams filtered through the mini-blinds, casting parallel patterns of light and shadows along the peach-swirled wallpaper.

Peach...

*"What is it with you women: always referring to colors as food?"* He'd asked. *"Suddenly purple's eggplant or grape, green's lime or avocado, and orange can be anything from salmon to carrot to—"*

*"Peach"*, she'd interrupted.

*"Yeah, peach."*

God, he had it bad. *Peach ...? Really...?*

His thoughts drifted to that night—the night he'd held Lana in his arms in the middle of the dance floor at The Saloon. His memory was sharp, vivid—like he was reliving the moment again: the way the blue lights settled on her satiny skin, the way she'd felt pressed against him, the wanton look in her eyes. In fact when he closed his lids, he could practically smell the subtle scent of vanilla that always seemed to linger on her soft body...

"I think you might've outdone Olivia's infamous Jet Ski joyride this time", Kendall remarked as she stepped into the room. "At least she came back in one piece."

Randall's eyes flew open, his gaze landing on the raven-haired exotic beauty. A stab of disappointment bit into his chest, vibrating his wounded soul.

Crazy, really. It'd never occurred to him that the nurse had been referring to Kendall when she'd mentioned the cute brunette.

*My, how times have changed...*

He wasn't necessarily disappointed by Kendall's presence, per se. He'd just been expecting someone else.

*Wishful thinking, buddy. You walked out on Lana, remember?*

Yeah, unfortunately he did.

Forcing a smile he didn't quite feel, Randall gestured toward his body. "I am in one piece."

"Barely", she whispered as she dropped into the chair at his bedside. "Damn it, Rand, of all the crazy, stupid things you've done over the years, this tops the list."

"Can't disagree with you there." Pressing his palms against the lumpy mattress he carefully sought a position that didn't aggravate his tender ribs, wincing slightly as he stirred.

"So how do you feel?"

"Like I rolled my truck in the middle of a tropical storm", he revealed wryly. Kendall didn't seem to find his attempt at sarcasm very amusing, however. Crossing her arms, her amber eyes narrowed. "All right, all right—I feel like shit."

Satisfied with his honesty Kendall reached for his hand and gave it a gentle squeeze. "You have no idea how worried we've been."

"We?"

"Yes, '*we*'... There's an entire waiting room"—she gestured with a tilt of her head—" filled with people that love you, Rand."

But not Lana. He didn't blame her for not being here; he hadn't exactly given her a reason to believe that loving him mattered. Because sometimes actions did speak louder than words, and walking out on her yesterday while she'd begged him not to spoke volumes.

"I've known for a while, you know."

Jolted from the memory of yesterday, Randall regarded her with uncertainty. "Impossible."

"Okay, let me rephrase, then: I've had my suspicions for a while. It all started with the scuffle at the station with Tommy. And the following month my suspicion was confirmed when I saw the two of you dancing at The Saloon. The way you looked at her... It's the same way Ty looks at me. That's when I knew."

"Knew what, exactly?"

Kendall smiled for the first time since she'd stepped into the room. "You love her."

God, did he ever. He loved her something fierce. Lana Phillips was his kryptonite, his biggest weakness. Everything about her—from her contagious smile, to her incredible body, to the way she picked at her polished nails, to her unyielding faith in him. A wounded man lost in a black hole of nothingness, Lana was his beacon in the dark, the mesmerizing light luring him to safety. She was his everything.

"Yeah", he admitted just above a whisper. Briefly pinching the bridge of his nose, his gaze settled on Kendall once again. "God, Ken, I really fucked up this time. She told me she loved me, and what did I do?—I turned my back on her, left her sitting on the floor, crying, begging me not to leave." Sighing in frustration, he tilted his head back against the nearly flat pillow. "No wonder she's not here; can't say I blame her."

Kendall shook her head. "Rand—she was here all night. She left first thing this morning, said she had something she had to take care of. I called her the moment Dr. Conrad informed us you'd made it out of surgery." Kendall's dark brows drew together. "Come to think of it, she should've been here by now..."

# Chapter 34

A blast of cool air rushed over Lana's skin as she entered the lobby at Mainland Hospital. The soles of her sandals clapped against the linoleum floor.

Click. Click. Click. Click.

She'd just made it back to her car at the cemetery when Kendall had phoned with the news: Randall was in Recovery. His ankle surgery had been a success. She'd sat behind the wheel of her idling Corolla for roughly ten minutes before her composure returned. A swell of relief had flooded her insides, because she knew all too well how close she'd come to losing him—how close she'd come to burying the man she loved. Again.

She wasn't going to go there. Simply couldn't. He was going to be okay. And although his recovery was going to be long and painful, it certainly beat the alternative. Death.

Rounding the corner Lana moved toward the elevators, so deep in gratitude for the second chance she'd been given, she'd failed to notice the woman leaning against the wall near the elevator entrance. That is until the woman pushed off the wall and headed toward her.

"Well, it's about time."

Lana halted immediately, clapping eyes on the woman responsible for outing her relationship with Randall in front of the entire town. Rage boiled inside her depths, red-hot and festering. "Get out of my way", she ground out, clenching her fists at her side.

Steering her body around her former friend Lana took a step, reaching for the call button next to the elevator—only, Jenny took a step, too, thwarting her hasty getaway.

"Wait, there's something you need to hear first."

"There's nothing you could possibly say to me that I'd want to hear right now, Jenny."

"Trust me", Jenny said as she reached into her purse for the small voice recorder, "You'll definitely want to hear this." Gripping the small device, she pressed PLAY.

*"We need to talk."*

*"What're you doing here? I thought I was pretty clear about you lying low for a few days."*

*"I needed more details."*

*"Then you should've called. Anybody see you come in here?"*

*"Relax. The building is nearly empty this morning."*

*"Yes, but the Public Services Department is—"*

*"The Public Services Department is buzzing with post-storm clean up coordination. Trust me, no one saw me."*

*"You shouldn't be here. It's too risky."*

*"Then I'll get right to the point. You promised me a job in exchange for my performance yesterday. I'm here to collect."*

A stretch of silence, and then…

*"Well, obviously I need some time to make good on my end of the deal. Everything has to appear convincing, Jenny. Timing is key."*

Jenny stopped the recording and inhaled a deep breath. "I know this is probably hard for you to believe, but… I'm sorry—for everything." She explained how Mayor Cliffburg had contacted her last week with what seemed like the perfect solution to all her problems.

"I just… wanted to take the focus off me and all of the rotten choices I've made this year. That was my chief motive, here. Mayor Cliffburg offering me a job—well, that was just icing on the cake.

"When I stood up in front of everyone yesterday and publicly humiliated you, I expected to feel some sort of... redemption, I guess. But I didn't. The moment you stepped foot off that stage the guilt started eating at me." Shifting her weight, she went on. "And then after the auction ended, when I got a *job-well-done* from the mayor, I suddenly wanted no part of it. I promise you, Lana", she pleaded, "if there was any way I could reverse time and undo all the damage I created yesterday, I would!"

Lana watched as tears trickled down Jenny's cheek. She didn't want to feel compassion for her former friend—lord knows the woman's selfishness was part of the reason they were standing here. Jenny had made some poor choices since the new year began.

And according to many, so had Lana.

Quick to judge and slow to forgive, the residents of Butler Island had unknowingly initiated yesterday's outcome. Months of contempt and humiliation had sucked the liveliness from Jenny, leaving behind a bitter and spiteful shell. The woman wasn't an innocent bystander by any means, but Lana understood—probably better than anyone—that sometimes life's toughest choices weren't presented in black and white. More often than not options were murky and gray.

Lana wanted to believe that Jenny's remorse was sincere. The woman was a lot of things, yes—but she wasn't a liar. She'd made her feelings for Lana blatantly clear the last several months.

Crystal clear.

"I just don't get it, Jenny. Your misery-loves-company motive is twisted and sick, but straightforward. What has me completely baffled is Mayor Cliffburg's motive. Why?—why would *he* do this?"

"Honey, isn't it obvious? The man's completely captivated by you. Needless to say, when he found out that you'd been secretly seeing Randall, he didn't take the news well."

With quivering hands, Jenny ran her fingertips over the tender skin near her mouth where the mayor had grabbed her face earlier. "He's not the caring, charismatic man he leads the public to believe, Lana. He's cold. Conniving. Downright scary. He's waiting for public outrage to peak. He wants you to feel like the only thing you have left is your position at city hall. And when that happens, he plans to take that away from you, too."

"And you're my replacement", Lana stated just above a whisper.

Jenny nodded. "But... things change, Lana. I have a new plan, and if you're willing, I think we can attempt to make this right. What do you say?"

A high-pitched *DING* announced the elevator's arrival a moment before the heavy metallic doors slid open. Part of her wanted to turn her back on Jenny, the part that felt mauled and betrayed. But something kept her feet planted firmly in place.

"You ladies going up?" asked the kind, middle-aged gentleman that'd just stepped aboard.

Mayor Cliffburg had everyone fooled, claiming to be honorable and good, when truthfully he was anything but. He'd mastered his craft, disguising his poisonous and corrupt insides with flashy suits and phony smiles.

He could ruin her reputation, deliver her walking papers, but his evil scheme couldn't take what mattered to her most. Family.

She wasn't afraid of Michael Cliffburg.

But Michael Cliffburg should be afraid of *her*.

The people in this town deserved better. They deserved to know their beloved leader was crooked to the core.

"No", Lana finally said, "we're not. Thank you for asking." Nodding firmly once, the chivalrous man removed his hand from the impatient door, disappearing a moment later behind a sheet of sliding heavy metal.

Crossing her arms, Lana's eye's returned to Jenny. "So"— she shrugged—"what now?"

Feeding her starved lungs with a liter of antiseptic-scented air, Jenny's rigid shoulders relaxed. "Two things", she gestured with her fingers, "a computer and some of your time."

\* \* \* \* \*

"Having any gas pains?" Chief Handler's wife, Debbie, asked. "When I had my gallbladder removed a few years ago, the surgeon pumped my body full of air—I was tootin' like a New York City cab driver in rush hour traffic for the next three days!"

Randall's dark brows lifted briefly in surprise. "Nope, no gas pains." But suddenly he *was* sensing a sharp pain in his ass. Chatty Debbie meant well, he knew, but damn... Where did she come up with this shit?

"Do you have any idea how embarrassing it is to have zero control over your body?"

*Probably no more embarrassing than hearing you talk about it.*

"Seemed to happen every time someone came into my room. Kind of reminded me of those movies set in medieval times—you know, the ones where horns announce the arrival of royalty? Anyhow, I..."

Chief Handler scrubbed a chubby hand down his face before mouthing the words *I'm sorry* to Randall. How the man had survived thirty years of peculiar conversation, he'd never know.

"...They don't tell you these things beforehand, you know. I mean, what woman in her right mind would agree to have an elective surgery, knowin' her rear end would come down with a case of Tourette's syndrome?"

*Probably the same kind of woman that openly talked about it.*

Randall eyed the clock: almost noon. *Damn it, Lana, where are you...*

"Uh, honey", Chief Handler interjected before she started again. "Would you mind gettin' me a cup of coffee from the cafeteria? After the night we all had, I could use another jolt of caffeine."

"I reckon", she said, planting a kiss on the top of his nearly bald head. "But you'll have to drink it black this time; you've already had three candy bars this morning."

"Yes, Dear." Chief Handler waited for the door to close before he released a frustrated breath. "The woman has too much time on her hands. Drives me damn nuts, sometimes", he uttered wryly.

*You're not the only one.*

Randall studied him for a beat. Chatty Debbie may occasionally drive the man berserk, but there was no mistaking how much Chief adored his wife. "Yeah, but you still love her anyway."

"Sure do." Shifting his large derriere in the narrow seat, his eyes settled on Randall. "You gave us all quite a scare last night, you know—*especially* Lana. For the second time, I had to stand on her front porch and deliver bad news. I don't *ever* want to have to do that again."

"Then we both want the same thing."

"Good." Chief jutted his chin in the direction of Randall's ankle. "Doc say how long before you're back on your feet?"

"If he did, I was too doped up to remem—"

"I'm sorry", Lana announced as she stepped into the room. "I didn't realize you had a visitor. I can come back lat—"

"No!" Randall blurted. His sudden outburst rattled his cracked ribs; palming his left side he winced, sucking air through his mouth through clenched teeth. He'd waited all morning for Lana to arrive, and if experiencing a little pain's what it'd take for her to stay, he'd gladly do it again.

"But you're—"

"It's okay, Darlin' ", Chief uttered, rocking in his chair until he gained enough momentum to stand. "I was gettin' ready to head down to the cafeteria, anyhow." Shuffling to the door, he gave Lana a friendly pat on the shoulder and murmured something that sounded an awful lot like *go easy on him* before vanishing into the hall.

Lana stood several paces in front of the door, her arms wrapped around her middle for comfort. Feet fixed to the linoleum floor, her eyes swept over his body, carefully surveying the damage.

"I'm okay", he reassured her when her blue eyes began to fill with tears. A quivering hand briefly covered her mouth before her composure returned. The piercing sharp pain exploding behind his breastbone had nothing to do with his injuries, this time. The fact that he'd done this to her—*again*—didn't sit right with him. "C' mere", he uttered quietly, patting the mattress.

In roughly two strides Lana rushed forward, carefully shrouding him with her soft body. The sensation felt good, natural, leaving no doubt that this—this life, *this woman*—was what he wanted.

"I'm sorry", he whispered, nuzzling her neck with the tip of his nose. Subtle hints of vanilla drifted into his awareness, immediately putting his weary mind at ease.

Lana raised her upper body a bit, aiming her glassy blue eyes at his. "When I opened the door last night and saw Grant and Chief Handler, I-I thought—"

"I know", he murmured, tucking a strand of light brown hair behind her ear. "I'm so sorry. Guess I just thought if I left town for a day or two it'd make things easier on you."

"I can handle the looks and the crude comments, Randall. Because at the end of the day what people think of me and the choices I've made, don't matter. *But you do*. You matter to Connor... to me."

"I never meant to hurt you. God", he sighed, letting the back of his head rest against the pillow again, "That's all I seem to be good at these days."

For the first time in days he saw the corners of Lana's mouth lift into a radiant smile. "Well, that's not *all* you're good at; I can think of quite a few things, actually."

Randall smiled too. "A few, eh?"

Laughter fled her pink lips, filling him with a sense of purpose. God, he loved hearing it, loved how her full lips spanned across her slender face, how her deep-blue gaze danced buoyantly, as though she didn't have a care in the world.

"I still have a few moves you haven't seen yet, you know."

"*Yet?*" One of Lana's dark brows raised before her eyes raked over his wounded body. "I don't think you're in the best condition to—"

"I think I can still manage", he commented wryly. "It would have to take a full body cast to keep me from showing you." Hell, just the thought of sinking into Lana's sweet body right now had blood suddenly rushing south. At least he knew everything still worked.

Staring at her hands, Lana's expression gradually turned serious. There was definitely something on her mind. And with a multitude of misfortunes in the last twenty-four hours alone, her weary brain had been working overtime. "A penny for your thoughts..."

Silence stretched for a few beats, leaving him to wonder whether she'd answer. "I ran into Jenny this morning", she finally murmured.

"Really?"

Lana nodded. She explained how the mayor had pitched the idea to Jenny, offering her Lana's position at city hall in return for her performance.

"What makes you think she's telling the truth? She'd probably say just about anything to—"

"She engaged the mayor in a very incriminating conversation this morning and got it all on tape... That's actually why it took me so long to get to you today; I loaded the audio on the town's website."

Lana shrugged as if bringing down corrupt politicians was all in a day's work. "Jimmy never liked the guy", she shared, picking at the remnants of coral polish leftover from the night before. "Guess now I know why..."

*Living beings tend to overcomplicate things. Doesn't have to be that way, though. The secret to life really is simple. It all comes down to love: the love you give and the love others give you.*

It was time—hell, past time—to tell her how he really felt. Jimmy was right: the secret to life is love. And he planned on giving his to Lana until his last breath. "I saw him, you know."

"Who, the mayor?"

"No... *Jimmy*." Set to a timer, the blood pressure cuff tightened around his left bicep with a low hum. He stared into Lana's hopeful gaze until the cuff hissed, slipping into a slumber-like phase

"How'd...how'd he look?"

Just one of the many things he loved about this woman. He knew how crazy it probably sounded, and to most people what he'd experienced had been nothing more than a dream, a vivid hallucination brought on by the narcotic cocktail he'd received after paramedics extracted him from his mangled Ford.

But not Lana. Because irrational or not, she believed him.

"He looked good—sarcastic as ever, too. He couldn't help but point out how he'd rescued me for the second time." Lana covered her mouth with her fingertips, but the half-laugh/half-sob escaped anyhow. "He asked me if I was in love with you."

"And what di-did you tell him?"

"The truth…" Randall palmed her face, wiping a fleeing tear with the pad of his thumb. "Because I am. Have been for a long time."

The hint of a smile curved her lips. "This you or the drugs talkin'?" she teased.

Randall chuckled under his breath, the subtle vibration reminding him immediately of his injuries. "Ahhh… don't make me laugh", he managed, smiling. "It hurts."

"I'm so sorry!" she amended. "I didn't mean to—"

"It's okay. For the first time in a long time, everything feels… okay."

"Just *okay*?" she asked, nibbling on her bottom lip.

Randall carefully tugged her a little closer, planting a soft kiss to the sweet spot just below her right ear. "Better than okay: perfect…"

Pulling back slightly, Lana's blue gaze homed in on his. "You know… I've always believed life was deliberate, that the highs and lows we experience are mapped out far in advance. That people enter and exit our lives for a reason. And so for the life of me, I couldn't understand how losing Jimmy fit into that equation. It just seemed so… random."

Wiping a falling tear, she smiled. "But I think I get it, now", she whispered. "Jimmy rescued you that day, making it possible for you to rescue me."

He'd never thought of it that way, but maybe she was partly right. Because through the tragedy of losing Jimmy, he and Lana had discovered each other. They'd managed to transform something awful and unfathomable into something beautiful and treasured. "You know, as your rescuer, you owe me."

"That so? And what is it that you want, Randall Burns?"

His eyes followed his fingers as he nudged a lock of light brown hair that'd fallen across her left cheek. "You... Forever..."

The next few seconds felt like centuries. He searched her delicate features for clues as to what she was thinking, but her expression gave nothing away.

"You sure about that?" she finally asked. "Because it's not just me—Connor and I are *sort of* a package deal."

"Good. Because I was *sort of* counting on that. I love Connor... and I love you, too." Lana silently chewed on her bottom lip for a few beats, her midnight eyes connecting with his. "You're killing me, here", he whispered.

Finally, a hint of a smile.

"*Me?*" she asked, placing her palm against her chest. "*Forever?*"

"Please."

"A simple thank you won't suffice?"

Randall's head gently shook from side-to-side as another bout of silence slipped between them. And then...

"Well... since you said 'please', I guess I can't refuse."

Not willing to give Lana another second to rethink his marriage proposal, Randall pressed his lips against her soft, smiling mouth. The moment he tasted her, he wanted more. Tilting his head, he deepened the kiss just as the pad of his thumb brushed against the front of her white blouse.

"What do you think you're doing?" she mumbled against his mouth.

With a wry grin, Randall grazed the hard nub again. "*Multi-tasking...*"

# Epilogue

"The end."

Randall closed the book he'd been reading and placed it on the wood nightstand. Connor had dozed halfway through the story, but Randall had pressed on, anyhow. Tugging on the covers, he hauled the sports-themed quilt over Connor's shoulders and shuffled to the door, killing the light with a flip of a switch before quietly closing the door behind him.

Tucking Connor into bed had become a nightly ritual. The little squirt really seemed to enjoy it, and truth be told, so did Randall.

Reading to him took roughly five minutes, but for five minutes every night, Randall felt Jimmy's presence—like he was actually there, listening to the story alongside Connor, smiling his signature ear-to-ear grin.

The notion resonated with him.

Trekking into the kitchen, he poured a glass of white zinfandel and snagged a Miller Lite from the fridge, closing the door with his left foot.

Roughly three months post-op his limp was barely noticeable, the four-inch scar along the outside of his left ankle looking better every day. The pink ridge was a constant reminder of how close he'd come to death; how grateful he was to be alive. He'd just placed Lana's wine on the coffee table when she appeared at the front door.

"Honey, I'm home", she teased as her purse strap slid down her arm. Placing the faux leather bag on the entry table, she gestured to the glass, "That for me?"

"Yes ma'am."

"Good. After the day I had, I need a drink." Scooping the pink concoction into her hand she caught the glass between her lips, swallowing a sip before collapsing onto the couch next to him. Planting a brief peck on Randall's lips, she swallowed another sip of white zinfandel. "Connor sleeping?"

"Yeah, just tucked him in about fifteen minutes ago."

"Did he make it to the end this time?"

Randall took a pull from his Miller Lite and shook his head, "Only halfway."

She angled her body to face him, propping her elbow against the back of the couch. "You know, for the first time ever, I think he actually looks forward to bedtime. He loves it when you read to him."

"Me too." He felt Lana's smile all the way to his toes. *God, she was really somethin'.* A brilliant blend of angelic beauty, easy confidence and effortless grace. "So, how'd it go tonight?"

"Surprisingly well, actually. I only had to interrupt the meeting twice to make reference to the agenda."

Michael Cliffburg resigned as Mayor of Butler Island less than a week after his devious plot was exposed on the town's website. Betrayed by their acclaimed leader, residents had all but forgotten the subject matter of Jenny's outburst at the inaugural *Jimmy Phillips, Jr. Charity Auction* and had chosen instead to focus their requital on the man that'd orchestrated it. With the town's executive chair vacant, a special election had been conducted in early July, awarding Debbie Handler the uncontested title of Madam Mayor.

Residents embraced her platform of honesty and integrity, believing Debbie's transparent-approach to governing was just what the small island had been lacking in their former leader. Because whether one liked what she had to say or not, no one could deny that Chatty Debbie was a straight shooter. She told it like it was—*often in great detail.*

"So she only went off-topic twice, eh? Not too bad for her first city commission meeting."

"Yeah, I suppose it could've been much worse", she agreed before swallowing another sip of wine. Setting the glass on the coffee table, she kicked off her navy heels and tucked her legs underneath her. "I mean, the woman can change subjects on you in the blink of an eye! One minute, she was discussing the budget for the Oyster Festival next month, and the next thing I know she was advising everyone to be on the lookout for peeping Toms."

He couldn't take it anymore. Setting his beer beside her wine glass, he hauled her onto his lap, her legs flanking his powerful thighs. "Oysters are an aphrodisiac, you know."

"So I've heard." Wiggling her bottom against the hard bulge expanding behind his fly, Lana captured her bottom lip between her teeth. "Mmm, did somebody have oysters for dinner tonight?"

"Sweetheart, I don't need any help in that department, thank-you-very-much. Just lookin' at you gets me hard." His hands disappeared beneath the hem of her white dress, sweeping up her smooth legs. When he reached the apex of her thighs, he found her hot core already wet.

"What do we have here?" he asked as the pad of his thumb brushed the damp satin of her panties. "Looks like maybe somebody else had oysters."

"I don't like oysters", she practically moaned, gently rocking her hips.

"That so?"

"Yes."

"What *do* you like, then?"

"This... You being here... *Us...*"

Randall observed her through hooded eyes, noting how her heavy lids mirrored his own. Lana's lips parted on a sigh as she ground her wet core against him. Firm. Steady. Slow. He could sense her heat through his fly, could feel his denim jeans dampen with her sweet honey.

Thick strands of silky caramel hair surrounded him as her lips drew nearer, tickling his face. The immensity of Lana's beauty punched him in the gut, sending shockwaves of tenderness, gratitude, and warmth surging across his body.

Because he was living the dream.

A dream he prayed he never woke from.

## A note from the author:

To my readers,

Thank you for spending time with me and the characters of Butler Island. It has truly been an unforgettable journey for me and I hope it was for you, as well.

For roughly sixteen months my mind inhabited the small island: helping Olivia Everitt overcome her fear of commitment in *Picture Perfect*, guiding Kendall Porter down a path of personal and professional bliss in *Addicted to You*, and finally ending with the difficult journey Lana Phillips faced after the sudden death of her husband in *Rescue Me*.

Though the characters were imaginary, their struggles are real. And that's precisely what I wanted: for readers to feel a connection—to feel they could relate to the insecurities and strife plaguing the lives of the characters in this series.

I hope I was able to accomplish that on some level.

This trilogy will always hold a special place in my heart, as will each and every one of you.

*Thank you, thank you, thank you*!

Until we meet again,
*Nikki Rittenberry*

Please visit www.nikkirittenberry.com for a complete booklist, news about upcoming novels and appearances, and the author's bio.